F Doolittle
Doolittle, Sean, 1971–
Lake country: a novel

SPARTANBURG COUNTY PUBLIC LIBRARY

W9-AYN-999

SPT   AUG – – 2012

Praise for the novels of Sean Doolittle

SAFER

"I loved *Safer*. The best thing I've read in a long time." —LEE CHILD

"*Safer* is a high-octane, rip-roaring page-turner. I read it in one sitting—and loved every minute."
—HARLAN COBEN

"In *Safer,* Sean Doolittle has crafted a taut, claustrophobic thriller in which our safe world of home and neighborhood becomes instead something terrifying and deadly. Safer made me look twice at my neighbors and check the locks on my doors, and that earns Doolittle a solid A+ in skin-crawling suspense."
—KAY HOOPER

"Doolittle produces a smart, funny and powerfully suspenseful thriller. Sometimes, *Safer* reminds us, home can be the most dangerous place on earth."
—*People* (3½ stars)

"Doolittle cleverly articulates the vulnerability of a close-knit community where those friendly people who know your name also know your darkest secrets." —*The New York Times Book Review*

"[An] enthralling and unsettling story . . . Doolittle has written four previous novels, and *Safer* is good enough to make me want to catch up with them all."
—*The Washington Post*

"Doolittle's outstanding *Safer* is a harrowing tale of suburbia at its ugliest. [*Safer*] proves that he's a writer to watch." —*The Kansas City Star*

"Superb . . . The gut-wrenching *Safer* presents a terrifying portrait of suburban paranoia and the dangerous downside of pursuing security at all costs. A stunner." —*The Providence Journal*

THE CLEANUP

Winner of the Barry Award

"*The Cleanup* is a wonderful discovery. Tight, taut and tough, this is the work of a writer who knows the territory inside and out. This is a great read."
—MICHAEL CONNELLY

"[Doolittle's] novels are stylishly written and refreshing in their quirky originality. . . . [*The Cleanup* is] a terrifying nightmare seen from the inside—and absurdly funny when you're lucky enough to be just looking in." —*The New York Times Book Review*

"Sean Doolittle is one of the bright stars among the galaxy of talented young authors who write with style and authority. . . . [*The Cleanup* is] the perfect noir movie without sound or pictures."
—*The New York Sun*

"Another standout effort . . . [Doolittle's] understated novels are real gems, fine examples of timeless crime writing." —*Chicago Sun-Times*

"Doolittle has become, over the course of three previous novels, a steadily assured voice with enough genuine good humor and humanity to balance the nihilism and gunplay . . . [he has] become a 'must-read' author." —*San Francisco Chronicle*

RAIN DOGS

"As long as there are writers like Sean Doolittle out there, American crime fiction has got a sterling future ahead of it. *Rain Dogs* is tense, evocative, and anchored by a main character, Tom Coleman, who I'd love to see more of. A terrific novel."
—Dennis Lehane

"A superb, suspenseful tale filled with the droll expressions and ambiguous gestures of Nebraska natives. . . . A beautifully written work with idiosyncratic humor and a lot of heart."
—*The Wall Street Journal*

"[Readers will be] drawn in by the quality and authenticity of the writing. Doolittle's lean, mean prose evokes the hardscrabble territory of the Nebraska badlands that serve as the story's setting. His style is likewise stark and spare, casting the story in the hard-boiled tradition of James M. Cain and Jim Thompson." —*Chicago Sun-Times*

"Sean Doolittle is a young writer with serious chops. With *Rain Dogs* he brings it strong."
—GEORGE PELECANOS

BURN

"An exceptionally well-crafted and well-told tale of arson, police work, misplaced zeal, bad relationships, good relationships, family bonds and, oh yes, exercise videos. Quirky, compelling, intelligent, and funny . . . If you like Elmore Leonard, do yourself a favor and pick up *Burn*." —*Lincoln Journal Star*

"Sean Doolittle has been winning high praise from crime fiction readers, and *Burn* will show you why—it's deftly written, tense and intelligent, and bound to make you scramble to find his other work."
—JAN BURKE, *New York Times* bestselling author

"A cult writer for the masses—hip, smart and so mordantly funny that the casual reader might be laughing too hard to realize just how thoughtful Doolittle's work is. Get on the bandwagon now."
—LAURA LIPPMAN, *New York Times* bestselling author

"Sean Doolittle combines wit, good humor, and a generosity of spirit rare in mystery fiction to create novels that are both engrossing and strangely uplifting. He deserves to take his place among the best in the genre."
—JOHN CONNOLLY, *New York Times* bestselling author

DIRT

"Uproarious." —*Publishers Weekly*

"In a passionate flurry of curious motives, seedy characters, and a touch of the heroic, Doolittle delivers an A+ effort that should be considered one of the top crime novels of the year. . . . Highly recommended."
—*Cemetery Dance*

LAKE COUNTRY

Sean Doolittle

Spartanburg County Public Libraries
151 S. Church Street
Spartanburg, SC 29306-3241

BANTAM BOOKS TRADE PAPERBACKS

NEW YORK

Lake Country is a work of fiction. Names, characters, places, and incidents either are the product of the author's imagination or are used fictitiously. Any resemblance to actual persons, living or dead, events, or locales is entirely coincidental.

A Bantam Books Trade Paperback Original

Copyright © 2012 by Sean Doolittle

All rights reserved.

Published in the United States by Bantam Books, an imprint of The Random House Publishing Group, a division of Random House, Inc., New York.

BANTAM BOOKS and the rooster colophon are registered trademarks of Random House, Inc.

Library of Congress Cataloging-in-Publication Data

Doolittle, Sean
Lake country: a novel/Sean Doolittle.
p. cm.
ISBN 978-0-345-53392-0
ebook ISBN 978-0-345-53214-5
1. Missing persons—Fiction. 2. Veterans—Fiction. I. Title.
PS3604.O568L35 2012
813'.6—dc23
2011040262

Printed in the United States of America

www.bantamdell.com

9 8 7 6 5 4 3 2 1

Book design by Caron Harris

For Brian Hodge, sojourner

ANNIVERSARY STORIES

I. POTTER AND BARLOWE

Darryl had been in one of his moods for a week, and he seemed to find a valve for it that night at the bar. "All you clowns pipe down," he said.

Nobody paid much attention. Glen Campbell kept playing on the jukebox. Pool balls clacked around the table in back. A couple of guys from the garage across the street threw darts in the corner, still in their grease-stained coveralls. The old-timers down the bar went right on bitching about whatever they figured needed bitching about today, and Mike Barlowe sat on his stool, nursing a beer, wondering what it would take to fix his life. More or less Tuesday at the Elbow Room.

Darryl said, "Hal, gimme the thing." Hal wiped the bar with one hand, slid the remote over with the other. Darryl gave Mike a nudge and punched up the volume on the Elbow's only television, a raggedy Magnavox Hal kept bolted over the back-bar mirror on a shelf made out of angle iron and a plank of warped plywood.

Mike looked and saw that they were doing a story

about Becky Morse on the ten o'clock news. At first he wondered why, and then the reporter told him: April 7. Five years tomorrow since the crash.

"Tell you right now where the hell this is going," Darryl Potter said.

Mike watched as they reran the same bygone photo from the Morse kid's senior yearbook: same honey hair, same pretty smile. A heartbreaker. The picture cut to file footage of cops and EMTs, a dark highway strewn with wreckage, emergency lights strobing wet pavement and scattered glass.

Now came the girl's mother, Lily Morse, looking older than Mike remembered. She spoke to the reporter from a couch in a living room he remembered better than he'd have preferred. In a minute the picture cut again to some white-haired state senator with a face full of eyebrows, talking to the camera about whether or not they'd ever pass a new law.

Finally, a little business on the other driver: Benson, his name was, though Mike wouldn't have remembered that if he hadn't been watching the news. Late forties or so by now. Sharp-looking guy with a sharp-looking wife and a sharp-looking daughter of his own.

"Son of a bitch," Darryl said. He shoved the remote back down the bar with his knuckles and lit a cigarette.

Mike felt a dull pang of shame.

April.

Jesus. He'd been out of work since the last week in March, too much of that time spent right here at the Elbow with Darryl, and the days had started running together. He sat back on his stool and rubbed his eyes. Thought: *Hell*.

"What's with you two mopes?" Hal put down new beers and changed out their ashtray. No such thing as a smoking ban at the Elbow Room.

"Got a joke for you," Darryl told him. "Knock knock."

"Who's there?"

"Asshole falls asleep driving and kills your kid sister."

"Asshole falls asleep driving and kills my kid sister who?"

Darryl jetted smoke through his nose. "Some fuckin' joke, ain't it?"

Hal looked at Mike.

"I don't get it either," Mike said.

II. LAMB

After the party had broken up, and the rain tapered off, and most of the others from the dayside crew had found their coats and umbrellas and headed for home, Rose Ann Carmody took the stool next to Maya's, ordered a Sapphire martini for each of them, and said, "Happy birthday to me."

Maya smiled. "Happy birthday, Rose Ann. You're supposed to let us buy the drinks."

"This one's not for me, kiddo. It's for you."

"What did I do?"

"Hush," Rose Ann said. "The news is starting."

Maya glanced at the nearest television. It wasn't hard to find one; the Fox and Hound sat around the corner from the station, and all umpteen flat screens played the same thing every night at six and ten.

Like clockwork, all around the room, News7 logos came spinning into frame, trumpeted in on a fanfare so familiar by now that Maya imagined she'd need surgery if she wanted it removed. The intro peeled away, revealing Rick Gavigan and Carmen Brashear behind the anchor desk, live, in high-definition, not half a block from where Maya sat—in somewhat less than regular definition, at this point—sipping call gin with Rose Ann. Rick and Carmen had been teetotaling here themselves an hour ago, wishing Rose Ann a happy fiftieth along with everyone else. Maya expected they'd see at least Gavigan back here in the bar in approximately thirty-seven minutes, ready to cover lost ground.

Meanwhile, tonight's top story: ruptured sewer main in Eden Prairie. Rush-hour traffic held at a standstill.

"The shit we cover," Rose Ann said.

Maya went back to her drink. At the first commercial, Rose Ann noticed Maya's glass, already empty, and said, "Oops." She ordered another.

"Okay," Maya said. "What do you want?"

"Want?"

"You're plying me with alcohol for some reason."

"I'm waiting to make a toast, you lousy sponge."

Maya narrowed her eyes. "What kind of toast?"

"Good grief, the regular kind," Rose Ann said. "Or is tomorrow not your anniversary?"

As if Rose Ann had cued it, the broadcast returned: second segment, lead story, Maya Lamb reporting.

"Ah," Rose Ann said. "Here we are now."

The story was a follow-up on Becky Morse and Wade Benson. Benson was the local architect who had worked past midnight too many nights in a row, fallen asleep behind the wheel of his Range Rover, and crossed the center line on a stretch of State 169 that normally had a barrier but happened, that rainy spring night five years ago, to be serving as an undivided two-lane due to road construction. Becky Morse had been the Mankato State University sophomore he'd met more or less grille-to-grille in the oncoming lane.

Alcohol hadn't been a factor on either side, only fatigue and dreadful timing, and the architect had come through with a concussion and minor bangups. Becky Morse, on the other hand, had been driving a compact hybrid, and not an expedition-class four-by-four. She'd lingered two days in a coma at the Hennepin County Medical Center before succumbing to her injuries, which included ruptured everything, fractured you-name-it, and massive head trauma.

For years now, the girl's mother had been pushing for legislation to mandate stiffer sentences for so-called "drowsy driving," and a version of her bill had finally made it through committee. Five years since the crash that had given the bill its nickname, Becky's Law now awaited hearing on the Senate floor. Maya had been working on the piece for a few days, tonight's installment being the first in a two-part package tying in with the state patrol's Highway Safety Week.

"Well done," Rose Ann said when it was over. She raised her glass. "Welcome to the Five Minnesota Winters Club."

Maya was surprised. A little touched, even, in spite of her mood. Becky Morse had been the first story she'd ever covered at News7. Maya hadn't mentioned this to a soul, but Rose Ann hadn't missed it.

She clinked stemware with her news director. Thin glass chimed beneath the sports report. After they'd taken their medicine, Maya said, "Tell me something."

"Happy to," Rose Ann said.

"When the hell did half a decade go by?"

Rose Ann laughed. "Honey, I stopped counting 'em two decades ago. Now. Speaking of plying a reporter with alcohol."

Maya followed Rose Ann's gaze to a booth in the corner, where two other daysiders had lingered. Kimberly Cross, tiny and blond, fresh cosmo in hand, flirting up a storm with Justin Murdock, the hot kid just in from some market in Idaho. Suddenly Maya felt ancient. "Who's plying whom?"

"I don't know," Rose Ann said. "It's impossible to be certain from this distance."

They watched. It was a regular *National Geographic* special over there: *The male of the species displays his plumage; the flushed cheeks and tousled forelocks of the female signal her interest.* After a minute, Maya said, "Isn't Kimberly engaged?"

"Mm," Rose Ann said, sipping her drink.

Maya turned on an elbow. "Isn't Kimberly engaged to a left defender for the Wild?"

"When last I'd heard," Rose Ann said. She tilted her head in thought. "That's a nice smile on our young Justin Murdock. It'd be a shame if someone came along and knocked all his teeth out."

"Or even most of them," Maya agreed.

Across the room, in the dim pocket of the booth, Kimberly Cross finally glanced up and noticed her audience. Maya and Rose Ann waved in unison from the bar. Kimberly looked away quickly, the bloom in her creamy cheeks spreading to the rest of her face.

God, Maya thought. She'd been Kimberly's age when she'd come up to the Cities from Clark Falls, Iowa, ready to take on the world, or at least Minneapolis. The twenty-six-year-old Maya had imagined herself somewhere in New York City by now, a string of Justin Murdocks bobbing in her wake like channel markers in a wide river of accomplishment.

"Cheer up," Rose Ann said, misreading Maya's mind. "You're still young. And we're leading a 14 market. And you're the only reporter in town speaking for Becky Morse tonight."

Is that what I'm doing? Maya thought.

"Becky Morse," she said, leaning her glass once more toward Rose Ann.

"I was going to say dental insurance," Rose Ann said, shaking her head sadly at the Cross–Murdock booth. She pinged the rim of her glass against Maya's. "But whatever makes you feel better."

III. LANCE CORPORAL MORSE

Mike watched Hal Macklin set up three empty shot glasses in a line. He filled them straight across the top, one two three. While Hal poured, Mike pondered the cloudy green blob of old tattoo ink nestled amid the wiry hair of the man's grizzled forearm. The tattoo had been a bulldog, once upon a time. Now only its initials remained legible: U.S.M.C.

"Hal," he said. "When's the last time we paid for a drink in this dump?"

Hal flopped his rag over a shoulder. "Already paid for 'em, kid." He dealt the full glasses out: one for Mike, one for Darryl, one for himself. "How'd you know the girl?"

If Darryl registered any of this, he didn't let on. If he noticed the free shooter full of Old Crow sitting on the bar in front of him, he didn't announce that either. He'd gone dark since the news went to sports. For the past few minutes he'd been sitting on his stool, hunched over his beer, generating his own surly atmosphere.

Mike said, "We knew her brother."

"You don't know him anymore?"

"Not anymore."

Looking at Darryl, Hal put two and two together. "This brother have a name?"

"Lance Corporal Morse," Mike said. He'd actually graduated Sibley High a year ahead of the guy, though they hadn't known each other in school. Hadn't once met, in fact, before landing in the Sunni Triangle together with the 4/8 Marines. "First name Evan."

"Lance Corporal Morse," Hal repeated. "Final rank, I take it."

"E-3 for life," Mike said. He took a pull from his beer. "Died the same day, the way it went. How's that for a story?"

"Same day as what?"

"As his sister."

Hal glanced at the television, where the girl's picture had been a few minutes ago. Nothing about a brother.

"They weren't together at the time," Mike told him.

Hal waited for the story, which sounded more mysterious than what it was. The 4/8 had been banging full tilt inside sunny Ramadi for three days straight when word came in through forward command that Morse's sister had been in a car wreck back home. The kid's company commander had cleared him to take the ten-day emergency leave, but Morse decided to stay put with his squad, which had lost guys already. He'd figured he could keep in touch with his family from outpost until they had more news.

More news came two days later, when a team from Fox Company—Sergeant Mike Barlowe, a machine gunner from West Virginia named Darryl Potter, and a couple of other available grunts—had pulled Morse from his team's position in a shelled-out café in the market square. They'd shuttled him back to command, where a lieutenant colonel informed him that his sister had died stateside that morning.

Morse hitched a ride from the forward operating base back to Camp Ramadi with a returning supply convoy after nightfall. The rear gun truck—the same up-armored Humvee Morse had climbed into—hit a roadside IED on the edge of town, and that had more or less been that.

"Christ," Hal said.

"Their old man went so low over it that he offed himself after the funerals."

Hal raised an eyebrow. "No shit?"

"Negative shit," Mike said. "Drove himself to this little place they had up in the lake country. Paddled a canoe out to the middle of the water, sat up on the gunwale, and shot himself in the gourd."

After a minute, Hal said, "Congratulations. That's the saddest goddamn story I've heard this week."

"Yeah, well," Mike said. "It's only Tuesday."

Pool balls clacked around the tables. The wrench monkeys threw darts and the old-timers bitched. The jukebox played Springsteen now. On the television, the weather guy called for more rain tomorrow.

Hal picked up his glass. He studied it a moment, then said, "Lance Corporal Morse."

Mike sighed. "And his kid sister."

"Ooh rah," Darryl muttered, and knocked back his shot without waiting for them.

They drank more to Lance Corporal Morse as the night wore on. And his kid sister. They drank to the 4th Battalion, 8th Marines. They drank to Lily Morse, who'd lost her family one member at a time until she'd woken up all alone one morning in a tidy house in West St. Paul. Nobody could decide whether to drink to Bill Morse or not, checking out the way he had, but they erred on the side of sympathy. They made the rounds again every so often, just to be thorough. By closing time, Darryl was only getting warmed up.

"Guy straight up kills somebody," he said, still talking about the architect driving the other car. Wouldn't let it go. "And he does ten days for it."

"Yeah, well." Mike shambled over to the wall and racked his cue stick. They hadn't really been playing anyway. "I'm sure he's sorry."

"Hell. Killed three people, if you look at it."

"Depends how you look at it, I guess."

"Get more'n ten days for a bar fight," Darryl said. "That's how I look at it."

"Good point," Mike agreed. He could have made the counterpoint that Darryl had started that bar fight, and he'd broken a guy's cheek, and there was his record to contend with, and he'd also called the judge a not-so-nice name at the arraignment. But it was getting late.

"Guy's still got his wife and kid. Still got his nifty address. Bet he's made himself a pile more dough than he had five years ago too. What's Lily Morse got?"

"I don't know, man." Mike didn't really know Lily Morse, and neither did Darryl. "I gotta hit the head."

By the time Mike came back, Hal had turned on the lights. He caught Mike's eye from behind the bar, then glanced toward the rear. His expression delivered the message: *Better deal with him.*

Darryl was leaning on his pool cue, beer in hand, staring at the eight ball as if daring it to look back.

"Come on," Mike said. "Man says it's time to clear out." He'd wanted to go home for an hour, and his leg was killing him.

But Darryl felt like driving around. And since Darryl had filched the keys out of Mike's unattended jacket while Mike had been in the men's, they drove around.

"Tell me another thing," Darryl said at one point, waiting at a red light on Fairmount, over by the college. "You see anything about the kid's big bro on that news story? One word about any dead Marines at all?"

"Not a one," Mike said. He couldn't see any reason why there should have been, but arguing with Darryl only made him stubborn, and Mike wanted to avoid making Darryl stubborn tonight. He only wanted a Vicodin and some sleep.

At some point, they crossed the river. At some point after that, Mike nodded off.

When he woke up, they were parked at a curb on a leafy, darkened street on the south shore of Lake Calhoun. Not that Mike knew where the hell they were, until Darryl told him. The clock in the dash said 3:35 a.m.

"Right there he lives," Darryl said, looking out his window.

"There who lives?"

"The asshole."

"Who?" Mike yawned. His mouth had gone dry, and his tongue felt thick. He leaned forward, looked at the house Darryl was watching. It was one of those stylish modern-looking things, set back on a wooded rise, all geometric planes and cantilevered sections and floor-to-ceiling views of the lake. All at once Mike felt nervous. "You mean the architect?"

Darryl made a rough sound in his throat. He swiveled his head, nodded out Mike's window. Across the dark water, beyond the far shore, downtown Minneapolis glittered in full view against the night sky. It looked nice.

"Some punishment, huh?" Darryl said.

He'd gotten into the glove box while they were rolling, Mike saw. Darryl sat with an elbow on his door, resting the open pint of Old Crow on his knee. His eyes had taken on that loose, liquid sheen Mike knew for what it was: a warning sign. Like clear oil shimmering in a hot pan. It seemed to Mike that he'd been seeing this look of Darryl's more often than he used to.

"Jesus," he said. Rubbed his face. "We gotta get better jobs, man."

Darryl was quiet. After a bit his mouth twitched. Not quite a grin, but closer than a few seconds ago. "Speak for yourself," he said.

Mike glanced at his friend's eyes and breathed a little easier. The storm had passed. "Gimme the damn keys," he said. "You lose your turn."

He opened his door and got out. It was a clean night, scrubbed fresh by the rain. The cloud cover had pulled apart in spots overhead, showing starry black patches here and there, and the moon looked like a puddle of silver on the water. The tangy spring air felt good on his face.

Mike breathed it in. Limping around the car, he checked up and down the empty street, hoping nobody happened to look out the window at a quarter of four in the morning, see two guys casing houses in a rust-bucket Skylark, and call the cops.

As he rounded the front bumper, he glanced through the cracked windshield and saw Darryl, already shoved over into the passenger seat, washed in the light from the overhead dome. Darryl's eyes looked red and his hair stood on end. If Mike had been closer to sober and more than half awake himself, it might have occurred to him to ask how the guy had known where the architect lived in the first place. But he didn't think about that until later.

CITIZEN CON

1

For the first time in as long as he could remember, Mike Barlowe woke up from one of the old dreams.

He'd been sighting down his rifle from the edge of a rooftop, unable to see the ground below. A hot wind blew in from the desert, obscuring his view. He could feel the tension mounting beneath his trigger finger. He couldn't make out his target in the void.

The moment he fired, Mike bolted up in a clench of panic, heart hammering, unaware of his position.

Then, little by little, the hollow, scouring sound of sand blowing against his helmet resolved itself into the soft patter of rain on the bedroom window. Gray daylight seeped in through the curtains. As his surroundings slowly came into focus, so did the real-world noise that had roused him:

Somebody banging on the front door.

Mike dragged in a rattling breath, dimly recalling the echo of distant artillery as the last of the dream fell away. He looked around and found himself on top of his own unmade covers, still in his clothes. He glanced at the clock beside the bed and saw that Wednesday morning had already come and gone. It was nearly three o'clock in the afternoon.

A fresh barrage thudded through the walls while he sat there, still blinking away the fog. Mike hauled himself out of the rack and shambled down the hall in his stocking feet, thinking, *All right, already. Don't break it down.*

He was halfway across the living room when the door fell silent, then thundered once in reply.

Mike stopped in his tracks as the jamb splintered. For a moment, standing there frozen, watching the door burst inward on its hinges, he wondered if he was still dreaming after all.

A guy Mike had never seen before came strolling into the house like he had an invitation: Mid thirties, dressed in jeans, a leather sport-bike jacket, and lug boots. He was built low and lean, with a Kevlar bulge under a black nylon T-shirt and a face that looked like it had been broken and healed wrong. Seeing Mike, the guy's eyes went hard. "Got him," he yelled over his shoulder.

"Really?" another voice said from out on the stoop.

A new face appeared in the doorway, and this one Mike recognized. The expression on this face changed from relieved to surprised to disappointed, all in a few seconds.

"Oh, crap," the newcomer said. "Mike. Sorry, man. We sort of thought nobody was home."

Mike stood in his spot, flat-footed, still scrambling to assess the situation in front of him. He couldn't seem to untangle his reflexes. It occurred to him that if the dream had been real and he'd been back in the desert, he'd have had his ass shot off by now.

"Toby," he said. It came out like a croak.

The first guy through the door rolled his eyes.

Toby Lunden shook rainwater from the sleeves of his windbreaker. He looked embarrassed. "We tried knocking."

"Oh," Mike said. He released the breath he'd been holding, still waiting for his pulse to settle. "In that case, come on in."

Mike wasn't a gambler, but he'd known a few book-ies, and Toby Lunden wasn't like any of them.

He was a kid, for one thing, barely twenty years old, with bad eyes and thin bones and a complexion like pancake batter. If the stories Mike had heard about Toby were true, Toby started up his first sports book as a sophomore in high school. By the time he was a senior, he had faculty from across the public school district on his weekly bottom sheet.

Toby's facility with numbers was said to be such that he'd pulled straight Ds in math class, yet he'd been able to pay cash for a restored '64 Shelby Cobra on graduation day (the same car he'd supposedly driven into an overpass abutment on graduation night). Even if those stories weren't true, they summed up Mike's impression of Toby Lunden well enough: a young guy with big ideas and all the smarts he needed to get himself more horsepower than he knew what to do with.

"I can get a guy to fix that," he told Mike, nodding at the busted door frame as he stepped through. He dried his shoes politely on the crusty bath towel laid down as a mat in the entryway. He took a look around and said, "Did we get you out of bed?"

"That's okay," Mike said. "I had to get up to answer the door anyway."

The guy with the brutal face and the ballistic undershirt seemed impatient. "Where's your roommate?" he said.

Mike looked at him.

The guy looked back.

"I didn't get your name," Mike said.

"You don't want it."

"That's Bryce," Toby jumped in. He turned to his man and said, "Mike's okay."

"Hey, what a relief." Bryce watched Mike but spoke to Toby. "Future reference, you could have mentioned there might be two in the house."

"Sorry."

Mike waited.

"So . . . yeah," Toby said. He looked around some more, shifted his feet, and said, "Hey, Mike? You haven't by any chance seen Darryl around, have you?" He paused. "I mean like today?"

"You mean like in the five minutes I've been awake?" Beyond Toby's shoulder, the open front door gave a view to the street; through spits of rain Mike could see a black Lincoln Navigator with Minnesota plates parked at the curb in front of the house, blocking the driveway. To his left, he had an angle on the window overlooking the empty carport alongside the house. No Skylark. Mike couldn't help wondering why they'd bothered blocking the driveway.

"Like, maybe he rolled over and nudged you before he slipped out of bed this morning," Bryce suggested. "Nibbled on your ear, made spoons, told you where he was off to? No?"

Mike reminded himself that he didn't know this guy Bryce from a hole in the ground. But he knew this game: pick a fight, establish dominance, make sure the other guy knew when he'd been alpha-dogged. Barracks Douche Bags 101.

"Darryl's old-fashioned," he said, ignoring the bait. "He never talks to me about his work."

"How could he with your knob in his mouth?"

"Hey, okay," Toby jumped in. "Let's just, you know. Right? Bryce, I've got this." His eyes said, *Please?*

Bryce smirked. "Whatever you say, boss. I'll give myself the tour." He brushed past Mike on his way into the house. His eyes said, *Stop me.*

Mike caught a glimpse of a shoulder holster under the bike jacket as Bryce passed. None of this seemed like a promising way to start a day.

"Sorry," Toby said when they were alone. "Bryce has an intensity."

"I got that," Mike said. "Where'd you find him?"

"Works for my uncle." Toby shrugged. "He's sort of on loan for the day."

"No kidding." Toby's uncle was a bail bondsman with billboards all over town. Television commercials too. Late at night it was hard to miss them. "Real live bounty hunter, huh?"

"Fugitive Recovery Specialist," Toby said. "He has business cards and everything."

"Neat. Why did he kick my door in?"

Toby sighed. "Maybe we could sit a minute?"

"Sure," Mike said.

As they arranged themselves like civil people, Mike

could hear Bryce the Fugitive Recovery Specialist moving room to room through the house, sweep-searching. Mike did his best to let it go for now.

He left the beat-up couch for Toby, took the beat-up recliner for himself, observing the state of the place as he picked his way through the mess. The coffee table, and the floor all around the coffee table, were littered with half-crumpled beer cans. Mike saw the Old Crow bottle from the kitchen cupboard, more than half full last he remembered, empty now. The ashtray, which he'd dumped yesterday, overflowed with butts. By the look of things, Darryl had kept right on drinking after they'd come in at 0-dark-30 and parted company. That, or he'd gotten an early start. Either way, he'd put some work into it.

"Let me guess," Mike said. "You lost Darryl's cell number?"

"Hey, I've been calling it," Toby said. "Believe me, Mike, he hasn't been answering."

"What's so urgent?"

"Finding Darryl, at the moment."

"Feel free to elaborate."

Toby leaned forward on the edge of the sofa cushion, elbows on his knees. He seemed unsure how to begin.

"Okay," he finally said. "A couple hours ago, I get this call from one of my regulars. Lunchtime or so. Nice guy, owns a steak and chops place on Nicollet. Chevalier. You ever been there?"

"Can't say that I have."

"Serve a mad porterhouse," Toby said. "Anyway, this guy, he's a good customer, been on my sheet for, I don't know, two, three years? He wins, he loses, I let him ride, it evens out. He owns his place but he's also the head chef, works like a dog; he's at the restaurant all the time. So I send a guy to him every week. He's always ready with the commission, lays whatever action he wants that week, on we go. No problems."

"Okay, less elaboration," Mike said. He couldn't listen to Toby while listening to the rest of the house with his other ear; he couldn't hear anything out of Toby's man Bryce, and he didn't like the quiet. The house wasn't exactly big enough to get lost in. "Fast forward to lunch."

Toby nodded. "Like I said. My guy calls me. This is during his busy hour. He tells me that Darryl came by the restaurant this morning, regular time or so, early, when the place was empty."

"In other words, like normal."

"Well, that's the thing," Toby said. "Normal, yes and no."

"Yes and no like how?"

"Like, normally Darryl wouldn't take eight hours to deliver me a collection, for starters."

"Jesus, Toby. You're kicking in doors now?"

"I know, right?" Toby said. "I'm a numbers guy. You know I'm not cut out for this hardball stuff. That's why I use guys like Darryl in the first place." He gave a weak smile. "I guess that's probably what they call irony, right?"

Mike yawned. He rubbed his face. His head felt cracked, and his mouth tasted like a dry sewer line. He wanted a glass of water and a shower. And his door fixed. "I think you can relax. The Skylark's a hunk of junk. Maybe he broke down somewhere, forgot to charge his phone. You know Darryl."

"Yeah," Toby said. "That's part of the problem." He was quiet, then added, "Thing is, Mike, I sent a guy to Chevalier this week already."

"Oh."

"Monday morning."

Mike thought he was finally getting the picture. Considering the rubble of empties between them on the coffee table, it wasn't difficult to imagine what must have happened. Only the night before, at the Elbow Room, a news reporter had to remind him that April was a week old already, and, compared to Darryl, Mike was organized. He said, "So mistakes were made."

"You could say that," Toby said. "If by mistakes you mean putting a gun up to my best customer's eye and pretty much flat out robbing him, in broad daylight, in his own place, then, yeah. It sounds like definitely mistakes were made."

Mike looked at him. "Say that again?"

"Eleven o'clock this morning, my customer calls and tells me Darryl comes to his place around daybreak, pulls out a hand cannon, and tells him he'll shoot his face off if he doesn't settle his sheet." Toby's voice rose as he talked. "And not just the weekly juice either, which, remember, he already paid. I mean the whole balance."

Mike didn't know if he'd ever heard quite this tone out of Toby. Hand cannon? Juice?

Even Toby seemed to hear how he sounded. He released a long breath. "Apparently my guy was in his office, batching up tickets," he said. "Most of what he would have owed me was stacked in cash on the desk, all ready to go to the bank. He said Darryl shoved a bag at him, like a gym bag, told him to stuff it all in, and just, you know. Walked out with it."

"That's what your guy told you?"

"He was pretty rattled," Toby said. "Took him all morning to pull himself together, the way he tells it. Lucky thing he called me instead of the cops."

"Did you talk to him in person or only on the phone?"

"Both," Toby said. "Can't see any reason not to believe him, Mike. He's never lied to me before, as far as I know."

Mike thought a minute. "There's no way you and Darryl could have crossed wires?" he said. "He messed up the day, went in there with the wrong idea?"

"I don't think so."

"But it's possible."

"Thing is, Mike? Darryl doesn't exactly work for me anymore."

That definitely didn't make sense. "Doesn't exactly?"

"Doesn't at all." Toby seemed to be sizing him up. "I'm getting the impression you didn't know that."

"It's new information," Mike admitted. "Since when?"

"About a week ago," Toby said.

"He quit?"

"Not so much quit." Mike got the impression that Toby wished he didn't have to be the one to explain. "Mike, you know I like the guy, but lately? I don't know, man. It kind of seems like he's been coming unglued."

"How do you mean?" Mike said, even though, being maybe the closest thing to a friend Darryl Potter had left on planet earth, he thought he knew well enough what Toby meant. Unglued was as good a way to put it as any.

"Getting rough on people, for one thing."

"A bookie's worried because one of his collectors is getting rough on people?"

Toby's cheeks flushed. "More than need be."

"How much more?"

"More enough," Toby said. "Okay? My sheet, Mike, the regulars, they mostly always pay. I wouldn't keep taking their action if they didn't. Guns? Who am I, Tony Soprano? I'm a numbers guy."

Mike tried to think. What came to him was a picture of Darryl in the passenger seat of the Buick twelve hours ago, sitting in the dome light with bloodshot eyes and a thousand-yard stare, and all Mike could think was, *What the hell have you started this time, you dumb grunt?*

"And you know for a fact it was Darryl," he said. "At the restaurant this morning. Not one of your other guys?"

"I've only got one other guy, and he's answering his phone," Toby said. "Besides, this customer's seen Darryl a time or two. If he didn't remember him before, he sure remembers him now."

Bryce came back into the living room then, cracking his knuckles. "No wonder this genius took your money," he said to Toby, scanning his surroundings. "This place is a shithole."

At the mention of money, it occurred to Mike to ask, "How much was he into you? Your restaurant guy."

Toby shrugged. "Ten grand or so."

"Jesus."

"His Final Four bracket didn't work out."

Mike sat and thought about ten thousand dollars.

Toby added, "He told me Darryl walked out with more like eleven."

"Eleven?"

"Thousand, yeah."

Mike thought about eleven thousand dollars.

"Look, Mike, I'm really sorry," Toby said. "I know he's your boy and all. I'm not exactly in my comfort zone here."

By now Mike was only half listening again. A bad feeling had crawled into his stomach and curled up there.

"Anyway." Toby stood. He produced a smartphone, looked at the screen a minute, tapped it a few times with his index finger, then put the phone back in the pocket of his windbreaker. "If you see him . . . I guess, you know. Could you tell him to call me?"

"Sure," Mike said.

Toby seemed ready to say something else before deciding that there wasn't much else to say. He rejoined the muscle he'd borrowed from his uncle and headed for the door.

As they let themselves out, Mike said, "Hey, Toby?"

Toby looked back.

"You haven't heard from any of your other customers today, have you?"

"Not so far," Toby said. "Believe me, we've been checking."

"If you do," Mike said, "would you let me know?"

"Sure thing, Mike. Thanks. And, you know. Sorry again about the door."

Mike felt himself nod.

"See you around," the bounty hunter said.

2

By the time her simple highway-safety story turned into breaking coverage of a felony kidnapping, Maya Lamb remained the only reporter in the state of Minnesota who'd spoken with Wade Benson's daughter in the hours before she disappeared.

She encountered the girl first thing Wednesday at the sleek, modern house in Linden Hills, where Juliet Benson still lived with her folks and where Maya arrived, with a station photographer, for the in-home interview Benson had granted them.

It was half-past eight in the morning. Cheryl Benson had escorted Deon into the breakfast area to set up his gear for the piece; Wade Benson had excused himself briefly to take a phone call in his office down the hall. Maya, for the moment, had been standing alone at the wall of glass with the rain-streaked view over Lake Calhoun. The house was every bit the pad she might have conjured for the successful architect, if anyone had asked her to imagine one, and in five minutes she'd already composed the intro to her ten o'clock package in her head:

Once each year, on the anniversary of the roadway collision that ended Rebecca Morse's life, Wade Ben-

son says goodbye to his family, hands his longtime business partner the reins to Benson Granger Architecture and Design, gathers together a small bag of personal toiletries, and goes to jail.

"You know, I can't help feeling like I owe you an apology," a voice behind her said.

Maya hadn't been aware she had company. She turned and smiled, wondering how long Juliet Benson had been standing there behind the Barcelona lounge. "An apology?" she said. "What on earth for?"

"For hating you."

How to respond?

"Not just you." Juliet came over and joined Maya at the window. She had intelligent brown eyes and pretty dark hair, cut a fashionable length. Skinny jeans, a light hooded top, a hint of fragrance. Everything tasteful. Even her tone was pleasant. "I hated all of you for a while."

Good morning to you too, Maya thought. She said, "All of us?"

"You and everybody else with a news camera." Juliet folded her arms and took in the view as though she didn't take time to notice it every day. "I was fifteen the first time we met. Do you remember?"

"I do," Maya told her. "I remember very well, actually." The mildly bug-eyed high schooler with braces on her teeth had grown into quite an arresting young woman in the time since. Maya knew from her research that Juliet Benson was now in her second year at the Minneapolis College of Art and Design, but somehow it hadn't occurred to her until just then, standing there at the glass together, that five years made Juliet twenty years old. The same age Becky Morse had been when she died.

"I mean, I sort of admired you. I thought you were smart," Juliet said. "Nicer than the others. But I still hated you."

"I'm sorry to hear that," Maya said, and she meant it. Regarding Juliet Benson in profile, for the first time she began to consider this side of her highway-safety story from a different angle. "If it means anything, I think I understand how you could feel that way."

"You guys used to set up camp out there." Juliet nodded toward the world outside the window. "Every night that my dad showed up on the news, I'd walk through school the next day feeling everyone's eyes. Even the teachers. Heck, the janitors. I wanted to climb into a locker and not come out."

"Of course you did."

"When I think of what Mrs. Morse and her family went through, I'm ashamed of myself for complaining, but back then? I just wanted you guys to go away." Juliet turned from the window and faced Maya with such an utterly guile-free expression that Maya liked her instinctively. "Want to know what seems funny?"

"What seems funny?"

"Now I'm standing here thinking, Where is everybody?" She quirked her mouth. "I know. Pick a gripe, right?"

It hadn't struck Maya as an unreasonable question. "Minneapolis architect avoids criminal charges, receives unusual sentence," she offered. "If it was such big news in the beginning, why not at the end?"

"Something like that, I guess."

Reporters move on to new markets, Maya could have told her. Assignment editors retire. New stories crowd out old ones—sometimes even stories as terrible as this one. All true statements. Were they answers?

"I saw your piece last night," Juliet said. "I thought you were fair."

"Thank you," Maya said. "I try to be."

"And Mom let you in the door. So I gather you must be okay there too."

"I appreciate you saying that." Maya took a chance and added, "Does that mean you don't hate me anymore?"

Looking back, she'd remembered the way Juliet Benson had smiled at her. It was a nice smile. Genuine. Something in her eyes seemed older than twenty. "Let's see how tonight goes," she'd said.

"You feel sorry for the dude," Deon told her later, in the van, as they followed Wade Benson's silver Audi through the misty drizzle along Calhoun Parkway. "I can tell."

Maya sipped cold coffee from a paper Go Shop cup and watched the lakeshore pass by her window. "Can you, now."

"I can read people."

"Who told you that?"

Deon chuckled, leaning over the wheel as he drove. "That ain't a denial."

"Yeah, well," Maya said. "It's not my job to feel sorry for him."

"Never said it was your job. Just said you feel sorry for the dude."

They'd gotten good sound around the Benson family breakfast table, a little more than fifty minutes to work with back at the station. Now they were accompanying Benson to his downtown office to shoot B-roll for the piece. This afternoon, by arrangement with jail officials—and against the flinty objections of Wade Benson's attorney, who seemed exasperated with his client's willingness to subject himself to renewed public scrutiny—they'd be meeting their subject again, this time at the Hennepin County Adult Corrections Facility in Plymouth, where they'd shoot him booking in for his final stay. It would make a good visual, Maya thought: the downtown architect, and the county inmate. Same guy, different clothes.

She considered the lone silhouette behind the wheel of the car ahead of them. It wasn't her job to like Wade Benson either, though Wade Benson happened to be a likable man. He had the sort of understated, put-together quality she associated with people who designed things for a living, and she sensed in the way he carried himself a humility that had come at a dreadful price. Between the two of them—Benson and his wife, Cheryl, who worked in corporate relations for St. Jude Medical—it wasn't difficult to see where Juliet had come by her general self-possession.

"Fine, I feel sorry for him," she said. "Why, don't you?"

"Where I come from?" Deon glanced at the image of Wade Benson's graceful home receding in the rear-view mirror. "Little hard to feel sorry for a guy with that guy's view. Know what I'm saying?"

"Try looking at your daughter and seeing the kid you killed. How about that view?"

"I got four boys."

Maya finally turned in her seat and appraised her photographer, with whom she'd worked maybe a dozen times since he started with the station in February. Deon wore a different Timberwolves jersey each day of the week, had already picked up three speeding tickets driving the news vans, smoked cigarettes in front of their call sign when out on stories, and could set up a live mast shot faster than any camera jockey Maya knew. He also seemed to get a kick out of trying to hook her for some reason.

"Tell you what, though," he added. "A brother from Hawthorne killed that kid? Instead of some white dude from Linden Hills? They'd send him up more than two days a year."

And if Grandma had balls she'd be Grandpa, Maya thought, but it was a fair enough point. "Maybe so."

"Anyhow. Mix in a Red Bull, that's all I'm saying."

"You never fell asleep driving, huh?"

"Nope."

"Nodded off? Never once?"

"Guess I never been that tired."

Maya rode along, listening to the clockwork thud of the windshield wipers, the whisper of mist on the roof over their heads. As they followed Benson off the parkway, turning right onto West Lake, she said, "We don't know how to measure tired."

"Say what, now?"

"That's what a state patrol lieutenant told me at Benson's trial," she said. "He said you can pull a guy over and have him blow into a machine, and the machine tells you if he's had too much to drink according to the law." She looked at Deon. "But how's a trooper in the field supposed to write down a guy's legal level of tired?"

"How do I know?"

"Exactly," Maya said.

The county grand jury hadn't been able to answer that question either. Nor had they found, in Wade Benson's case, the gross negligence required for a charge of criminal motor-vehicle homicide under Minnesota law. For his role in Becky Morse's death, Benson had been convicted of misdemeanor reckless driving and sentenced to five years' probation. In a final twist—which had made for splashy coverage at the time—the judge in the case had expressed her own opinion by imposing the following condition:

Each year for the duration of his probation term, on the anniversary of the accident, Wade Benson was bound to report to Hennepin County ACF, where he would spend the ensuing forty-eight hours incarcerated—a period of time roughly corresponding to Becky Morse's hours in critical care before she'd expired.

Deon shook his head slowly. "Don't know how to measure tired, huh?"

"That's what I was told."

He cracked his window, tossed out his ragged toothpick, and popped in a fresh one. "They know how to measure dead, though."

Maya sighed. "That they do."

They drove on in silence. The windshield wipers thumped along. On the north side of Loring Park,

Deon cocked his head and said, "Something buggin' you over there, Maya Lamb?"

Something was bugging her, in fact, though Maya couldn't seem to put her finger on it. Just then she'd been replaying her conversation with Juliet Benson, but the truth was, something had been bugging her ever since she'd started working on this story—this bookend to the past half decade of Wade Benson's life. Of Lily Morse's. Of her own. Something she'd seen in Juliet Benson's eyes seemed to boil it all down somehow, though Maya couldn't decide how or down to what.

She gave Deon a disappointed look and said, "I thought you said you could read people?"

It wasn't hard to follow the bounty hunter's tracks through the house. Bryce hadn't exactly tidied up after himself.

The first thing Mike noticed about Darryl's room as he passed it—after the open closet, and the bureau drawers emptied all over the floor—was the blank square in the dust next to the little TV on the dresser. Wherever Darryl had gone, apparently he'd taken his Xbox with him.

Then Mike did something he'd never done before. He went into Darryl's room and looked around himself. Also missing: Darryl's rucksack, the .45 he normally kept between the mattress and the box spring, and the last of Mike's optimism.

Back in his own room, he found more or less the same state of disarray. The cheap leather jewelry case he kept in the bottom drawer of the night table lay on the floor a couple of feet away, opened and upside down. The case was smaller than a shoe box, obviously not big enough to hold eleven grand in cash, and the message there seemed clear enough: *Here's what I think of you, fella.*

Mike went around policing up the scattered contents of the box. He found his combat ribbon in a pile of socks, Purple Heart against the baseboard under the window. Bronze Star caught in the heating vent. He found his dog tags under the bed.

There were half a dozen curled photos he hadn't looked at in a while. The last one he picked up showed two guys he barely recognized in BDUs and brain buckets, smoking cigarettes on the hood of a Humvee. Their faces were streaked with sweat and covered in grime. Light wisps of smoke from their cigarettes trailed off to one side of the snapshot, mimicking the heavy ropes of smoke still trailing from the empty window of the shell-pocked building in the background.

Ten minutes before that photo had been taken, inside the same building, Mike Barlowe had killed two people. He sat on the edge of the bed with the box on his lap and looked at the photo. Five years, he kept thinking; that was all that stood between the Marine he saw in the picture and the sad sack he saw looking back at him from the dresser mirror on the other side of the room.

Mike confronted his own reflection: a blotchy, stubbled wreck, sitting on the edge of an unmade bed with a photograph in his hand. *That's you,* he thought.

He almost didn't believe himself. His face looked too hard, his eyes too hollow. In a month and a half he'd be twenty-seven years old, and he was already starting to resemble one of the middle-aged burnouts who held down the the bar at Hal's place every night of their slump-shouldered lives. *If it's not me,* he thought, *then who the hell is it?*

A guy who had better things to do than sitting around looking in the mirror, that was who. Things like tracking down the other grunt on the Humvee in the photograph, for example. Preferably before somebody wound up getting hurt.

It seemed like enough to figure out for one day. Mike dropped the photos into the box, closed the lid, and put it all back in the bottom drawer where it belonged. The clock on the night table read a quarter of four in the afternoon. He'd be asked to remember that later.

3

Mike started with the obvious: Darryl's mobile phone. No answer. He tried twice more, but Darryl still wasn't biting. He stood around thinking for a minute, then tried the number on the side of the fridge. Three rings, four, then five; as he was preparing to hang up, Tanya Ellerbe finally answered.

"Hello?" She sounded out of breath. Mike could hear something whirring and thumping in the background. He guessed laundry.

"Hey, Tanya. You sound busy."

"Oh, hi, Mike. Nah. Just on the treadmill. How's it going?"

"Well, I'm not on a treadmill," he said. "So I guess that part's going okay."

She panted a laugh. "What's up? I haven't talked to you in forever."

It hadn't been forever, but Mike guessed it had been a while. He thought of Tanya as a friend, or at least as a friendly, although primarily she was their land-lady. She'd gotten the house in her divorce—a two-bedroom North End cracker box with sagging gutters and a leaky basement—but she hadn't wanted to live there anymore, alone or otherwise; instead of selling, she'd moved to a studio apartment near Marydale Park and listed the place in the City Pages.

In the year or so he and Darryl had been Tanya's tenants, Mike had taken to looking after what needed attention on the house, and Darryl had taken to looking after what needed attention on Tanya, and Tanya cut them breaks on the rent when they needed it. Between Mike's VA benefits, work when he had it, and what Darryl earned running collections for Toby, they didn't need it often. But then, April wasn't shaping up all that well so far.

"I'm looking for Darryl," he said.

"Oh." The treadmill hummed along, Tanya's footfalls keeping time. "He wander off his leash again?"

"Something like that. You haven't seen him, have you?"

"Seen him?"

She gave the word *seen* a little extra inflection, and Mike felt sudden heat in his face. He couldn't see himself but knew he was blushing. This was stupid. "He hasn't been by your place, then."

"Not today," Tanya said.

"Any chance you've talked to him?"

"Not recently."

"Oh. Okay." It was nice to hear Tanya's voice, but he wished he hadn't called. "Look, sorry to bug you."

"Cut it out. You're not bugging anybody."

"Okay. Go back to your workout."

"I'm done, so there." The mechanical hum shut down in the background, and Tanya's breathing lightened up. Pretty soon Mike heard the crinkle of plastic and the sound of gulping over the line. Listening, it was easy to imagine Tanya on her end of the call:

damp with sweat, flushed from exertion, towel on her shoulder, tipping back a water bottle. She looked healthy.

"So you can't find Darryl," she said.

"Well, I just started looking."

Gulp. "He's in some kind of trouble, isn't he?"

"Trouble?" Mike didn't want to get into it. "Not that I know about."

"You've never called here looking for him before."

"Actually, I need the car," Mike told her. "Deakins laid off some guys a couple weeks back, so I don't have the truck anymore, and I thought he'd be back a while ago. Darryl."

"That's who I figured we were still talking about." Tanya's tone sounded skeptical, but she didn't press. "Mike, the truth is, I haven't seen Darryl in a while. Or, you know. Talked to him."

"No?"

"Not in a while."

"Can I be nosy?"

"You're not being nosy."

"How long's a while?"

"About a month?" Tanya said. "He didn't mention it, obviously."

"No," Mike said, feeling more awkward as this conversation went on. "Sorry."

"Nothing to be sorry about."

"I didn't realize."

"Hey, don't get me wrong," she said. "I've always known what it was and what it wasn't. Darryl and me. We're all grown-ups."

"Sure," Mike said.

"Frankly, I liked things fine the way they were. But

lately, with his moods . . ." She trailed off. Drank some more water. "Listen, if I wanted a sullen asshole and angry sex, I could have stayed married. You know?"

He was out of his depth. "Makes sense to me."

"Anyway, besides that, I sort of met somebody." Tanya's voice softened a bit. "He's nice. Lives in the building."

"No kidding?"

"I know. Sounds like a sitcom, right?"

"People like a good sitcom," Mike said. "How long has this been going on?"

"Who keeps track?" Tanya said. He could almost hear her smiling. "About a month."

A month. Mike put that with what Toby had told him about cutting Darryl loose. About a week ago, Toby had said. If there was a pattern to this timeline, Mike didn't love the look of it.

"I mean, who knows," she said. "But so far it's been . . . refreshing."

"Tanya, that's great," he told her, and he meant it. "You deserve it."

"Hell, I don't know what I deserve, Mike. But I'll take what I can get. You know?"

He knew. Or he thought he knew. Anyway, good for Tanya.

"As far as Darryl," she said, "I don't know what's going on there."

Mike rubbed his eyes, pinched the bridge of his nose. His headache felt like it was getting worse instead of better. "Yeah."

The line went quiet for a bit, but Mike was so lost

in thought that he didn't notice the silence until Tanya said, "Hey, Mike?"

"Still here."

"Did you really lose your job?"

"Yeah." The truth. "But I've got a couple things lined up." A lie.

"That sucks," Tanya said. "Listen, don't sweat this month, okay? Maybe go down and look at the sump pump if you get a chance. Or whatever."

The sump pump. He'd fixed it when the snow thawed, but the mention of it reminded him that the rent was a week late already. If he'd felt awkward before, now he just felt shitty. "Thanks, Tanya. But everything's fine. I forgot to mail the check, that's all. I'll get it to you."

"Whenever," she said. "Listen, I need to clean up, and then I have to go run around a little. You need a ride somewhere? I can come by and pick you up."

"Nah. But thanks. Hit the showers."

Tanya seemed hesitant. More silence. This time he noticed it.

"I feel like I want to say something," she finally announced. "It isn't my place, but maybe I'll go ahead and say it anyway."

"I live in your place, Tanya. Say whatever you want."

"Then here I go." She paused. "Look, I know Darryl's your friend. You've been through a lot together, and I can't imagine what any of it must have been like, but I know you feel like you owe him."

Only because I owe him, Mike thought, automatically annoyed by the commentary. But Tanya meant no ill. And he'd been the one who invited her to speak her mind. So he said, "We go back a bit."

"Well, I feel like your friend too," Tanya said. "Maybe that's dumb, we haven't known each other that long, but it's where this is coming from. Okay?"

"Sure."

"You're a nice guy, Mike." She started to add something more to that, then sighed, backed up, and took a different tack. "Remember when you said you weren't on a treadmill?"

"I guess so."

"I'm just saying." He heard plastic crinkling as Tanya drank her water. "You sure about that?"

Half an hour before Maya packed up her things for the trip out to Plymouth, a shadow fell across the doorway to the editing bay where she sat reviewing old tape. She looked over her shoulder to find Rose Ann Carmody watching her.

"Well, look at that." Rose Ann lifted her chin toward the video monitor. "Who's the little girl with the microphone up there?"

Maya glanced back at the frozen warp of her own image on the screen. The tape was one of the masters she'd pulled from the newsroom morgue, most of her original reporting on the Morse/Benson story. She barely remembered the outfit she was wearing in the piece. She remembered the haircut, though she couldn't remember what she'd been thinking when she'd paid for it.

"Dunno," she said. "I hardly recognize her."

Rose Ann examined the Maya on-screen, seemingly

bemused. "How'd the interview at Benson Manor go?"

"Fine," Maya said. "I asked him to describe the hardest part about going to jail. Want to hear what he told me?"

"What did he say?"

"He said it was so easy any fool could do it."

"Did he." Rose Ann considered that. "I like it. Where are we?"

"Ninety percent in the can. Except for what they'll let us shoot at county in an hour." Maya checked her watch. "Hour and change. I had Deon cut what we've got to fit the last bits in."

"Good. Plan a live shot at the jail for the six if nothing breaks late. I'll tell Miles." Rose Ann removed her reading glasses and gestured with them. "You look like hell, by the way."

"Gee, thanks. You look like a spring daisy."

"Don't be sensitive. Trouble sleeping?"

"Not particularly," Maya said. "Why?"

"Because you look dog tired, that's why."

"I'm hungover, Rose Ann. You drank me under the table at your birthday party."

A smirk. "Is that how you remember it?"

"It's fuzzy, thanks."

Rose Ann crossed her arms and observed Maya clinically, one stem of her glasses notched in her teeth. After a moment, she stepped in and slid the sound-proof glass door closed behind her. "Frankly, my dear," she said, "you've looked dog tired since January. Care to comment?"

Maya sensed a trap. "Have I?"

"At first I assumed you were pregnant, but you

don't appear to be showing. And there was all that gin."

"Jesus, Rose Ann. No, I'm not pregnant."

"That's reassuring. No terminal illness, one assumes."

"I'm fine," Maya said. "Everything's fine."

Rose Ann glanced at the archives stacked on the deck, representing Maya's first six-odd months in the Twin Cities. "I wonder," she said.

"Why are you asking me all this?"

"You mean besides the fact that you're hiding out mooning over auld lang syne in the middle of a working news day?"

"Hiding?" *The door was open,* Maya thought. She tilted her head. "Mooning?"

"Think up your own words if you like."

"Then, yeah," Maya said. "Besides that."

Rose Ann came over and sat down against the edge of the console. She took a moment to arrange herself, then settled her hands in her lap. "Culling from my vast and varied experience, there's only one other condition I can think of that makes a good reporter look the way you do. Perhaps it's time we paused to evaluate the situation."

"You say that like there's a situation."

"A manageable one, I hope."

"And what is it you think we're up against?"

Once more, Rose Ann looked at the younger Maya frozen on the monitor screen, half blurred. She looked at the Maya in the chair. Eyeglasses folded in one hand, battle-scarred BlackBerry in the other, she smiled a little too kindly and said, "We all get tired."

We don't know how to measure tired, Maya

thought, but she said nothing. The air in the sound-sealed pod suddenly felt too compressed. Tupperware for newspeople.

"Want to talk about it?"

"I thought you wanted this for the six?"

"I think we can safely spare a few minutes."

Maya pretended to check her watch. Rose Ann waited. After the silence had stretched to a point she deemed long enough, Rose Ann said, "Do you want to know what I think?"

"Sure," Maya said.

"I think we reach . . . points. Mile markers, call them. Fiftieth birthdays, five year anniversaries. These are random examples."

"Of mile markers. I'm following you."

"Places where it seems perfectly natural to stop and look back." Rose Ann shrugged. "I think that News7's Maya Lamb has reached a mile marker."

News7's Maya Lamb said nothing.

"The question is, when you look around, what do you see?"

That was the question, Maya thought, mildly annoyed with Rose Ann for hitting the target with so little effort. The truth was, she'd been sitting here wondering where that other Maya on the monitor screen had gone. And she didn't know the answer.

Looking at the monitor, what she saw was a dewy young hotshot filled to the brim with ambition and goals. At the time this piece had aired, she'd just arrived from her previous station, serving a much smaller market in the bluffs of western Iowa, where she'd broken a career story involving vigilante cops, an accused pedophile, and a teenager who'd thrown herself from a bridge. That earlier Maya had barely gotten her desk here in order when Wade Benson swerved into Becky Morse's path.

In the five years since, she'd covered all manner of human suffering: rapes, stabbings, shootings, beatings, fatal car wrecks, fatal boat wrecks, and fatal fires. She'd made a living out of being the first person to show up on people's doorsteps on the worst days of their lives, and Rose Ann was right: She was good at it.

But somewhere along the way, the Maya on the screen had turned into the Maya sitting here in the chair. The Maya who couldn't remember the last time she'd been able to fall asleep at night without Ambien, or gin, or—more and more regularly these days, it seemed—a helping of both. The Maya who hadn't been a bit surprised to learn that Juliet Benson hated her.

The truth? She'd have been surprised to learn otherwise.

"This Benson story," Rose Ann said. "You've covered worse."

Maya thought of the I-35 bridge collapse during rush hour. She thought of the young couple in New Hope who'd found their infant son cold and blue in his crib. She thought all the way back to her teen bridge-jumper in Clark Falls. Worse? Better? Equally bad?

"Why does this one get under your skin, do you think? Apart from being a mile marker."

For a mile marker, it looks a lot like the same place I started, Maya thought.

What she said was, "I don't know." Then she gave

it an honest thought and added, "But I could use a happy ending for a change."

Rose Ann held her gaze a moment. Grinned. "I was going to say a raise and a vacation," she said. "But whatever makes you feel better."

Maya stuck out her tongue, not realizing that it would be more than ten hours before she laid eyes on Wade Benson again, without a happy ending anywhere in sight. A vacation would have been nice. Starting a week ago. It was 3:41 p.m.

The Hennepin County Adult Corrections Facility housed six hundred residents and an institutional worm farm on an eighty-acre tract of land between two small lakes, some twelve miles northwest, and a world apart, from privileged Linden Hills.

Deon got them there in the live truck at ten minutes past four. They rolled up through the line of young budding trees on either side of Shenandoah Lane. They parked in the visitor's lot of the main building: a squat, art deco brick edifice that rose from two wings in a chevron-tipped tower and accommodated, alongside various administrative units, the men's detention section. At 4:15, they entered the public lobby through the big double doors in front, right on schedule.

By 4:30, Maya smelled something rotten.

At 4:45, she began to lose patience. By 4:55, she'd lost diplomacy.

"We're scheduled to meet with Officer Hanscomb," she told the detention officer now stonewalling them. Officer Brooks, according to the nameplate pinned to the right chest of his duty shirt. He looked like a slab of beef with a mustache and behaved, Maya couldn't help noticing, like a total penis. "Corrections approved this three days ago."

"I'm not aware of that schedule," he said.

"Which is why I'm asking to speak with Officer Hanscomb."

"Yeah, but you're not asking nice, though."

"May I please speak with Officer Hanscomb?"

"If she had anything to speak to you about, I expect she'd be the one out here speaking to you," Brooks said. "Instead of lucky lucky me."

What was it with this guy? In Maya's view they could have been perfectly civil with one another, but, no, he wanted to break her balls for some reason. She shone her brightest TV smile in his face and motioned to Deon, who put the camera on his shoulder. "In that case, should I be talking to you instead?"

"I wasn't aware you'd stopped." The two-way radio on the detention officer's belt beeped twice, then chattered softly. Brooks batted his eyelashes for the camera and stepped a few paces away to answer the call.

Deon said, "I don't think he wants to talk to you, Maya Lamb."

"You got that, huh?" In the past quarter hour, a pair of uniformed sherrif's deputies had materialized outside, in front of the building. They appeared to be standing post on either side of the entrance doors. Maya looked around the empty wooden benches lining the vacant waiting area and said, "What's going on around here?"

Deon shrugged, working a ragged toothpick from one corner of his mouth to the other. He turned with the camera and found the cops outside through his viewfinder.

Officer Brooks came back, radio on his belt. "Congratulations," he said. "Officer Hanscomb is en route."

"En route?"

"That's a law-enforcement word. It means you can wait over there."

"Actually it's two words," Maya said. "A phrase, if you want to get technical."

"Hey, I know another phrase," Brooks said, but he was interrupted by the door to the secure area behind them, which buzzed, then opened. A woman emerged into the waiting area, striding briskly beneath the arm of another officer holding the door for her. Her ID badge jounced on a lanyard around her neck.

"Well, that wasn't such a long wait," Maya said.

Brooks smirked at her.

"Miss Lamb," the woman said, extending a hand as she approached. She stood five feet flat and weighed all of fourteen ounces in slacks and a blouse, with a springy mop of curly blond hair, owlish eyeglasses, and straight white teeth that seemed half a size too large for her mouth. "Jackie Hanscomb. I apologize for the confusion. And for making you wait."

"Not at all," Maya said. She felt like a giant shaking Hanscomb's small hand. "Has something come up?"

"You could say that." Hanscomb pressed her lips together in a grim line, and Maya got a good look at her eyes. Efficient posture aside, the diminutive media officer looked as though she'd come through some kind of wringer this afternoon. "I'm afraid I won't be able to grant your interview after all."

It wasn't even supposed to have been an interview, Maya thought. Just a quick bit of B-roll, then done. She said, "Can you tell me why?"

"If you're able to spare fifteen minutes, I have somebody you can talk to." She nodded politely at Deon. "But not the camera. I'm sorry."

Maya glanced at Deon. He worked his toothpick, shrugged, lowered his camera. She turned back to Hanscomb and said, "I'm all yours."

"All right, then. Please come with me."

To Deon, Maya said, "Call the station, will you? Tell Miles I'll touch base in fifteen."

"Happy to," Deon said, crumpled pack of smokes already in hand. "Let's see if I can get a better signal outside."

The detective from the Hennepin County Sheriff's Office was a new face to Maya. He looked to be somewhere in his forties, wore shirtsleeves and dress pants, a clip holster and a wedding ring, apparently took care of himself, and met her with a far more collegial disposition than had Officer Brooks in the waiting area. "Roger Barnhill," he said, shaking her hand. "Nice to meet you."

"Likewise," she said, still gaining her bearings. Hanscomb had brought her down a hall and up a flight of stairs to the jail superintendent's office, which had a bank of security monitors on one wall, leather-bound volumes of the *Annotated Minnesota Statutes* going back to the 1950s on another, and a massive old wooden office desk in between. Against the edge of the desk leaned the superintendent himself, Terry Spilker, whom Maya had met a couple of times before. "Terry, nice to see you again."

"Always," Spilker said. He unfolded his arms and stepped over to join in on the hand-shaking. "Apart from the circumstances."

"Yeah, I was wondering about those." Maya looked around the faces in the room: Spilker, Detective Barnhill, Jackie Hanscomb, and a tall, well-heeled man she knew to be Morton Clay, Benson family attorney. Clay, who hadn't approved of Maya's presence in the first place, appeared to have softened on that point. Other than that, none of the faces told her much. "I can't help feeling like I'm missing something."

"I think we're all still getting up to speed," Barnhill said. "Thanks for the time, I know you're short on it. Frankly, so am I, and I believe we may be in a position to help each other."

"Is there something News7 can do for the sheriff's office today?"

"That's what I'd like to talk to you about. Officer Hanscomb tells me you came to the facility in a broadcast truck. Is that right?"

"Yes, that's right. I'm scheduled to go live from here top of the hour."

"I'm going to share some information with you," Barnhill said. "Some of it I need to go out on the air to the public as soon as possible. Most of it I need to stay in this office. For now."

"That's not something police normally say to reporters," Maya said.

"No, I don't suppose it is. But I want you to understand the situation fully."

Her senses were on full tingle now. "I appreciate that."

"First, some ground rules."

"What kind of ground rules?"

"If you agree to keep a tight lid on everything I want you to hold back, then I won't hold back anything," Detective Barnhill said. "And when your competition from the other affiliates and the print outlets show up, I'll remember all the trust you and I have established."

"By observing the ground rules," she said.

Barnhill touched a finger to his nose. "As long as you hold up your end of the deal, no other reporter gets any information from me that you didn't get first. I'll give you my word on that. Your thoughts?"

Maya thought that this man Barnhill from the sheriff's detectives was already planning a press conference in his head, and he didn't appear to be enjoying it. She glanced at Morton Clay in the corner. Benson's attorney didn't appear to be enjoying it either. She said, "I'd say that sounds doable."

"Then we have an agreement." Without further preamble, the detective walked over to the desk, where Maya saw two matching BlackBerry mobile phones sitting side by side on top of a plain manila file folder. "What I'm about to show you falls under the stuff-we-keep-in-this-office category."

Maya nodded.

Barnhill picked up one of the phones. "This is Cheryl Benson's PDA." He picked up the other phone, so that he now held one in each hand. "This one belongs to her husband. Mr. Benson arrived here at the facility just over an hour ago. Shortly after that time, both phones received the same transmission, copied simultaneously."

"What kind of transmission?"

Barnhill fiddled with one of the phones, then brought it over to Maya. "Remember," he said. "Inside this office only."

Maya took the device and looked at the screen. At first she couldn't make sense of what she saw there. "Is that . . ." She looked closer. Her pulse spiked. "Is this Juliet Benson?"

"Her parents assure me it is."

Maya drew in a breath.

"What you see there was sent from Juliet's phone," Barnhill told her. "Whoever sent it went through and picked *Mom* and *Dad* out of the girl's contact list. That phone, hers, is now offline."

"Holy shit." Maya stared at the image in the palm of her hand: a digital photo, presumably taken with the camera on board Juliet Benson's phone. The resolution wasn't great, but the image was legible enough for Maya to recognize Wade Benson's daughter, bound and gagged in the trunk of a car. "When did you say this came in?"

"Three fifty-seven this afternoon, according to the time stamp."

Maya took another look at the image. It was difficult to absorb the details; her mind kept straining to run ahead of her. *I just talked to you,* she thought.

As if reading her mind, Barnhill said, "I understand that you also may have video images of Miss Benson from earlier today. Her general appearance, what she was wearing, et cetera. Is that correct?"

Maya felt herself nodding. She couldn't stop looking at the PDA screen. In the photo, Juliet Benson's pretty dark hair clung to the grimy carpet of the trunk floor beneath her head in wet, matted tendrils. Her mouth had been stuffed with some kind of rag and tied with what appeared to be the belt of her own raincoat. Above the gag, her eyes swam with fear.

"Around her wrists," Maya said, squinting. "Are those flex cuffs?"

"Possibly," Barnhill said. He didn't elaborate. Maya finally noticed him standing patiently, palm out.

She pulled herself together, shook her head, handed the BlackBerry back to him. "And that's all there is?"

"That's all."

"No note? Anything?"

"Just what I've showed you," Barnhill said. "Our office is preparing a press release to the other outlets now. But you're here, and I'm new to this county, and I believe it's time I made a friend in the TV business."

"I feel like we're old pals already," Maya said. "What do you know that won't be in the press release?"

"I haven't seen a draft yet, so I'd say that determination is ongoing," Barnhill said. "What we know so far is that Juliet Benson has a two-o'clock class on Wednesdays and that she attended class today. We know that she missed a study date at a coffee shop off campus at four o'clock. I have deputies on campus now, and Minneapolis PD is supporting us there. Personnel from that group have determined that the girl's car is not currently located in the student parking lot she normally uses. According to Mr. Benson, it could be her car in the photo, but there's not enough for him to make a positive ID. Either way, the Bolo call on that vehicle went out over police channels twenty minutes ago."

Listening to all of this, Maya couldn't help extrapolating time frames in her head. A two-o'clock class, a four-o'clock study date. It was entirely possible, she realized, that at the very time she and Rose Ann had been sitting around at the station, chatting about happy endings, Juliet Benson was being forced into the trunk of her own car.

Detective Barnhill went back to the desk, replaced the phones, and picked up the file folder. From inside the folder he took a sheet of paper with another photograph—a good old-fashioned print this time—paper-clipped to the corner.

"This is part of what's going out to everybody," he said, handing the page to Maya. "Juliet Benson's full description, our hotline info, so forth. This photograph came from her mother's purse and I'm told it's recent, though certainly not as recent as whatever footage you've obtained. You've done the rest before, I assume."

"Police are seeking the public's assistance in locating a Minneapolis woman," Maya said, appraising the new photo: Cheryl Benson and her daughter in tennis dresses, arm in arm. Juliet had her dad's eyes and her mother's smile. Maya looked at Detective Barnhill. "Surely we're using the word missing?"

"Missing and endangered," Barnhill said. "We'll want to name the campus as her last known location, mark the time at three p.m. this afternoon. Everything else . . ."

"Authorities have yet to disclose further details," Maya said.

At last, Benson's attorney spoke up from his spot in the corner. "Detective, about the reward."

Maya looked at Clay. Looked at Barnhill. Detective Barnhill took what seemed like a measured breath, then nodded toward the page in Maya's hand. "Mr. Clay's firm wishes to secure a private cash reward for any information leading to Miss Benson's safe return. That information is also included on the sheet you have there."

Maya looked back at Morton Clay. He seemed unsatisfied but remained silent. She slipped the photograph free of its clip. "Do you have a soft copy of this?"

"Our public-information office does. Give me an email address and I'll tell them where to send it."

Maya was already eyeballing the multifunction office printer on Terry Spilker's desk. "That has a scanner, right?"

Spilker nodded. "If you know how to run the thing. I don't."

"May I?"

"By all means."

Five minutes later, from behind Terry Spilker's computer monitor, Maya used the superintendent's office phone to call Miles Oltman at the station.

"Ticktock," her assignment editor said. "How we doing?"

"I sent you something," Maya told him. "Check your mail, you should be—"

"It just popped up. Hang on." A pause. She heard Miles tapping away on his laptop in the background. In a moment he came back on the line. "Okay, what am I looking at?"

"Tonight's top story, I'd think," Maya said.

5

By five o'clock Mike felt more or less human. He took three Vicodins for his leg and stayed a long time in the shower, then shaved, brushed his teeth, and got dressed. By the time he was finished, he'd organized a rough order of business in his head. First item on the list: Eat something.

The cupboards were bare, so Mike grabbed his jacket, locked up the house, and walked over to Hal's place. The Elbow Room wasn't licensed to serve food, but each day Hal made up a couple dozen ham sandwiches with mayo and mustard, wrapped them in plastic, and loaded them into the cooler under the bar. Hal didn't advertise the sandwiches, but if you knew to ask, he'd sell you one on a napkin with a beer or whatever you were drinking for a buck or two extra. What he didn't sell by last call he took the next morning to the soup kitchen over by Como Park Lutheran. Mike had gotten to like those sandwiches.

The rain had quit, and the air smelled like early morning instead of late afternoon. Mike breathed it in through the nose as he walked, let it freshen up the inside of his head. It was still cool for April, but they'd finally turned the corner on winter; he could hear the ground sucking and popping beneath the hump-backed lawns along Front Avenue, thirsty after an early thaw and a cold, sunless March. The robins were out in numbers, hopping about in the wet grass, hunting for earthworms. Mealtime for everybody.

By the time he made it to the Elbow, Mike's stomach was rumbling. He pulled open the door to the clack of pool balls, *Jeopardy!* on the television over the bar, and the scattered voices of a few other early birds getting a head start on happy hour.

"That was a quick trip," Hal said as Mike took a stool. "Fish weren't biting, huh?"

Mike felt like he'd walked in on somebody else's conversation. "Fish?"

Hal brought up a sandwich, pulled a beer to go with it. "I guess you stayed home."

"You lost me at *trip,* Hal. Thanks for the grub." He put a fiver on the bar, which Hal ignored. Mike left the money anyway. He slid the sandwich toward him by the napkin, began undoing the plastic wrap. "What are we talking about?"

Hal chuckled. "Potter came by first thing this morning, asked if he could borrow my place a couple days. Said he needed to dry out, thought he'd see what the walleye were up to. Hell, I didn't have the heart to tell him walleye season don't open 'til May."

Hal owned a little place up in the lake country, a ramshackle cabin on a pretty piece of water he'd inherited from his grandfather twenty years ago. Rockhaven, the older man had named the spot, planting the sign at the end of the long narrow lane that stood today. Mike had used the place himself on occasion, at Hal's invitation, and he'd hauled Darryl along up there one weekend last August, after Darryl got off probation, thinking the peace and quiet could be good medicine for both of them. They'd run out of booze, and then cigarettes, and Darryl had spent the last day sweating, slapping bugs, and crawling out of his skin.

Mike evaluated this news with mixed feelings. On one hand, his chore for the day had gotten easier. On the other hand, Darryl didn't fish.

"That's funny," he told Hal. "I was about to ask if you'd seen him around here today."

"Uh huh." Hal smirked and wiped down the bar. "You ain't the first either."

Shit. Mike took a bite of his sandwich. It tasted better than eleven thousand dollars. "I guess Toby Lunden's been by."

"That's his name? Milky-lookin' kid, glasses like Coke bottles?"

"That's his name," Mike said.

"So that's Mr. Big, huh?" Hal shook his head slowly. "Jesus, I must be older than I thought."

Mike said, "I suppose he probably had a friend with him."

"Shoulder holster. Face like he got in a fistfight with some guy who had hatchets for hands."

"That'd be Bryce. We only just met."

"Yeah, well, they both met the end of my foot kickin' their asses outta here."

Mike couldn't help smiling. "Yeah?"

"You don't bring a gun into my place. Not unless you're a cop. And that asshole wasn't a cop."

"Not to my knowledge, no."

"So," Hal said, ignoring the guy down the bar trying to flag him for another beer. "Who is he? Besides the reason Potter figured he ought to get the hell out of town."

Mike thought about how to answer. He felt bad that any of this horseshit had gotten tracked into Hal's place of business. "I gather there was a miscommunication at the day job," he said.

"I guess there must have been." Hal flopped his towel over a shoulder. "What's he gotten himself into this time?"

"No clue," Mike lied. "You know Darryl."

"Not as well as I know you," Hal said. He went to pull a refill for the guy down the bar, leaving Mike to wonder what that was supposed to mean.

While Hal tended the paying customers, Mike sat on his stool and finished his sandwich and tried to figure out what the hell Darryl thought he was doing up in vacation land with Mike's car and Toby Lunden's money.

But there was just no damn telling. The Skylark might be a piece of crap, but it was the only piece of crap Mike owned, and while on a given day Darryl Potter could have been liable to uncork all sorts of havoc you wouldn't have seen coming, he'd never left Mike stranded before. And that was saying something.

"Hey, look at that," Hal said, wandering back Mike's way. He grabbed the remote from the bar and punched up the volume on the Magnavox. "Speaking of Babe Winkelman Junior. Ain't that his new favorite reporter?"

Mike looked. *Jeopardy!* had given way to the six o'clock news. Hal was right: On-screen was the same reporter they'd all been watching the night before. Maya something—an animal name. Mike couldn't remember. Lamb.

The way she looked, Mike figured she was probably lots of guys' favorite reporter around this time of day. He washed down the last of his sandwich with a gulp of beer, licked mustard off his thumb, and waited to hear what sunny piece of good cheer she had for them today.

Deon got them from Plymouth, through downtown rush-hour traffic, and to the MCAD campus on Stevens Avenue by 5:45. They set up in front of the student parking areas off Third Avenue and 25th, squad cars and yellow cordon tape in the background. At 5:52, Maya held a blank notebook page in front of Deon's lens so he could white-balance the camera. At 5:54, she popped in her earpiece and tested the audio link with her producer at the station.

Fifteen seconds before Rick Gavigan made the toss to her live shot, her producer came back over the link. "Give me an ask to lead you out."

Maya scrambled. Ten seconds. Into the mike, she said, "After I give the hotline number, have Carmen ask me if the police have any further instructions. I'll mention the reward again."

Lame. Whatever. Five seconds.

Her producer's voice came back in her ear: "Instructions, reward, got it. Go."

"Rick, Carmen, thanks," Maya said. Behind the

camera, Deon gave her a thumbs-up. She had the same moment of throat-clenching panic she always felt at the top of a live remote, no matter how many she'd delivered: mind a sudden blank, notes forgotten, wondering how the words would come out of her mouth. Then she took a breath and said, "I'm standing in front of the student parking facilities at the campus of the Minneapolis College of Art and Design," and they were off and running.

Three minutes later, they were out. Deon said, "Way to go, pro."

Maya heard him in one ear, while in the other her producer said, "Stand by. If you get more, we'll break in after sports."

But she was already walking out of the shot.

Deon turned as she passed him. "Um . . . where ya going, Maya Lamb?"

Maya handed him the mike and stripped out the IFB, letting the earpiece hang over her shoulder by the cord. She kept walking toward Third Avenue. She waited for a break in traffic, then hustled across, picking up the tree-lined sidewalk on the opposite side of the street.

Behind her, Deon called, "You know the news is on now, right?"

She ignored him and kept walking, past the ivy-covered apartment buildings facing the college, scanning the cars parked along the east side of the avenue. Something had caught her eye on the way in, though she'd had her mind on more-immediate matters at the time.

But while Deon had set up the gear, she'd found herself looking back the way they'd come. Then, right in the middle of her stand-up, a disturbing thought had popped into her head.

Just beyond the Children's Theatre, she finally found the car she was looking for, still sitting where she'd noticed it the first time: a dented-up, rust-punched Buick Skylark with a cracked windshield and Minnesota plates, burgundy paint job baked dull by the sun.

Maya stood and looked at it. She walked all the way around and returned to the sidewalk.

Nah, she thought, then flashed to the view from Benson's house in Linden Hills. She saw herself standing alone at the wall of glass, looking out over Lake Calhoun, just before Juliet Benson announced herself in the room. Looking out over the lake, and the skyline beyond. And the street below.

She took one last long look at the beat-to-shit Skylark at the curb.

Then she turned and started running. Maya ran back up the sidewalk, back into Third Avenue, not waiting for traffic this time. Tires squealed. A horn blared. She hurried across, as fast as her heels would carry her, all the way to where Deon stood smoking a Parliament. Watching her with interest.

"This morning," she said. "You shot roll outside Benson's house, right?"

Deon nodded. "You know I did. We cut it in the pack."

"The master. Is it in the truck or at the station?"

"Brought it with," Deon said. He tossed his unfinished cigarette in the gutter, where it died with a hiss. "Why?"

Maya grabbed him by the shoulder and pulled him along after her, toward the truck. "Because I think I saw that car," she said.

"What car?"

"That one," she said, jerking a thumb toward the street, remembering the Skylark clearly now. It had looked just as out of place sitting at the curb in front of Benson's house as it looked camouflaged by its surroundings here.

"You mean that one?" Deon said five minutes later, as they crowded around the mobile deck inside the truck.

Maya was already on the phone. Three rings, then a voice in her ear: "Barnhill."

"Detective," she said, belly sizzling as she stared at the image Deon had found for her on the small monitor. "It's Maya Lamb. I think I have something you need to see."

When the news went to commercials, Hal picked up the remote, muted the sound, and stood for a moment, facing the back bar. When he finally turned to Mike, his eyes seemed to express Mike's own thoughts: *Did I see that right?*

The photo of the girl they'd just shown on the news hadn't come from any high school yearbook. But it put Mike immediately in mind of the photo of Becky Morse they'd shown last night. Wade Benson's daughter actually looked a little like her. Not sisters or anything, but not Abbott and Costello. They were even the same age.

The comparison didn't appear to be lost on Hal either. He looked like he was trying to figure out a math problem in his head. Mike didn't know if he wanted to hear the answer Hal came up with.

The bell over the door jingled then, and they both turned to see Regina hurry in, digging in her giant purse with one hand, applying an ambitious smear of candy-colored lipstick by feel with the other. Regina was a part-time waitress at the Elbow Room, a mother of two grown girls who lived away and rarely called, and Hal's third ex-wife. She came over to the bar and planted a fat, lipsticky smooch on Mike's cheek. "Look at you, all clean-shaved," she said. "Handsome devil. Where's Darryl?"

Mike eyed Hal and said nothing. Hal stood with his arms crossed, frowning at the bar. Regina looked back and forth between them. She cocked a hip and planted a fist on it, hoopy bracelets clattering together. "Okay, what did I miss?"

Hal glanced one time at Mike, just long enough to be noticed, and then changed faces. "The start of your damn shift," he said. "But what else is new?"

"Oh, shut up," Regina told him. "I had Jazzercise."

"Well, Jazzercise on back to the time clock and punch in already. Booth four needs a new pitcher."

"I'll punch something," she said, winking at Mike. "Good to see you, hon." She nodded at the five-dollar bill on the bar. "Put that back in your pocket before some old ugly bastard picks it up."

Hal leaned across and swatted Regina's ample backside with his rag. She gave him a smirk and headed toward the back, rooting in her purse all the way.

As soon as she was gone, Hal's expression changed

again. He acknowledged the guys from the garage across the street, who stood waiting for darts at the far end of the bar. Then he glanced at Mike one last time and said, "Stay put, friend. I want to talk to you."

6

Mike wasn't sure how long he sat there, feeling Regina's moist lipstick print on the side of his face, staring at the muted television as the rest of the bar noise faded to static in the background.

All he knew was that the evening news kept on playing up there on the dumbstruck Magnavox, as if you couldn't look out the window and see the weather for yourself, and at some point Regina took over for Hal behind the bar. Then Hal put a firm hand on Mike's shoulder, and Mike felt himself get up off the stool and follow the man. Past the wrench monkeys throwing darts in the corner. Past the game of eight ball clacking around the pool table in back. Down the cramped hall, past the bathrooms, through the dusty stock room stacked with cases of booze. All the way to the glorified supply closet Hal used for an office.

"Sit," Hal said. He pointed to a metal folding chair with most of the paint worn off. The voice he used was not the endearingly gruff barkeep who wouldn't let Mike Barlowe pay for drinks or ham sandwiches; this was the born-hard gunny sergeant Mike knew Hal Macklin to have been in his life but had never glimpsed for himself before just now.

Mike sat.

Hal shut the door. Firmly. He came around and leaned against the invoice-littered desk in the corner, facing Mike in the chair. He crossed his arms and studied the floor a minute, then looked up and said, "Tell me what you know."

"Hal, I know what you know," Mike said. It was mostly true but felt like mostly a lie, and he couldn't make himself meet Hal's eyes.

Right there he lives, Mike kept thinking. It was all he kept thinking, remembering the sight of Wade Benson's sleeping glass house from the curb between last call and dawn. The promising glimmer of the city beyond the lake. The look in Darryl's eyes. *Some punishment, huh?*

Had that actually been the last thing he'd heard the guy say?

Mike couldn't remember. He remembered it had been a quiet ride home.

"Son," Hal said. "I'm not asking."

Mike exhaled carefully. His leg was starting to hurt. He said, "He was bent out of shape about that architect when we left your place last night."

"Yeah, he was," Hal said. "I was here. And so were you."

Mike started to tell Hal about their after-hours joyride over to Lake Calhoun, but at the last minute he swerved away and said, "He was gone when I woke up today, and he's not answering his phone. It sounds like he took some money that didn't belong to him, and he took my car. After that I'm in the dark, Hal. Believe me."

Hal leaned against the desk with his arms folded,

scowling at the floor. The next time he spoke—and it took a minute, long enough that Mike started to hope maybe the conversation was over—he spoke very quietly, and he didn't raise his eyes.

"Is it possible he went and took that girl?"

Mike didn't know how to answer. He rubbed his eyes. "Possible covers a lot of ground."

"Don't hand me that shit. You served with him, kid. You fought next to him. You're the guy took him in when he showed up here without a pot to piss in or a goddamn friend in the world." Hal finally put Mike directly in his high beams. "So I'm asking you, and it's the last time I'm asking, so take a goddamn minute before you open your mouth. Could he have taken that man's daughter or not?"

Mike took more than a minute. He wanted to say that he couldn't imagine it. The only problem was that Mike had seen enough crazy shit in his time that he could imagine just about anything if he tried, and, deep down, he'd already answered Hal's question.

Hal didn't need to hear him say it. He shook his head. "Christ."

"Hal?" Mike sat up. "Where you going?"

"Where the hell you think I'm going?" Hal had already returned to the door. "I'm gonna write down that number they've got up there on the TV screen, come back here, and dial it." He paused and cocked his head. "Does that spook-eyed son of a bitch have it in his head that I wouldn't? Because we used to wear the same initials?" He held up his forearm and smacked the old tattoo there with the flat of his hand. "Do *you*?"

"No," Mike said. "Hal, wait a second."

"Wants to use my place. *My* goddamn place."

"That's what I mean." Maybe this was like a bad episode from one of those cops-and-lawyers shows on television: Some guy in a bar blurts out how he'd sure like to teach so-and-so a lesson. Next morning, so-and-so turns up dead, and who's the main suspect? Everybody goes apeshit looking for him, but then surprise: They all find that the guy who made the threat was really off screwing somebody's wife when the murder happened. "If Darryl was . . . Look, he sure as hell wouldn't tell anybody where he was going, right? Why would he do that?"

"Because he's a goddamn head case," Hal said.

"Yeah, well, who isn't?"

Hal snorted. But he was listening.

"Anyway, he's not stupid."

"You say."

"Pretty far from it, Hal. Trust me."

Hal shook his head again. Still listening.

"Give me a chance to get up there and see what's what," Mike said. He rose from the chair and joined Hal at the door. "He's probably just hacked off at Toby, trying to make a point."

"Yeah? What kind of a point would that be?"

"A memorable one?"

"Don't be a wiseass."

"I'm just saying, one thing might not have anything to do with the other."

"Might not," Hal said. "And if it does?"

"Hal, this girl's been missing, what, a couple hours? Come on. She could be anywhere."

"Yeah, and she could be somewhere real specific, too," Hal said. "Could be there right now while we're standing here talking about it. You'd better think about that, son."

Mike hadn't stopped thinking about it. None of it made any sense. Making sense wasn't always a priority with Darryl, but still. "It's a couple hours to Rockhaven," he said.

"I know where the hell it is."

"Hal, give me a head start. If he's up there alone, playing some game on Toby, I can sort it out. Without a bunch of cops."

The way the muscles in Hal's jaws rippled, Mike could tell that he was grinding his teeth. "If he's not?"

"Hal . . ."

"If it turns out he was up there helping himself to this girl while you and me were busy making deals? I guess you won't mind carrying that around, huh?" Hal gave Mike a withering look. "I guess you won't mind if I have to either."

Mike took care not to answer too quickly. He took care to stand straight and to address Hal without direct eye contact, indicating that he was at full attention, not at ease. He took care to make sure that he believed his own answer before he spoke it. He found that what he believed, in his gut, was that Darryl Potter was a lot of things, not all of them charming, and not many of them predictable. But he wasn't *this* thing.

"If I thought that was a possibility," he said, "this conversation wouldn't be happening. I promise you that."

Hal said nothing. He only grimaced. Folded his arms.

"I'll check in," Mike said. "You'll hear from me by closing time. Promise you that too."

"Closing time, huh? Is that all?"

Of course it was asking for too much, but Mike wanted room to negotiate if necessary. "Not a minute later."

Hal looked him over. "Tell me how I hear from you."

"I'll call, Hal. By closing time, if not before."

"You'll call?"

Mike started to repeat himself, to guarantee it, then understood the question for what it was: a trap.

No phones at Rockhaven. No cell signals either. He could have guessed Hal's next words: *Well, you've just thought this through up down and sideways, haven't you, son?*

"From town," he said. "Or the highway."

Hal stood with the same hard look on his face. "Got it all figured out. Is that right?"

"No, sir." Mike faced Hal. He took a breath, reached deep down and way back, and said, "But Corporal Potter served under my command, and I believe my judgment of his nature to be sound." He lowered his eyes to the door knob between them, waiting to be turned. "I wouldn't ask you if I didn't."

Hal was quiet a long time.

Mike waited.

Hal said, "I guess the next thing you'll tell me is you need to borrow a damn car."

7

Mike left the Elbow Room at a quarter past seven with the spare keys to Hal Macklin's old Dodge pickup in his jacket pocket. Hal lived over the bar but kept the truck on hand for errands and the occasional Sunday afternoon keg delivery, though, according to Hal, the truck needed plugs and a new solenoid before he'd trust it on a road trip. He made a deal with the grease monkeys throwing darts: free pitchers through the weekend if they could open the garage and get the work done inside the hour.

Mike walked to the end of the alley and found the Dodge in the lot behind the building, where Hal told him it would be. His plan: run the truck across the street, walk home, grab some cash, his Vicodin, some outerwear, maybe a coffee thermos, anything else he figured he'd need and could carry with him. With any luck, by the time he got back, the guys would have him ready to roll out of town.

He'd climbed into the cab when his jacket pocket chirped. Mike dug out his phone and saw a text message from Tanya Ellerbe:

Where r u??

Nobody he knew sent him text messages, including Tanya. Mike hated trying to string together an answer one character at a time, and by the time he finished he could have called the person. Hell, they were already using phones.

He fiddled with the buttons, looking for the command that let you automatically dial back the incoming number. While he was doing that, the phone chirped again.

Cops @ yr house rite now. 4 Darryl.

Mike had to read the words twice. He sat behind the wheel of Hal's truck in the fading daylight, staring into the bright glow of the phone's small display screen, thinking, *Shit*.

Chirp.

4 U 2!

Double shit.
Now what? Mike tried to think.
Chirp.

! ! !

"All right, cripes, gimme a second," he said to the phone. He looked around, as though anyone else might have reason to be back here on this weedy patch of asphalt. But there wasn't anybody else. He was alone.

Mike cobbled a reply as quickly as he could tap out the letters with this thumbs:

copy—call me soon as u can talk ok?

He hit SEND. In a few seconds, the screen told him the message had gone where it was supposed to go.

Mike couldn't think of anything else to do after that but sit there and wait, so he tossed the phone onto the seat beside him and started the truck. It took him two or three tries. He hoped those guys from the garage had finished their dart game.

Dobry Automotive opened at 6:00 a.m. and closed at 6:00 p.m. every day but Sunday, according to the sign out front. Apparently, exceptions could be made.

The guys were waiting for Mike when he arrived. Their names were Ray and Wayne, he learned. One of them rolled up the door to the service bay while the other brought him in with hand signals, stopping him with a show of his palms. When they were set, Mike cut the engine, got out, and said, "Guys, you're really helping me out here."

"Don't sweat it," Wayne told him. Or maybe it was Ray. One was taller, but they didn't have names on their coveralls, and they both had beards. Being distracted, Mike had already lost track. He felt bad meeting them this way; he'd seen them maybe three or four hundred times at the Elbow, always in the same corner after they got off work, and he'd never once bothered to exchange much more than a nod with either one of them. They didn't seem concerned about it.

"Take a load off," Wayne or Ray said, leading him through a door to a customer waiting area. "Parts are in stock, shouldn't be long."

"Thanks," Mike said, genuinely meaning it, but WayneRay had already left him. Mike caught the broadside of his back as he lumbered out into the shop, where RayWayne had his head under the hood of the Dodge.

Mike took a seat in the deserted lounge, which had a few chairs, a few issues of *Field & Stream* magazine, and a lonely, after-hours vibe. A cold, forgotten inch of complimentary coffee sat in the pot on the counter. A girl in a bikini smiled at him from the muscle car calendar on the wall. He could hear a faint electric buzz coming from the ancient yellowed *Drink Dr Pepper!* clock hanging over the coffeepot. The clock said it was 7:36.

At 7:53, the door to the service bay opened again. WayneRay leaned in, held out Mike's phone between two thick, grime-stained fingers, and said, "This rang a couple times."

Crap, Mike thought, only then realizing he'd left the phone behind in the truck. He had to get his head screwed on straight. He went over to the door, took the phone. "Sorry about that."

"Don't sweat it," WayneRay said. Back to work.

Mike flipped the phone open. Tanya had tried him three times in the past three minutes, according to the caller-ID log. Mike wasn't sure whether to call her back or wait, but the phone rang in his hand while he was standing there wondering.

"Hey," he answered. "I'm here."

"Mike, good grief," Tanya said. "Where are you?"

"Not far," he said. "What's going on?"

"You tell me," she said. The way she paused, it sounded to Mike as if she was smoking a cigarette.

Last he knew, she'd quit a while ago. "The house is totally crawling with cops."

"Yeah, I got your message. You went by there?"

"They called me," she said. "To come open the place up."

"The cops called you?"

"An hour ago. I'm at the curb out front right now, watching them go in and out. So are all the neighbors."

"Jesus, Tanya. I'm sorry." Mike tried to run through possibilities. There seemed like a lot of them all of a sudden. "Did they show you a warrant?"

"Oh, they showed me a warrant." Puff. Exhale. "They showed me a warrant, all right."

"What does it say?"

"It says your name, Mike. On the first page." Puff. "Want to know what else it says?"

"Tell me."

Tanya was quiet a moment. "You already know," she said. "Don't you? I can hear it in your voice."

The house is totally crawling, she'd said. Not exactly a standard police response for a guy wanted in connection with sticking up a steakhouse. His heart sank. "I have a guess."

"Jesus God," she said softly.

"I don't think he's involved," Mike said, believing it less now than when he'd said the same thing to Hal. But then the logic in what Tanya was telling him fell apart. "Wait, back up a minute. Before you told me they were looking for Darryl."

"They are now," Tanya said. "I told them why you called me this afternoon. They asked me all kinds of questions about you, and I haven't said much, Mike, but I'm not liking this. I'm not liking this at all."

"Why are they looking for me?"

"Because they found your car."

"The Skylark?"

"No, the Rolls."

Mike felt something click in his throat. "Where?"

"I don't know, but they found it somewhere. Does it really matter?"

No, Mike thought. He supposed it probably didn't. Wherever they'd found his car, he was forced to accept the obvious: The police had tied the Skylark to Juliet Benson somehow. Which pretty much blew his hopes of a coincidence out of the water once and for all.

"Your address is on the registration," Tanya said. "I guess they checked the county records, found out who owned the house. Woo-hoo, here I am." Puff. Exhale. "I'm sorry, I don't mean to be a bitch, but this is . . . I don't even know what this is. They asked me what I knew about the girl too. Juliet?"

"Yeah," Mike said.

"Mike, what have you gotten yourself into?"

I haven't done anything, he wanted to say, but that seemed beside the point.

"The place was already a wreck when I got here, by the way," Tanya said. "It looked like somebody had come in and turned everything upside down."

Mike spoke by rote, mind elsewhere. "We had to let the maid go."

"I'm glad you think this is so funny."

"I'm sorry," he said. "It's not funny."

"No, it isn't. At all." Tanya dropped her voice again. "Did you find Darryl or not?"

"Not," he said. It was technically the truth, and he was starting to get paranoid, talking on the phone. "I'll make all this up to you, Tanya. I promise. Thanks for the heads-up."

"Hey, you wait a minute," Tanya said. "You're on your way over here, right? You're going to tell these guys Darryl took your car hours ago, and you haven't talked to him, and you have no idea where he is. Right?"

Mike was quiet too long.

"Because if you don't," Tanya said, "then I'm washing my hands. Are you listening? I'm not covering for anybody on this. Not for Mr. You-Know-Who. And not for you either, Mike. Not for this."

"Tanya—"

"Look, I know there's something you're not telling me, but I'm not going to be in this position. Okay? And you shouldn't be either."

"Tanya, I'm not asking you to cover for anyone," Mike told her. "Not for me or Mr. Anybody."

"Good, because I won't."

"I'm just sort of tied up right now."

"Bullshit. Who is this girl they're trying to find?"

"I don't know her."

"Bullshit. Where are you?"

"I really am sorry, Tanya. Thanks for the info. I'll sort this thing out."

"Mike—"

"Just cooperate and tell them whatever you can tell them. Okay? I'll take care of it."

"Goddammit, you'd better not hang up on me."

"Gotta go," he said, and hung up on her.

Mike pinched the bridge of his nose until his eyes watered. He felt like an asshole, but more talk wasn't going to get anybody anywhere; if anything, the longer he kept Tanya on the phone, sucking down cigarettes and stealing glances over her shoulder, the worse it would look for her to any cop who happened to be watching.

What had they found in the house? What had he overlooked? How long before these cops found their way over to Hal's place?

What the hell was happening at Rockhaven?

Tanya was right. The thing to do—the only thing he should even be thinking about doing—was to get back to the house, find whoever was in charge over there, and spill all he could. Starting with Darryl at the bar last night, and ending with the directions to Hal's cabin. He should stop by the Elbow first, long enough to bring Hal up to speed. The man had trusted him against his better judgment; if he'd known the new score, he'd never have gone along.

Mike knew all these things in his gut, the same way he knew to back off from a growling dog. The way he knew right from wrong.

The same way he knew you didn't leave a buddy in the soup. The way Darryl had known the same thing, in another life, on the other side of the world. Known it *without* standing around thinking about it. Like breathing.

Christ, what a mess.

Mike turned off the phone. As an afterthought, he removed the battery too. In case of what, he didn't know, but he'd heard tales about what the cops could do about locating cell phones. He didn't really know what was true and what was bullshit, but there was no sense taking any chances.

He checked the Dr Pepper clock—8:13.

Behind him there came the muffled sound of an engine turning over, followed by the steady grumble of a big old V8. He went over to the door and looked out the window into the service bay. WayneRay sat behind the wheel of the Dodge, one leg hanging out the open door. RayWayne stood by the front bumper, wiping his hands on a greasy rag. When he held his thumb up, WayneRay cut the motor.

Mike pulled open the door and went out. "You guys are fast," he said.

RayWayne nodded. "Cheap too."

"Don't fill out the customer-satisfaction card or anything," WayneRay said, climbing out of the cab. "Boss don't normally give out free starters."

"I can pay for the parts," Mike said. He thought of the five-dollar bill in his wallet. Then he thought of his bank account. He said, "You know, next time I see you."

RayWayne took down the prop arm and let the hood drop. The sound of the slam echoed tightly in the space. WayneRay waved a hand. "Don't sweat it," he said. "Boss is a dick anyway."

Toby Lunden didn't know who made him more nervous: the guy he'd been looking for all day, or the guy his uncle had sent to help find him.

Bryce sat in the passenger seat of the Navigator, watching Potter's place through a pair of compact field binoculars. "You know what?" he said. "I sorta can't wait to meet this fuckhead."

"Maybe we should just, you know. Get out of here," Toby said.

Bryce smirked beneath the binocs. "Don't want your money anymore, huh?"

They were parked curbside at the far end of the block, around the corner, off the radar. At least Toby hoped they were off the radar. He was starting to feel sick to his stomach.

Since this afternoon, cops had descended on Potter and Barlowe's place like ants on a candy bar; from where they sat, Toby could see uniforms talking to the neighbors, eyeballing the street. There were squad units parked around, from the county and St. Paul PD both, plus an unmarked in the driveway, poking out from the carport. A couple of the squads still had their flashers going, strobing the neighborhood red and blue. Toby didn't like any of it. He was a numbers guy.

"I can't believe he called the cops," he said. "What an asshole."

"Who?"

"Nathaniel."

"Who?"

Toby said, "What do you mean, who? My guy."

"Your guy."

"From the restaurant. The whole reason we're out here?"

Bryce didn't lower the binoculars. "This is something different."

"What else could it be?"

"There's a question," Bryce said. "By the way, kid? Piece of advice?"

"What?"

Bryce looked at him. "Mind your tone when you speak to me."

Toby felt his scalp tingle. His mouth went dry. Bryce said it sort of casual, but, Jesus, something about this guy's eyes. Toby dropped his own automatically. "Yeah, man, sure. Sorry."

Silence. Toby sat still. He felt the car getting smaller.

"Apology accepted," Bryce said, and raised the binocs again.

They'd been there maybe another ten minutes, watching the action down the street, when Toby's mobile went off. He jumped so hard at the sudden ring in the quiet of the car that his seat belt locked, holding him in place. Jesus, he was on edge.

Bryce chuckled. The phone kept ringing. Bryce said, "You thinking about getting that?"

Toby took a breath, grabbed the phone out of its cradle. He saw who was calling and answered, "Hey, Uncle Buck."

"How's the hunting?" his uncle said.

Toby wasn't quite sure what to tell him. "Um . . . it sort of got kind of weird."

"Oh?"

"Kind of."

For some reason Uncle Buck didn't sound surprised. "I just got a tip from a state patrol buddy of mine," he said. "Tell me again, what's the name of this nut you're lookin' for?"

"Darryl," Toby said.

"There a last name goes with that?"

"Potter. Darryl Potter."

"Huh," Uncle Buck said. "That's what I thought you told me."

Toby didn't understand. "You got a what from who?"

"A tip," Uncle Buck repeated. "From a buddy of mine. With the state patrol."

"A tip about Darryl?"

"That's the name I got here, yeah."

"Why?"

"For the show," Uncle Buck said.

"Oh," Toby said. "Wait. What?"

"One thing at a time, champ. Where are you now?"

"St. Paul," Toby said. "North End, where Potter lives. There's cops all over his house."

"I expect there would be." Uncle Buck seemed inexplicably pleased to be hearing this. "Bryce still with you?"

"Yeah."

"Good. Put him on a sec."

Toby wanted to ask what was going on, but he knew Uncle Buck. It was better if you didn't make him ask twice for things. He handed the phone to Bryce and said, "It's my uncle."

"So I gathered," Bryce said, still watching the house through the binoculars.

"He wants to talk to you."

Bryce took the phone with one hand, kept the binoculars in place with the other. He put the phone to his ear and said, "I'm here."

Toby tried to make out the conversation by listening to Bryce's end of it, but Bryce didn't give him anything to go on besides an occasional *yeah* or an *uh-huh* and one sort of vague-sounding *no shit.*

After a minute he finally said, "Got it," and handed the phone back to Toby. Toby put the phone to his ear, but the line had already gone dead.

He looked at Bryce. "What did he say?"

Bryce smirked under the binoculars. "He said he'd keep in touch."

"Come on, man," Toby said. "Seriously. What about Darryl?"

"Yep," Bryce said. "Still the question."

Mike killed twenty minutes at the Go Shop on the corner. He gassed up the Dodge, then hit the ATM inside and withdrew as much cash as he could without tripping the twenty-dollar minimum on the account. He used some of the cash to buy a bottle of ibuprofen, a thermal travel mug full of coffee, a fistful of energy shots, and a Minnesota state road map.

At the last minute, on his way to the counter, he veered and added two more items: an adjustable Twins cap from the general-goods aisle and a pair of sunglasses from the revolving rack inside the door.

Don't even think about it, said a reasonable voice in his head. *Just go.*

Mike ignored the voice and climbed into the truck. After tearing into the ibuprofen and chasing a few caplets with one of the energy shots, he bit the tags off the hat and glasses. He put the glasses on, pulled the ball cap down low on his head, and checked himself in the rearview mirror.

He looked like a jackass. A regular master of disguise. Sure.

Forget it, the reasonable voice said. *Get on the road.*

But his leg had a different opinion, Mike reasoned back. With the drive he had ahead of him, stuck in the same position for two hours, ibuprofen wasn't going to cut the mustard. Not when it got like this, with the throb in his knee already climbing up through his thigh bone, all the way into his hip.

Mike told himself that he had to be able to focus. To do that, he was going to need what was left of his Vicodin prescription, back at the house.

At that point his leg and the reasonable voice seemed to join. Each thump felt like a warning: *Don't be an idiot. Don't be an idiot. Don't be an idiot.*

Anyway, it had been at least forty minutes since he'd spoken to Tanya. Who knew? Maybe by now the coast was clear.

It wasn't.

A full block before he rolled past the north end of his street, Mike saw the steady pulse of flashers strobing the bare tree limbs in the dusky light. He slowed down as much as he dared, tried to glimpse as much as he could from a distance.

What he saw were cops. A whole convention of them in his driveway, more going in and out of the house. He saw patrol units with a couple of different sets of markings. He saw people standing around on the sidewalks, watching the show. He saw more or less the scene he'd imagined based on Tanya's description, clearly still in full swing.

He was trying to pick out Tanya from the crowd of

onlookers when someone tapped a horn behind him. Mike checked the rearview and saw headlights stacked up back there. It was the first time he noticed that he'd slowed all the way to a stop.

How about now? the reasonable voice said. *Now can we go?*

Or was the reasonable voice the one telling him to stay?

It was a minute past nine, according to the clock in the dash. If Hal could have seen what Mike was seeing now, he'd never have loaned out the truck.

But then, Mike wouldn't be looking at anything at all if not for Darryl. Both were equal realities, leaving him with a choice he didn't know how to make: turn right, down his own street, or keep on rolling. All the way up to Rockhaven.

The horn sounded again behind him, not so polite this time.

Screw it.

The Dodge grumbled and heaved as Mike punched the gas. With fifty-seven bucks in his wallet, the mouthy throb in his leg, and the clothes on his back, he set out for the lake country.

SOLDIERS OF
MISFORTUNE

9

"Jesus, buddy," Deon said. "Sometime today."

Maya checked her watch. Even with Deon driving, they'd been hung up in traffic for nearly an hour, stuck behind a jackknifed semi-trailer on I-94, and now here they sat: a hundred feet from their final turn.

"Hey," she said into the windshield, calling to the guy in the pickup hogging the street in front of them. "Looky Lou. Get with the program."

Off to her right, she could see squad cars crowding a small house on the east side of the cross street, several houses up from their corner, which remained just beyond reach. She could see Barnhill's unmarked unit in the driveway. Even as they sat there, she saw something else: a van from Channel 9, approaching the scene from the opposite end of the street.

At the sight of the competition, all Maya's reflexes kicked in: the jump in her pulse rate, the urgent pull in her gut, the stubborn clench in her jaw. She shifted impatiently in the passenger seat and said, "What the hell is this guy's deal?"

Through the back window of the pickup she could see the driver sitting there, half turned. He sat with an elbow on the steering wheel, one hand on his chin, pondering the action half a block up as if the whole street was his personal property. He wore a ball cap and sunglasses, even though it was dark outside, and something about his posture struck Maya oddly. He knew they were behind him—he'd looked in his mirror when Deon honked—and yet he just sat there, like a sculpture. Rodin's *The Thinker* in a cap and sunglasses, manning a thirty-year-old Dodge Power Wagon.

She looked back up the street and saw their doppelgangers from Channel 9 already parked and setting up shop. Another photographer, another reporter sniffing the ground.

"Oh, you're killing me," she said, reaching across Deon to lean on the horn with the heel of her hand. "Dude! Move your ass!"

The guy straightened in his seat as though she'd woken him from a nap.

"There we go," Deon said, moving at last, as the truck lurched forward ahead of them and sped away down the street.

Something about the whole thing gave her a tingle. Maya watched the truck's taillights bank and disappear around the first corner going left as Deon turned the corner going right. By the time Deon rolled up to the news already in progress, she saw that she'd scribbled down the truck's license number in her notebook without being fully aware she was doing it. It was stupid, but Maya didn't care. After this morning? No more overlooking suspicious vehicles. No more overlooking anything.

Their arrival was in no way overlooked by Channel 9. As Maya piled out, she saw the reporter—some kid she didn't recognize—making urgent hand gestures to his photographer, pointing to a spot up the curb. The reporter looked as though he were trying to box out an opponent for a clutch rebound.

The photographer looked bored. When he saw them coming, he nodded and said, "Hey, D."

"Randy," Deon said, popping a new toothpick. "What'd we miss?"

While the other reporter tried to decide whether or not to be friendly, Maya saw Roger Barnhill emerge from the side door of the house. The detective spoke briefly with a uniformed deputy and then headed for his car. She left 9 and 7 standing together at the curb and hustled over.

A St. Paul cop stopped her at the mouth of the driveway, palm out. "Nope," he said. "Sorry."

She stood on tiptoe, looking past him. "Detective!"

Barnhill saw her. He checked his watch, gave instructions to another deputy, then came down the driveway, walking quickly.

"It's okay," he told the St. Paul cop. "Thanks."

The St. Paul cop shrugged and stepped aside.

"Listen," Maya said, on impulse tearing out the page from her notebook with the tag number of the goofy-acting gawker in the pickup truck. "I'm sure I'm being paranoid, but . . ."

"Tell me on the way," Barnhill said. "You've still got my mobile number?"

Standing within paper-handing reach, she could feel a grim tension radiating off the detective in waves. "I've got it," she said. "On the way where?"

"I can't speak to you now," Barnhill said. He folded

the paper once and shoved it inside his sport coat. "You can follow my car if you keep up."

His demeanor gave Maya another tingle. A deep and unpleasant one. Something about the set in his jaw, the drawn look in his eyes, the tone in his voice. All at once, she felt tight in her chest.

"You found her," she said. The way the uniforms within earshot perked up, the way Barnhill reacted, she knew her intuition was correct. "Didn't you?"

Barnhill was already halfway up the driveway. "Let's hope not," he said, though it didn't sound to Maya like he had much hope left in supply.

She glanced for a reaction toward the St. Paul cop who had stopped her. He was nowhere to be found.

So she stopped standing there. Deon caught her signal and met her back at the truck. Inside, strapped into his seat belt once more, Deon fired up the engine, glanced over, and said, "What'd he say?"

Maya sat in her seat and felt her heart wilting and somehow couldn't bring herself to answer the question. *Please not like this*, she thought. *Not her, too.* She pointed ahead at Barnhill's car, now zipping away, flashers pulsing in the windows, already leaving them behind.

10

They watched a news rig from Channel 9 cruise by them, turn at the corner, and scoot down the street toward the action. Pretty soon they watched another rig, from News7, turn in at the other end of the block. The whole time Bryce sat there with the binoculars like he was watching his favorite show on TV, and when he finally spilled the beans about the call from Uncle Buck, Toby didn't believe him.

"Suit yourself," Bryce said. "Just telling you what the boss told me."

"Yeah, but that's crazy."

Never once did Bryce lower the binoculars. "Your point?"

"I'm just saying."

"Look it up on your space phone," Bryce suggested.

Toby looked at his mobile, on standby in its dash cradle, and sighed.

It was only a phone. Obviously he needed something that could get the sports feeds, and the lines from Vegas, and, besides, if you wanted to stay competitive, it was smart business to keep up with the top gear available. Seemed like something a respectable modern bounty hunter might like to consider, in fact.

So earlier, to pass the time, Toby had made the mistake of showing Bryce the GPS app that could track their position on a satellite map of the Cities—in real time, while they were driving, like in the movies—and Bryce had done nothing but give him shit about it ever since.

That, Toby had learned, was the thing about Bryce. Even when the guy didn't say anything or look at you, he had this way about him that made you feel like every single thing you did or said was weak and silly.

On the other hand, he had a point.

While Bryce went on surveilling through his window, Toby grabbed the mobile and fired it up. He went out to the online sites for Channels 9 and 7. Sure enough, it was the top story in both places: the rich girl from Lake Calhoun who'd gone missing this afternoon. Not long after Toby and Bryce had been here talking to Barlowe, if the Web feeds had it right.

"Damn," Toby said.

Bryce didn't look over, but he did seem interested. "What does it say?"

"Nothing about Potter," Bryce said, still scanning. "But you're right about the girl."

"Name again?"

"Huh?"

"The girl," Bryce said. "What's her name?"

"Benson," Toby said. "Juliet Benson. You see the thing on the news last night? About that architect?"

"Nope."

"Anyway, he's her dad."

"That's what your uncle said."

"Huh," Toby said. "There's a reward, sounds like."

"Yeah?" Bryce lowered the binoculars an inch. "What kind of reward?"

"For info on the girl."

"I figured that," Bryce said. "I mean how much?"

For a moment, Toby thought about ignoring him. Let the guy get his own space phone. Then he folded and said, "Twenty-five K."

"No shit?"

"That's what it says."

Bryce gave a low whistle. He raised the binoculars again.

Toby tried the online site for the *Star Tribune*, but he didn't find anything more there than he'd found already. He tried to imagine what this girl from up-market Minneapolis could have to do with a low-rent bully like Darryl Potter, and while he couldn't come up with anything, Toby had a sinking feeling that his odds of seeing any of his eleven grand come back into his pocket had stretched considerably.

Pretty soon he'd found everything it looked like he was going to find on the missing girl. Toby took a minute, set up an auto-alert with the keywords *Juliet Benson, Minneapolis, St. Paul, Minnesota, police,* and *authorities*. He thought about it and added the name *Darryl Potter*. He thought about it some more. Added the name *Barlowe*.

Then he put the mobile back in its cradle and said, "So what now?"

Bryce adjusted the focus knob on the binocs. "What now what?"

"I mean what do we do?"

"We're doing it."

Toby sighed and settled back in his seat. He was

tired, and he couldn't get comfortable. He wanted to go home, make a bowl of cereal, pop in a DVD, and pretend he didn't know about any of this. But he felt trapped. In his own ride, no less.

How had it happened? One minute, Bryce was just some guy working for him, on loan from Uncle Buck, and the next thing Toby knew, it felt the other way around.

It didn't seem fair. This was supposed to be *his* show. It was his money they were after. It was even his car. He was the one sitting in the driver's seat. But Toby was starting to get the message loud and clear: Sitting in the driver's seat only made him the driver.

They sat without talking for a while. Bryce kept watching through the binoculars until an unmarked car backed out of the driveway of Potter's house and drove off down the street, lights flashing in the rear window. They watched as the news crews piled back into their rigs and drove off the same way.

After a while, things seemed to be winding down. The neighbors had more or less dispersed. The uniforms had thinned out on the ground. Lights went dark in the house. Pretty soon, one by one, the squad units began peeling away. Before long the whole street looked quiet again. If you hadn't been sitting there watching, Toby thought, you wouldn't have known anyone had been there at all.

His mobile went off. Toby grabbed it, saw the screen, and said, "Hey, Uncle Buck."

"Howdy, sport," Uncle Buck said. "Listen, put Bryce . . ."

Toby was already handing the phone over.

Bryce took it and said, "I'm here."

Toby didn't even bother trying to listen this time. It was no use. He sat there behind the wheel, looking out the window at nothing in particular, until Bryce said, "I'll let you know," and handed the phone back.

Toby took it. Waited.

Silence.

Then Bryce said, "Barlowe's in the wind."

In the wind. It sounded mystical. "He's where?"

"Exactly," Bryce said.

Whatever. More silence.

Toby waited.

"So here's what I'm thinking," Bryce finally said. Talking like they were partners again all of a sudden. "You and me, we split that eleven grand of yours. What's left of it, anyway. Then we take that twenty-five-K reward money, and we split that too." Bryce winked. "You're the numbers guy, you tell me. What's that come to each?"

"Eighteen grand," Toby said.

"Yeah, that's what I got."

"Depending," Toby said.

"On?"

"On how much of my eleven grand there is left."

"Right," Bryce said. "Good point." He turned in his seat toward Toby, got comfortable. "So, figure we get no luck. There's nothing left of the dough Potter took from your restaurant guy. That leaves us with, what? Only twelve? Each?"

"Twelve and a half," Toby said.

"Hey. You really are a numbers guy."

Toby felt like he was having a perfectly logical conversation that made absolutely no sense. He sat a minute, wanting to avoid saying something dumb, which would only give Bryce something new to crack on him about, then said, "Tell me again how we get the reward money?"

"Same way we get your eleven grand back," Bryce said. "We find this Potter genius."

Who's the genius? Toby thought, but held his tongue. He took another moment, chose his words carefully, and said, "Isn't that sort of the whole problem?"

Bryce smiled. It looked like the bones in his face shifted position. "You be the numbers guy," he said. "Let me be the ideas guy."

11

Mike Barlowe had joined the Marine Corps straight out of high school because he couldn't think of anything better to do. He'd grown up in foster homes and had no blood siblings. His girlfriend—who he'd always known was out of his league anyway—had gone out east for college and met a new guy by Halloween. His buddies were good for laughs and trouble, but they were all going nowhere fast, and even though he'd never had much evidence to support it, Mike always had the idea that maybe he'd amount to something more.

He'd been a sophomore at Sibley when the towers came down in New York City. Though he'd never said so to anybody, inside he'd always admired the seniors he knew that year who signed up to go off and do something about it. Three years later, he signed up himself, one otherwise pointless Saturday afternoon, at a recruiting depot set up for the weekend at the Mall of America in Bloomington.

Three years after that, Mike came home from the Marine Corps with a plastic knee, 63 percent hearing loss in his left ear, and a bunch of grisly sludge where his nighttime dreams used to be. And if not for Darryl

Potter, he most likely would not have come home at all.

They'd been getting ready to turn over Ramadi to the next bunch of Marines after six months in the combat zone. September in Anbar Province was nothing like early autumn in Minnesota, and Mike had been daydreaming about fishing for lunker northerns and watching the leaves change back home.

Two weeks before shipping back to the States, his team found an ambush on patrol and ended up in a hell of a jam. They'd been outpositioned, pinned down in a side street for a quarter of an hour by the time support arrived. From his cover in a doorway, Mike laid down rifle fire while his men piled into the Humvee, then he broke out after them.

He'd made it about three steps when an RPG round screamed over on a rope of exhaust from a ground-floor window across the street, detonating high on the wall above the doorway behind him. The next thing Mike knew, he was deaf, half blind, concussed out of his gourd. He found himself bound up in a pile of rubble with no feeling in his leg, AK-47 rounds kicking up silent puffs of sidewalk all around him.

Potter, they told him later, hadn't even waited for the big truck-mounted .50-cal to swing around and start hammering. They said he just jumped out of the Humvee and bolted straight into the hail. Pulled Mike out of there. Dragged him all the way back by his flak vest with one hand, firing his regulated M4 across the street with the other. Burst after burst, they said, straight out of the movies. They said all he needed was a chewed-up cigar clamped in his snarl.

But Mike couldn't remember any of that. The next

thing he remembered was bouncing around in the back of the Humvee, hauling ass out of the hot zone, looking up into Darryl's grime-caked face. He remembered how white Darryl's teeth had looked against the battle dirt. He remembered saying thanks, though he couldn't hear his own voice.

He couldn't hear Darryl's either, but he'd been able to read his grinning lips: *Don't worry about it. Next time you can save mine.*

The lane to Rockhaven was so grown up with brome-grass and sumac that Mike might not have seen it in the dark if he hadn't known where he was going. The Power Wagon's headlights found the break in the overgrowth, then fell across the familiar sign, the old barn door Hal's grandfather had nailed across a pair of gnarly hedge posts sometime during the Truman administration. Its last paint job was nearly scoured away by the elements, and Mike wondered how that could be. He was the one who'd last repainted it—a thank-you to Hal for letting him use the place—and it didn't seem like it had been all that long ago.

He sat there a minute at the mouth of the lane, engine idling, headlights illuminating the path ahead of him. He'd driven two and a half hours nonstop, and the truck's big dual tanks were nearly empty.

Mike's tank was nearly empty. His leg was stiff and aching. His eyes felt raw. After about a quart of bitter Go Stop coffee, his stomach was sour and full of acid, and his bladder felt ready to burst.

He killed the ignition, got out of the truck, and relieved himself in the tall grass. He limped a circle around the truck, tried to work the rigor out of his leg. He was miles from anything, and everything was quiet. No bugs, no night birds, not even the whisper of a breeze in the trees.

All he could hear was the sound of the truck's engine ticking under the hood. The sound of his own feet kicking through the gravel along the rutted lake road, swept down to hardpan by the winter melt. Drifting clouds of tree pollen swirled in the headlight beams, otherwise invisible to the eye.

You're stalling, he thought, and climbed back in the truck.

Ahead of him, just beyond the reach of the headlights, the rock-topped lane made a bend and disappeared into the trees. The lane wound through the timber another quarter mile, wide enough for a single vehicle abreast, and now that Mike was here, he realized he didn't want to go down this road after all. Didn't want to face whatever was waiting for him at the end of it.

Half an hour to midnight, according to the clock in the dash. Almost a new day.

Hal would be waiting for his call.

He forced his hand up to the ignition. Turned the key. The new starter fired up on the first try. The engine rumbled. No excuses.

Mike dropped the truck into gear. Rocks crunched heavily under the tires as he turned into the lane.

When this is over, he thought, *I'm repainting that sign.*

12

By the time the guys from Dobry Automotive came back across the street, jingled the bell over the door on their way in, and ordered their first free pitcher of Leinenkugel, Hal Macklin was about ready to crawl out of his own damned skin.

"What's the matter with you?" Regina finally wanted to know, drumming her nails across the damp cork of her drink tray while he made change out of the register for the guys in booth five. "You're even grouchier than normal."

"I got a pain in my ass, that's what," he said. "It costs me nine bucks an hour and keeps going, 'What's the matter with you?'"

"Fine, be that way," Regina said. "See if I give a shit."

"Like you don't give me enough shit already," Hal said, as if it was her fault he'd let himself get talked into waiting around here with his thumb up his ass while who knew what was happening up at the lake.

It wasn't right. He knew that now, only two hours along. Hell, he'd known it two hours ago.

But he'd given his word.

He gave Reggie her change, wiped down the bar for the hundredth time, and tried to stop checking the clock over the jukebox every five minutes.

When the ten o'clock news came on, Hal left Regina behind the bar and went back to watch on the little twelve-inch set on his desk in the office, where he could hear better.

Five minutes later, he came out, cut the juke, turned on the lights, and said, "Drink up, folks. Closing time."

It took half an hour to round everybody up and get their mopey asses all moving in the same direction. First nobody believed him. Then came the griping and the bellyaching.

"Tommorrow night, first round's on the house," Hal kept telling them, herding and prodding them along. "Sorry, Bill; sorry, Tom; sorry, fella. Can't be helped. Here's what you do: You come in tomorrow night, you order a drink, you tell me, 'This one's for last night.' Got that? Now your left. Right. Left. Attaboy."

On his way out, Wayne Miller from the garage winked and handed Hal most of an unfinished pitcher of free Leinenkugel. "I see how it is," he said.

Ray Duncan joined in, saying, "Gotta watch you all the time, huh, Mackie?"

"I'm sorry, boys." Hal nodded to Wayne, clapped Ray on his meaty shoulder. "I owe you. Mark it down."

Reggie was the last person out the door. She stood there with her purse and jacket, arms crossed, until Hal thought he was going to have to go back to the stockroom, get the hand truck and some bungee cords, and wheel her out to her car at the curb.

She said, "What's going on, you?"

"Nothing," he told her.

"Don't give me that."

"I got some business."

"What kind of business?"

"The none-of-your-business kind of business."

"Harold William," she said, and gave him that look of hers. It was one of the reasons he'd married her, that look. One of the reasons he'd given her the divorce, come to think of it.

"Regina Christine," he said. Left it there.

She stood planted like that and stared at him a minute before she finally gave up. Right before she walked out, she did the last thing Hal expected: She leaned at him quickly, planted a hard kiss on his cheek, and said, "I don't like the look on your face."

She smelled like lipstick and cigarettes. Hal missed her a little just then.

"Shoo," he said.

He watched her to the curb, digging around in that twenty-pound rucksack she called a purse until she found her keys. Reggie looked back at him once, shook her head, then opened up her little Honda and got in.

She needed a new muffler, Hal thought, watching her drive away. He decided he'd talk to Wayne and Ray about that next time he saw them. He flipped the OPEN sign to CLOSED and locked the door.

The place seemed too bright and too quiet, now that it was empty. Hal killed the main lights on his way to the office. When he got there, he grabbed the phone and the pad of notepaper he'd left next to it.

Barlowe wouldn't be more than halfway to the lake by now, he figured. Hal didn't like selling the boy out.

But that was how it was going to have to be. He couldn't let it go now. Not after what he'd just seen on the news.

Sorry, kid, he thought, and began dialing the Sheriff's hotline number he'd scribbled on the pad two hours ago. *This wasn't the deal.*

Halfway through the number, Hal heard a muffled jangle in the bar: the bell over the front door.

"Jesus H. Jones," he said, and slammed the phone down. He went up front to run off whoever had wandered in already, knowing as he went that he'd locked that front door.

He came out into the bar and stopped. Saw the guy in the front entrance, just now stepping out of the shadows. In the light from the back bar, Hal recognized him right off the bat.

"Gotta be hard staying in business," the guy said. "I mean, a bar? Closing at ten when everybody else in town stays open 'til two?"

The kid had said the guy's name before. Hal couldn't remember it.

The face was too ugly to forget. Hal didn't bother asking the guy how he'd gotten in; he could see him slipping a little flat black case inside his jacket as he strolled on in, helped himself to a bar stool. That would have been the lock picks.

Hal felt his heart beating. All his senses sharpened up. He said, "The hell do you want?"

The guy smiled. "How about a beer?"

13

"Hey, I got a joke for you," the guy said. "You like jokes?"

Bryce, Hal thought. That was his name.

Didn't look like a Bryce. Hal came around the bar, taking care where he put his eyes. He could play casual too. Son of a bitch was going to find that out soon enough, whatever his name was.

"Sure, I like jokes," he told him, pulling up a mug from the rack under the taps. "If they make me laugh."

"Here's a good one," Bryce said. "Guy's selling brains on the black market. Right?"

"Brains," Hal said.

"Human brains, yeah. Like for transplants." Bryce waved a hand. "It's a new science."

"Why not," Hal said. He set up the mug and started pulling a beer. Shittiest brand he carried.

"So he points to a jar with a brain floating in it and says to his customer, 'This one's from a schoolteacher. Cost you twenty thousand bucks.'"

Bryce pointed along in the air with his finger while he narrated, indicating imaginary jars.

"Guy points to the next jar and says, 'Now, this one

here? Belonged to a heart surgeon. Run you fifty thousand.' Well, sure, the customer thinks to himself. Heart surgeon, schoolteacher, that makes sense. Then the customer sees a third jar and says, 'Who'd that one belong to?' Guy tells him, 'United States Marine Corps, friend. That jar right there goes a million-two.'"

Bryce dropped his jaw and sat back on his stool, miming amazement. A regular performer, this one.

"The customer, he can't believe it. Says to the guy, 'You must be kidding. Why does a Marine cost so much more than a heart surgeon?' The guy looks at him and says, 'Pal, do you have any idea how many Marines it takes to come up with an ounce of brains?'"

At his own punch line, Bryce rapped the bar top with his knuckles, grinning like a crocodile. A crocodile, Hal thought, that had tried to eat a lawn mower. And just might have succeeded.

Hal put the beer down in front of him. "You're right," he said. "That's a good one."

"Makes me laugh every time I hear it." Bryce raised his beer. "Cheers."

Hal waited for him to finish off his victory chug, then said, "You got any more?"

Bryce sucked foam off his top lip. "More what?"

"Jokes."

"Can't think of any off the top."

"Then I guess you can answer my question now."

"What was the question again?"

Hal didn't repeat it.

"Wait, I remember," Bryce said. "You asked me what I wanted."

"Starting to think you didn't hear me," Hal said.

He made a show of stacking clean mugs in the rack below the bar, keeping his hands below bar level.

"Oh, I heard you. I just figured it was rhetorical." Bryce drained what was left of his beer in one long pull, then set the dregs on the bar. He slid the mug across. "I figured, we're both smart guys. We know why I'm here."

"For a smart guy, you don't listen so good," Hal said. "I told you once already. When you came around here the first time."

"Yeah, but see, I'm thinking you weren't being honest. I can tell that about people."

"Can you, now?"

"Hang on a sec," Bryce said. He held up a finger, fishing a cell phone out of his jacket pocket with his other hand. He slid the phone open, thumbed a few keys, put the phone to his ear, listened a minute. Pretty soon he nodded and said, "Sorry, I think I have the wrong number."

He snapped the phone closed, put it back in his pocket. Looked at Hal. Shrugged. "See what I mean?"

Hal couldn't wait to wipe the smile off this guy's fucked-up face. "I guess I ain't smart like a heart surgeon," he said.

Bryce arranged himself on the stool like he was willing to go nice and slow.

"Try and look at it from my perspective," he said. "I come in here before, ask you politely about this guy I'm trying to find. For business reasons. You tell me he hasn't been in all day—okay, maybe I can buy that. Except then you run me and my partner out of here like you're John Wayne and we're the Indians." He shrugged again. "I mean, fair enough, I've got a little Chippewa blood on my mother's side, but still. At that point I have to pause and ask myself: Being my bar, is this the way I handle a couple of clean, mostly white paying customers who aren't causing me any trouble? If I'm telling them the truth?"

Hal didn't respond. He only moved a little to his left.

"Then when I come back to try again," Bryce said, "I find the whole bar closed. At ten on a Wednesday, no less. And *then*," he said, nodding toward the counter, "when I call the number I see you have written down there?"

Hal followed his glance to the notepad he'd carried out with him from the office. He hadn't even realized he still had it in his hand.

"A gal from the sheriff's hotline answers," Bryce said. "Something about that missing girl they've been talking about on the news. Imagine my surprise."

Within view, Hal arranged bottles along the rail. Below view, he felt the smooth walnut stock of the 12-gauge coachman's gun he kept on hooks beneath the liquor well.

"So, couple things," Bryce said. "First, and this is important, you want to think twice about bringing up whatever kind of peacemaker you've got hiding back there." He reached inside his jacket, brought a nickel-and-black autoloader out from the shoulder holster Hal had glimpsed earlier. Gunmetal clunked heavily on wood as Bryce placed his hardware on the bar in front of him. "Mine's a lot closer."

Hal gritted his teeth. Thought, *Hell.*

He exhaled slowly. From his angle, the way the son of a bitch had positioned the gun on the bar, Hal could see straight up the pipe. Like a dark, empty round eye looking at him. The eye didn't blink.

He thought it over and changed his angle. Straightened his back. Crossed his arms.

"Better," Bryce said. He took his hand off the gun. Left the gun on the bar where it was. "Now, I can sense you're a man with some principles. I respect that. Problem is, me, not so much."

"Huh," Hal said. "Hard to believe."

"Could be genetic," Bryce said. "Or maybe just bad parenting. But you see the conflict we're left with. You being you and me being me."

While Bryce talked, Hal studied the guy's eyes. Not because he particularly wanted to, but because he couldn't make himself look away. Once, in '67, in Quang Tri, he'd run across a Force Recon sniper who carried half a dozen blood-crusted Vietcong teeth around with him in a cigar tin. He used to dream about that after the war. That guy then had the same kind of flat, cold light in his eyes as this guy now.

"Thing is, I already know I'm walking out of here with what I came in here to get," Bryce said. "You don't want to give it to me, but we can't both win. And I don't lose."

"First time for everything," Hal said. His voice came out sounding weaker than he liked.

Bryce nodded. "True. And I can see you've got a stubborn streak. Question is, how stubborn are you? Because if you're stubborn enough, we both lose. At that point, I won't feel like I have much choice but to give my partner a call. You remember him from before?"

"I remember him."

"Well. If we get to that point—and I hope we don't—I'll probably feel like I'll have to have him bring back that nice-looking lady in the Honda he followed away from here a bit ago. See if she can help us sort all this out."

Hal felt his pulse jump. He thought: *Goddamn son of a bitch.* "She can't help you," he said.

"Yeah, but you're stubborn, remember? How could I be sure?" Bryce shook his head. "I don't know. It looked awfully sweet to me, the way you two parted company. I'll bet if push came to shove, she wouldn't be as stubborn as you are."

In twenty-five years owning this place, Hal couldn't remember ever feeling the way he felt just then: trapped behind his own bar.

He couldn't stand the way his mouth had gone dry. Couldn't stand the way his blood hummed inside his ears. He couldn't stand *standing* there. Letting this guy talk to him.

"I think she needs a new muffler, by the way," Bryce said. He leaned back on his stool, put his hands on his knees. He patted an easy rhythm with his fingers, then held his hands very still.

This was an invitation, Hal understood. The way the guy was sitting: hands on his lap, gun sitting alone on the bar between them, unattended. A regular Old West routine. The barkeep and the gunslinger. Goddamned ridiculous.

"So, you tell me," Bryce said. "What's next?"

Hal looked at the gun. Looked at its owner. He wondered: Who was closer?

"Three bucks," he finally said.

Bryce tilted his head. "Pardon?"

"For the beer." Hal nodded to the empty mug still sitting on the bar near the gun. "You owe me three dollars."

"Oh," Bryce said. His crocodile eyes seemed to twinkle in the back-bar neon. "Right."

He reached into his back pocket and took out his wallet. Without looking down at his hands, he opened the wallet, pulled a bill, and handed it over.

"Sorry I don't have anything smaller," he said.

Hal looked at the bill. A twenty. "I'll get your change."

"Much obliged," Bryce said.

At the register, Hal traded the twenty for a ten, a five, and eight quarters. Something caught his eye as he counted the money into his hand, and an idea came to him. His pulse jumped again.

He forced himself steady. Thought, *Easy, now. Nice and easy does it.*

Hal finished counting coins, then made the same move he'd made a few hundred times a night for the past twenty-five years: He turned and slid the register drawer closed with his hip.

Only this time, in the half second his back was turned, using the clackity-shuck of the closing drawer for cover, he used his free hand to scoop a handful of margarita salt from the glass rimmer on the ledge.

"Funny," he said on his way back. "I'm out of singles myself."

"Perfect," Bryce said, watching him all the way. "I can use the change for parking meters."

Fast, Hal thought. *Just be fast, is all.*

"But I like how you're thinking business," Bryce added. He held out his hand deliberately. A symbolic

gesture, Hal interpreted. "We're making a transac-
tion, you and me. Simple as that. Business doesn't
have to be complicated."

*Yeah, that's what I'm thinking, you hatchet-faced
prick,* Hal thought.

He placed the bills in the guy's open palm. Weighted
them down with the quarters.

In the next motion, he flung the salt hard with his
other hand, aiming straight for those open eyes.

Damned if he didn't hit where he was aiming too.
Bryce gave a garbled shout and rocked back on his
stool, blinking and pawing at the stinging grit in his
face, as Hal went for the gun on the bar.

He grabbed it clean. Felt the weight of it come up in
his hand even as he heard two bucks' worth of quarters clattering down though the legs of the bar stool,
hitting the floor. His thumb found the safety switch
like it was the cash button on his register. Right there
where it belonged. The pebbled grip found its place in
Hal's palm. The smooth curve of the trigger found the
crease of his finger. All just as fast as that.

And still, even with salt in his eyes, the son of a
bitch was faster.

14

Later on, when it was too late to matter, Toby Lunden would wonder why he sat there in the Navigator, in the lot behind that bar, waiting like he'd been told, when his head and his gut told him to do differently.

Everything had swerved off in some new direction he hadn't seen coming. Somehow Toby had gone from calling the shots to feeling like he was in over his head; he didn't have a clue what the hell was going on anymore and didn't think he really wanted to know.

This would have been the perfect chance for him to cut loose of the whole situation. It would have been so easy: While Bryce was inside, doing whatever he was doing, Toby could have dropped the Navigator into gear and said sayonara. He could have left Bryce there.

So why hadn't he?

Was he really that pissed off at Darryl Potter? Or was he really just that scared of Bryce?

Or was he kidding himself?

Maybe somewhere deep down, he and Bryce weren't so different after all. Toby wasn't a gambler himself, but in running a book the way he ran it, he knew how to judge an opportunity. Maybe it really was about the dough.

Why else had he followed instructions when Bryce told him to pull into the alley, around back of the building, out of view of the street?

What else could have kept him sitting there even after he heard the muffled bang inside the building? Because it sure sounded a hell of a lot like a gunshot to Toby, and Toby didn't do gunshots. He was a numbers guy.

Yet he was still sitting there when Bryce let himself out the back door ten minutes later. He was still sitting there when Bryce climbed into the passenger seat and hauled the door shut behind him. He was still sitting there when Bryce looked over and said, "Now would be the part where you start driving."

Toby didn't need to be told that part twice. He cranked the engine and backed up too quickly, nearly clipping the garbage Dumpster with the rear bumper. He skidded the brakes, threw the truck into go, and mashed on the gas. He cornered out of the alley hard enough to make the tires whine.

"Chill, kid," Bryce said calmly. He leaned forward and checked himself in his visor mirror, probing the skin under his eyes with his fingers. "We'll look dumb on television if we get pulled over here."

"Oh, man, what the hell," Toby said. It took every bit of will he had to keep the needle on the speedometer under the limit. It felt like they were crawling. He felt like he was losing it. "Hell. What the hell, what the hell."

"What the hell what?"

"What the hell happened back there?" Toby said.

Bryce opened his eyes wide, angling his head back and forth like he was checking his mascara. "I miscalculated," he said. "I can admit it."

Toby took a left and kicked up his speed as much as he dared. Every oncoming car made him cringe and want to hide. "What does that mean, you miscalculated?"

"Old bastard had some gristle, I'll give him that." Bryce pushed up the visor and turned in his seat. "Can you believe he almost got the drop on me?"

Toby looked over as they passed under a streetlamp. Bryce's eyes looked raw, and his hairline was damp, as if he'd just washed his face. Toby felt like his throat was closing. With a catch in his voice, he said, "What did you do to him?"

"I didn't *do* anything *to* him," Bryce said, making imaginary quotation marks in the air. "He made choices that caused events to occur. Hang another left up here."

Toby did as he was told. He felt his mind shutting down, numbing over. How had he gotten himself into this?

Bryce rode along for a moment, studying the floor mats, then finally shook his head. "Guess it goes to show you," he said. "You never know what people might do." He reached out, grabbed Toby's phone from its cradle, and turned it over in his hand like a piece of alien technology.

Toby didn't like him holding his property for some reason. It seemed like a stupid thing, but he didn't like it. He said, "What are you doing?"

Bryce smiled and said, "I assume this thing has a good old-fashioned GPS map of planet earth?"

15

In northwest Minneapolis, just inside the city limits, tucked into the grassy nook of the intersection where Webber Parkway met Lyndale Avenue, there was a footpath. The path meandered away beneath Interstate 94, through the trees along Shingle Creek, and emerged into a seventy-acre surprise of densely wooded parkland, hidden by the freeway wall from car-bound view. These woods rambled north for a mile along the western bank of the Mississippi River, and if a person didn't know to look for the area, they might not know it was there at all.

Quite a number of people knew to look by the time Maya caught the toss from the anchor desk at the top of the ten o'clock newscast. Most of these people were sworn law-enforcement personnel from the Hennepin County Sheriff's Office, Minneapolis PD, and the Minnesota State Patrol.

She and Deon delivered their second live shot of the evening from the parking lot of the Camden Center strip mall, where crews from two of the remaining three network affiliates had assembled to do the same.

By the time Sheriff's Detective Roger Barnhill addressed the media formally, the circus had come to the Three Rivers Park District in full.

Mike followed the lane back into the woods, through dark tunnels of old reaching oaks and high walls of tall shaggy pine. The sky was inky black over the tree-tops, the moon bright and nearly full. Every so often he glimpsed ghostly white birches that looked like slashes of bone in the silvery light.

Little by little, the lane widened, then took a long, slow bend, finally spilling out of the woods into broad, open ground. Here, in this sudden clearing, sat a small cabin on a small, spring-fed lake. Hal Macklin's own private retreat hidden away in the trees. Rock-haven.

At the first sight of the water, Mike felt a thump in his chest. He rolled the truck to a stop and sat there, idling. The headlights illuminated a reedy stand of bulrushes clogging a jut in the shoreline, and for a moment he considered dousing the beams. Then he thought, *Why?*

The sooner Darrell saw him coming, the better.

On the far shore, across the moonlit water, lights blazed in the ground-floor windows of the cabin at the end of the lane. The cabin itself was nothing fancy—a simple gambrel-roofed cottage with a half-story loft, clad in weather-scoured wood that had come from the same barn, according to Hal, that had provided the sign at the mouth of the driveway. Chunks of rugged stone around the cabin's foundation mimicked the craggy riprap along the shore of the lake. According to Hal, all the rock had been trucked in from a nearby granite quarry a load at a time, a hedge against erosion that had given the place its name.

From where Mike sat, the whole scene seemed almost welcoming. Warm and familiar.

All except for the unfamiliar vehicle he saw parked in front of the cabin.

It was the sight of the strange car that dried Mike's throat and kicked up his pulse. He realized that he'd been hoping—however irrationally, given the scene he'd left behind at the house in St. Paul—that when he arrived here, he'd find find the crap-trap Skylark waiting for him after all. The hypnotic separation of the long drive up here had almost convinced him that this whole day had been some kind of dream.

But he wasn't dreaming. Mike took a breath and followed the lane around the wide curve of the lakeshore, vaguely noting the open door of the canoe shed as he rolled past. He pulled the truck in next to the car, a little 4x4 Subaru.

The car's vanity plates bore the initials JMB. Mike thought of the news report he'd watched with Hal back at the Elbow: *Police are seeking the public's help in locating Juliet Marie Benson, the twenty-two-year-old Twin Cities woman last seen this afternoon. . . .*

He killed the lights and cut the motor. He tapped the horn twice, blasting a pair of holes in the stillness. Then he sat and watched the porch. Waiting.

Nothing happened. Mike hit the horn again. He leaned on it this time.

The front door of the cabin didn't open. No shadows darkened the windows; none of the curtains moved. The Power Wagon took no small arms fire. Other than the honking, all was peaceful.

You're still stalling, he thought.

Mike took one last look at the little Subaru sitting next to him. It didn't belong here, that car. He shouldn't have been able to find it.

He braced himself, climbed out of the truck, and went to see what else he could find.

At five minutes past midnight, Maya stood near a picnic shelter in the cold, watching her new photographer shoot B-roll of the state patrol helicopter circling overhead.

It had been nearly three hours since members of the sheriff's volunteer emergency squad had tracked the GPS chip in Juliet Benson's cell phone to a drainage culvert feeding into Shingle Creek, two hundred yards upstream from where the creek fed into the Mighty Mississippi.

There they retrieved, stuffed an arm's reach inside the culvert, a black plastic garbage bag containing the phone, a mud-caked women's overcoat, and a pair of size 6 women's mules. According to the off-record text message Maya had received from Roger Barnhill an hour ago, the girl's parents had identified the sodden apparel as their daughter's.

The helicopter scanned a dark patch of woods with a bright column of light. Down the line, spotlight beams played along the banks of the swollen creek. Flashers strobed the scene in hot reds and cold blues. Beneath the rhythmic thump of the chopper's rotors, over the steady rush of tumbling water, Maya listened to the voices calling back and forth in the dark. She could hear the distant whine of the search dogs moving through the timber. Police radios squawked and chattered all around.

"Something tells me this gets worse before it gets better," the new photog said.

"Yep," Maya said, watching a pair of sheriff's deputies trudging up the near slope of the creek bank. "Definitely a good day to be in the news business."

New Guy glanced away from his viewfinder momentarily, trying to judge whether or not she was kidding. His name was Carter something. The station had sent him, along with the two additional nightside crews now working the other side of the park, after the ten o'clock broadcast.

He'd been with the station a year and a half, Carter had said on arrival, all of it on the nightside, and Maya had never worked with him before. Apart from an apparent knack for stating the obvious, he seemed okay. She didn't know why she was busting his chops.

"Sorry," she told him. "Long day, bad joke."

"Yeah," Carter said. He seemed genuinely empathetic, but even that annoyed her.

The truth was, Maya felt unreasonably abandoned since Deon Bledsoe had accepted his long-overdue shift change. She thought that she even envied him a little. Photographers got to go home, story or no story. But for a reporter, the news policy of most stations was not unlike the retail-merchandise policies of yesteryear: *You broke it, you own it.*

Like it or not, she was in this for the long haul. Carter came over, shrugged off the camera, and said, "Hey, Miss Lamb. You okay?"

Miss Lamb. Jesus. How many years did this kid think she had on him?

How many years *did* she have on him?

Maya hugged her arms, worked out a kink in her neck. She'd dressed for six o'clock in Plymouth, not midnight on the riverfront. "Cold," she said. "Tired." She smiled. It felt like a smile-shaped piece of cardboard stuck to her face. "Do I look that horrible?"

He was too smart to step into that trap, Maya had to give him credit. Carter set the camera down on the concrete slab of the shelter, took off his News7 wind jacket, and handed it to her.

Maya glanced at the jacket. She glanced at Carter. She almost declined the offer out of random stubbornness, then she sighed.

"Thank you," she said, and meant it. The jacket more or less swallowed her when she put it on over her suit. The lining was still warm and smelled like men's deodorant. "You win the Nice Guy Award."

"Hey," he said. "I'll take one of those."

"You earned it, mister."

He smiled and nodded at her hand. "I meant one of those."

Maya looked down and realized she was still holding the half-crumpled pack of Parliaments Deon had left with her an hour and a half ago. *Call it a hunch,* he'd said on his way out.

She'd quit smoking before she left Clark Falls. Unless she'd forgotten a drunken relapse at some point along the way, Maya hadn't had a cigarette since the last time she stood around waiting for a search party to pull a young girl's body out of the drink. Funny. Maybe Deon could have been the reporter.

Maya almost handed the whole pack over to Carter in trade for the jacket. Then, at the last minute, she shook one out for him and kept the pack in her hand instead.

"Thanks," he said, hanging the cigarette between his lips.

"I don't even know what I'm doing with these," she told him, slipping the matchbook out from between the pack and its cellophane wrapper. She struck one and cupped her hand around the flare. "I quit years ago."

"Yeah, me too," Carter said. He leaned in, cupping his own hands around hers to help shield the small flame against the breeze. Teamwork.

When he was lit, Carter straightened, pursed a stream of white smoke toward the black sky, and said, "Sweet mother, that's good."

Maya shook out the match and nodded toward a small crowd milling around one of the other picnic shelters. "What's going on there, I wonder?"

Carter looked and said, "I heard some people from the neighborhood association brought down coffee. Want me to bring you a cup?"

Coffee sounded good. Coffee sounded better than good. Coffee sounded better than anything Maya could think of at the moment, unless it was coffee and one of Deon's hand-me-down cigarettes. "I'll go with you," she said.

They were halfway to the spot when a lightbank fired up ahead of them, illuminating the picnic shelter in a sudden bright splash. Maya realized they weren't walking toward kindly members of the Webber–Camden Homeowners Association but yet another camera crew. A few yards closer, she saw the subject of the camera's attention.

"You've got to be kidding me," she said.

Carter said, "What?"

"This has to be a new record," Maya said. "Even for that douchebag."

"Who?" Carter said.

Maya looked at him with genuine surprise. "You don't recognize that guy?"

As they walked, she cocked her head toward the man standing in the center of the light ahead. He was sixty-something, square-shouldered, dressed in the full signature getup Maya had come to identify on sight, even from a hundred paces: cowboy boots, sheepskin jacket, rodeo buckle, straw Stetson. With his early-white hair and matching walrus mustache, he looked like a cross between Wilford Brimley and the Marlboro Man.

Carter took a moment, leaned forward, and said, "Is that Buck Morningside?"

"The one and only," Maya confirmed, walking faster. "Come on, I want to hear this."

16

Hubert Humphrey "Buck" Morningside, now holding court in the picnic area at North Mississippi Regional Park, was a billboard bail bondsman whose three-foot mustache and laser-whitened smile overlooked freeways and high-volume thoroughfares all across the Twin Cities metropolitan area.

Maya Lamb had first encountered the man in person during her second year at News7, while covering the story of a missing thirteen-year-old Richfield boy named Timothy Herman. Herman had disappeared without a trace one sunny May morning on his way to school, and for about a week it had seemed that nobody who knew the young teen had a clue where to find him. Foul play was quickly considered, then suspected, and finally presumed.

Then, several days into the investigation, Buck Morningside—working privately for the Herman family—had shown up the state and local authorities by tracking the inexplicably vanished seventh-grader to a Starlite Motel room in Apache Junction, Arizona.

Young Timmy Herman, it turned out, had been

on his way to California with Charlagne Meredith, the twenty-nine-year-old divorcée who worked day shift at one of the convenience stores along Herman's route to school. Minnesota law enforcement had taken a beating in the press over it. Charlagne Meredith, pregnant with the middle schooler's child, became national shock-news fodder for a brief period of time. And Buck Morningside had been finding new ways to get his cornball mug on television ever since.

Maya had crossed his path more than once since the Timmy Herman debacle. By virtue of repeated exposure and a little grapevine intelligence, she'd learned a few things that Morningside had somehow managed—miraculously, it seemed—to keep from smudging his hokey-folky public persona. Starting with his given name, which was not Hubert Humphrey Morningside.

It was McNally Owen Spooner III. Nor was he from Black Hills cattle-rancher stock, as the bio on his website claimed (the only website for a bail-bonding company Maya had ever seen that featured a downloadable press kit).

In truth, Spooner had been a lawman himself, once upon a time. A one-term sheriff, according to Maya's sources, voted out of Yellow Medicine County in the mid 1980s amidst unproven allegations of nepotism, graft, and general skulduggery. Spooner had disappeared for a while, largely unmissed, resurfacing under a new name several years later to become, figuratively and literally, the face of surety bail bonds in greater Hennepin County.

It would have been predictable to find him here eventually, Maya thought. A missing girl, an active search, lots of news cameras—it was all right there in the front window of Buck Morningside's favorite candy store. But this was moving quickly even for him.

Maya walked up to a young guy with artsy black-framed eyeglasses and a North Face fleece. He was standing a few feet behind the camera operator, holding a clipboard.

"Hey," she said quietly. "Who are you with, anyway?"

The guy flipped her a cursory glance. Then he took a second look, brightened a little, and said, "Oh, hey. Maya Lamb, right? News7?"

She touched the insignia on Carter's coat. "That's me."

He smiled, tucked his clipboard, held out his hand. "Eliott Martin," he said, automatically matching her volume; nearby sound gear picked up the sibilance of a whisper more easily than it did low, quiet voices. "Twin Cities Public Television. I watch you all the time."

"Nice to meet you," Maya said, thinking, *TPT? Seriously?* She nodded toward the proceedings, where Buck Morningside stood bright in the light, spouting some horseshit or other. "Just curious—what are you shooting here?"

"New series we're doing in the summer," Eliott Martin said. He angled his clipboard so that Maya could see. "Pilot episode airs in June."

Maya squinted, found the show title in a log

heading at the top of the page: *American Man-hunter: Northstar Justice*. She had to read the words twice before she was convinced she'd read them correctly.

"You absolutely have got to be shitting me," she said.

One of the sound guys looked their way. Close behind him came a glare from an unshaven thirty-something fellow standing near the boom mike. Thirty-something wore a peacoat, Chuck Taylors, a denim military cap. Maya took him to be the director.

Which made Eliott Martin a producer of some kind. Martin cringed a little, gave a thumbs-up, made a cranking motion with his index finger: *Sorry, gang, keep rolling.*

When everybody turned back to business, Maya said, "American Manhunter?"

"I know, right?" Eliott used his clipboard as a shield. "I totally thought the same thing."

"When did TPT start slumming?"

"Desperate times call for desperate measures," the young producer murmured, as though they were con-spirators. "You don't even want to see our pledge-drive numbers for last year."

"Come on," Maya said. "Buck Morningside?"

"Oh, he's an onion. Believe me. We haven't even started peeling the layers on that guy."

It's official, Maya thought. *The world has gone to hell.*

"You know, we should put our heads together," Eliott Martin said. "Who knows? Maybe we could help each other."

Words failed her. Maya tuned in to the monologue in progress.

". . . triazolam," Morningside was saying to the camera. In what context, Maya couldn't immediately guess. "Docs used to give it for trouble sleeping, anxiety, what have you. Nowadays you don't see it prescribed quite so much as you used to, but regular folks might remember the brand name Halcion. Which, 'course we know now, is the same stuff Jeffrey Dahmer used to slip his victims."

Holy Jesus, what an idiot, Maya thought. Morningside was surrounded by the TPT crew and miscellaneous onlookers. Reporters from a couple of her competing affiliates had, like Maya, wandered over to check out the fuss. If Buck Morningside sensed her private derision emanating from anywhere in the audience, it didn't slow him down.

"Now, triazolam," he said. "You mix this stuff with a little alcohol, and what you've basically got is a batch of homemade knockout drops."

Murmurs from the crowd.

"'Course, we can't know that's what's happened here," Morningside said. The voice of cautious reason. "All *we* know is, a police search found an empty prescription bottle for triazolam in this old boy's medicine chest. But right now we just can't know. That's why we're out here."

Maya honestly couldn't believe the fool crap she heard coming out of the guy's mouth, and she'd heard her share over the years. Jeffrey Dahmer was involved now? Whose medicine chest?

But the director seemed mighty pleased with his

star. Eliott Martin rolled his eyes for Maya's benefit, though she could see plainly on his face that he'd given himself over to the dark side. *Desperate times call for desperate measures,* he'd said. She didn't even want to see last year's pledge-drive numbers.

When the camera and the lightbank went dark and the production crew set about their gear, Buck Morningside cut a handshaking path through the cluster of people, ignoring the other reporters in attendance, and made a line directly toward Maya. Apparently he'd noticed her after all. She must have been special.

"'Mares eat oats and does eat oats but little lambs eat ivy,'" he said, closing the distance between them. His mustache lifted up at the corners as he touched the brim of his Stetson. "Didn't even recognize you under that big old coat. What's the news, darlin'?"

"Gee, I don't know," she said. "I guess you'll have to tell me."

"How's that?"

Maya caught a glimpse of Eliott Martin under the picnic canopy, talking to the director. She looked for Carter and saw him thirty feet away, talking with a photog from KARE 11. For the moment, it was just her and and the one-and-only Buck Morningside.

"Come on, Hubert."

"Buck to my friends, darlin'."

I'm not your darling, Maya thought, surprised at her sudden anger. "Where'd you come up with that Halcion routine, anyway? Top of your head?"

"Now, Miss Maya," he said. "You know I got my sources."

"What sources could those be?"

Morningside chuckled. "You know, these cops, I just naturally expect to come down here and do their jobs for 'em. Don't break my heart and tell me I got to do yours now too."

"Oh, so *that's* why you're here." It occurred to Maya that she was taking this personally. "To do the cops' jobs for them?"

"Wouldn't be the first time."

"Hey, I don't know if anybody told you." She pointed over Morningside's shoulder, toward the search party spreading out through the timber in the background. "But everybody's over there."

"Oh, don't you worry, I got some boys of mine in the mix." He cocked his head thoughtfully. "Then again, when you're right, you're right. Guess I'd better quit jawing and get to work, hadn't I?"

This morning, Maya kept thinking, she'd talked to a bright young woman with her future ahead of her. Tonight they were searching for her body. And here was this clown.

"Don't forget your cameras," she said.

He touched the brim of his hat again. "Same to you."

Maya said nothing.

"Always a pleasure, darlin'."

As she watched him go, a breadth of dun-colored sheepskin moving away through the gloom, Maya stabbed at her mobile with her thumb, texting a single word to Roger Barnhill:

Triazolam?

In moments, her phone buzzed in reply.

Who gave you that information?

Her head was starting to ache. She was grinding her molars. She forced herself to relax her jaw.

Maya looked up from the phone screen and let her eyes drift across the tableau before her. She observed the loose scrum of newspeople milling about in the picnic area, waiting for something to happen.

She watched the crew from Twin Cities Public Television mounting up and preparing to move. She watched the scruffy director in the peacoat and denim cap, now speaking to Buck Morningside in sweeping hand gestures, perhaps blocking out their next scene in the air between them. She looked around and thought, as if it had only just occurred to her: *I'm part of this.*

All at once a crushing fatigue swamped her. She saw another group of people working beneath yet another picnic shelter. A short line had formed there, and Maya recognized at once what she was seeing: members of the neighborhood association Carter had heard about, doling cups of coffee to cold and weary volunteers.

A memory came to her. A favorite professor, a particular afternoon lecture: Ethics in Journalism 452. On the day of this memory, the professor had projected a famous image for the class to consider and discuss.

Their subject had been an AP photograph from the Vietnam War: a young village girl running naked toward the camera, face contorted in fear and pain, her flesh burning all over with napalm. It was a haunting image that brought the horror and chaos of wartime straight into your belly from someplace far away. The question for the class:

If you're the photographer, do you take time to snap the picture?

The photograph in question won a Pulitzer prize, and it had been credited with changing public perception of the war; moments after capturing it, the photographer had delivered the girl personally to a Saigon hospital, where, against all odds, she'd survived. And Maya—that day in class, and every day since—had always answered the question the same way:

Of course you take the picture.

You take the picture because that's why you're there. You take the picture because it's your job.

But something happened just then, watching the coffee line in the distance. For the first time in her career—standing there by the picnic shelter, feeling like a little girl in Carter's oversize coat—Maya felt her answer changing.

Thinking of Juliet Benson standing at her father's window—remembering the sight of the girl's haggard parents huddled together like refugees near the state patrol post back at the Camden Center mall—she could almost feel the moment her perspective shifted. Like a twig snapping underfoot. A galvanizing surge of adrenaline followed; her surroundings seemed to shimmer with new clarity. She thought of Buck Morningside's face as he tipped his hat goodbye. Then she thought, *What the hell are you waiting for?*

Maya started walking. She squirmed out of Carter's

jacket on the way. When she reached him, she draped
the jacket over his shoulder and said, "Thanks."

Carter took one look at her and said, "You okay?"

"Never better," Maya told him, and kept walking.

There was a twenty-four-hour drugstore at the Camden Center shopping strip, the parking lot of which
now served as the cross-agency command hub for the
Juliet Benson search effort. Maya took the footpath
up the grassy slope, crossed Webber Parkway at the
corner, and strode across the lot, through the lights
and commotion.

She walked directly to Webber Drug and pulled
open the front door. She went in past a cluster of employees, all crowded around the front windows in
their smocks and name tags. She grabbed a red basket
from the stack in the entryway. Then she struck out
for supplies.

In aisle 9, she found wool socks. She grabbed two pair
and tossed them in the basket, then moved on to the
rack she spotted at the end of the aisle: heavy hooded
sweatshirts in plain solid colors, on sale for nine dollars each. She found the last size small on the rack, in
navy blue. Into the basket it went. In the adjacent rack
she found matching sweatpants. Only extra-large left in
navy, nothing in black, only double-extra-large in gray.
Her choices appeared to be fire engine red or canary
yellow.

Yellow, she thought.

Into the basket.

Maya clacked along from aisle to aisle in her kitten-heel pumps, hoping to run across a bin of cheap sneakers or even a pair of basic buckle overshoes. Everybody sold overshoes in Minnesota.

Everybody except the Webber Drug at Camden Center, apparently. She coursed up and back, heels clipping and clopping. At last, at the very end of the outdoor aisle, she struck pay dirt: a rack of lime-green Crocs-brand rubber sandals. She grabbed a pair in her size, thought again, and exchanged them for the next size larger. She'd need to double up on the socks.

She grabbed three energy bars from the rack in the checkout aisle and tossed them into the basket with the rest of her goods. She lifted the basket into the check stand and then, as an afterthought, reached back and added one last item: a white plastic Bic cigarette lighter.

Maya had to clear her throat loudly before an irritated-looking woman with ruddy cheeks pulled herself away from the view out the window, slouched over without a greeting, and began ringing her through. Phyllis, according to her name tag. At one point she glanced up, and her eyes flickered, and she said, "Oh, hi there. Don't I know who you are?"

"I don't know," Maya said.

As Maya swiped her credit card, Phyllis snapped her fingers and said, "I knew it. You're Maya Lamb, aren't you? From the news? You must be with them out there."

Maya smiled politely and said, "Do you have a public restroom?"

Phyllis smiled back and escorted Maya personally to the women's room in the back corner of the store, near the pharmacy. At the door she said, "Do you really think they'll find that girl's body down there in the park?"

"Let's hope for a happy ending," Maya said, thanked the woman for her help, and pushed her way into the ladies'.

Five minutes later, she emerged, dressed in her new hot-green sandals, both pairs of socks just in case, and the mismatched sweatpants/hoodie combo.

The whole ensemble had cost her forty-one dollars and felt comfortable as hell. She carried her six-hundred-dollar suit and heels in the crinkly plastic Webber Drug sack. A few employees gawked at her as she left the store, and Maya caught a glimpse of herself in the glass of the window front outside. She looked like a circus clown. And she felt better than she'd felt all day long.

Deon must have departed in whatever station vehicle Carter had driven here, because the live truck remained where she and Deon had left it after the ten o'clock: around the corner of the Joy Luck Restaurant at the end of the mall.

Maya detoured quickly past the truck, flung her things in the back, then made a beeline toward the command post. She stopped the first person she encountered who looked like he knew what he was doing, a stocky sheriff's deputy just coming off his radio.

"Deputy," she said, and when he didn't respond, she called out, "Deputy!"

He was trying his best to be on his way somewhere, but he stopped and said, "Help you, miss?"

"I'm here to join the volunteers," Maya said.

The deputy looked her up and down, seeming puzzled by something. Maya waited impatiently for the inevitable: *Aren't you Maya Lamb?* Then she remembered what she was wearing and understood that he wasn't trying to place her at all. He was merely amused by her appearance.

"We're grateful for any assistance from the public," the deputy said. "Follow me."

17

Rockhaven might not have had any phones or a cell tower within range, but as of two winters ago the place did have a twenty-seven-inch RCA flat-screen television with three hundred satellite channels, including HBO. The TV had been a Christmas present to Hal from Regina, who had won the set selling mail-order jewelry. Every time Mike saw it, the thought of the crappy Magnavox Hal still kept over the bar at the Elbow Room amused him.

The muffled yammer of the television was the first thing he heard as he approached the cabin. It wasn't quite so amusing tonight.

He thought about trying to get a look through the east windows to see if he could get the lay of the land in there, but he didn't care to break an ankle crawling around the piled, jagged rock apron in the dark. So he climbed the steps up to the porch, walked heavily across the pine boards, and announced himself in a loud, clear voice on his way through the front door: *It's Mike, I'm coming in, don't shoot my ass.*

The way it turned out, he didn't have to worry.

Mike found Minnesota Public Enemy #1 passed out on the old leather couch by the fireplace, snoring loudly over the cackle of an after-hours infomercial. He stopped with his hand on the latch and scanned the rest of the room. You could see the better part of the place from the entryway, the main room going maybe twenty by thirty feet corner to corner, opening up to the rail-lined half-story landing.

Every lamp was burning. Above the fireplace, a trophy walleye hung shellacked and gleaming in the yellow light, posed over an old cane fishing pole in a frozen mimic of its former glory. Most of the furniture sat around a large rag rug in the middle of the floor. There was a rough sideboard, some handmade shelves, a few other trophies mounted here and there on the walls. An old steamer trunk sat in one corner, an antique rocker in another.

No sign of the girl who belonged to the car outside. Only Darryl, sawing logs in the middle of it all.

Mike went over. Darryl was slouched half upright amid a scatter of empty beer cans and a spilled bag of Doritos, legs splayed in front of him, one hand resting on the .45 at his side. His unwashed hair stood up from his head in matted clumps. His mouth hung open. His stomach rose and fell. He sounded like a dump truck climbing a hill.

On the coffee table, Mike saw yet another fifth of Old Crow, this one already worn down to a couple inches in the bottom of the bottle. The bottle sat next to a yellowed stack of last season's newspapers: *The Lake Country Herald—Voice of Brainerd/Baxter Vacation Land.*

On the floor beneath the coffee table sat Darryl's rucksack, alongside a zipped gym bag. The gym bag Mike couldn't remember seeing before, but he didn't need to look to know that he'd find Toby Lunden's cash inside.

Jesus. Mike stepped forward. He leaned down into Darryl's atmosphere, a noxious cloud of body odor and ethyl fumes, and slipped the gun from beneath his limp fingers.

There came an immediate hitch in Darryl's snore. He closed his mouth, shifted position, and was silent a moment. Mike stood like stone and waited.

Slowly, Darryl's mouth fell open again, and the snoring resumed.

For the first time all day, Mike felt relieved. He'd seen Darryl sleep like the dead for twenty-four hours after a bender, and by his rough calculations— thinking back over the past two or three days—this one would go down as a bender for the books.

Maybe all of this would go easier than he'd expected. He checked his watch. An hour and change before he had to call Hal.

Mike thumbed the safety catch on the .45, tucked the gun in the back of his waistband, and went to find the girl. He knew she couldn't be far: The cabin was no more than a thousand square feet all told, twelve hundred square at the most. Downstairs there was the main room, a small farmhouse kitchen, one bedroom, and a mud porch in back. A varnished pine staircase led up to the loft, which had been divvied up into a pair of smaller bedrooms.

Mike followed a hunch up the creaking staircase and knew he'd guessed correctly. The door to the bedroom at the top of the stairs stood open, but the door to the second bedroom, across the landing, was closed.

On the floor near the second bedroom he saw the cordless DeWalt drill Hal kept in the boat shed with the rest of his away-from-home tools. On approach, Mike understood why the shed door had been standing open when he'd arrived:

Darryl had removed the latch and the padlock from the shed, brought the whole thing inside, and reinstalled it here, on the second bedroom door. Mike looked down and saw little piles of fresh sawdust from the drill holes in the door frame. No light showed through the crack at the bottom of the door.

He tapped the door softly with a knuckle and said, "Juliet?"

Nothing.

He tapped louder and said, "Juliet, my name is Mike. I'm a friend. Are you okay?"

Again, not a sound in reply. He pressed one ear against the door, plugged the other with a finger. He couldn't hear anything apart from his own pulse, the sound of the television, and Darryl snoring away downstairs.

He imagined the Benson girl in there, cowering at his voice, holding her breath. Quiet as a mouse.

Or maybe she was sleeping, just like Darryl.

Or maybe there was some other reason she was quiet.

Mike didn't want to overthink it. He stooped down and grabbed up the drill, still outfitted with the driver bit Darryl had used. To the closed door he said, "Juliet. I'm coming in to help you. Don't be scared, okay?"

With that he went to work, zipping out the screws with six long pulls of the drill trigger. He caught the screws one at a time in his palm, caught the assembly as it fell from the door frame. He set the drill and the hardware down on the floor, then stood and listened again. Still nothing. The snoring downstairs went on undisturbed.

"Okay," he said. "I'm coming in now. It's me, Mike. Don't be scared."

He pulled the door open slowly and stepped inside the darkened room. The moon shone in through the sash window, casting the room in lambent shapes and shadows. Mike reached in, found the light switch, and flipped it on.

For the next several moments he stood there, eyes adjusting to the sudden change in light, trying to make sense out of what he was seeing.

Then, without thinking about it, he said aloud to the empty room, "You're fucking kidding me."

18

Mike Barlowe had never been the smartest kid in class. He'd never been the dumbest, but he'd never been the smartest. He'd graduated high school somewhere in the back third of the pack, and instead of going to college or trade school, he'd gone to war.

But you didn't need a degree in anything to be able to see how things had happened here. The tiny loft bedroom looked like a crime scene: wall-to-wall upheaval, smeared all over with signs of violence. Then, once the initial visual shock subsided, what first looked like grim chaos assembled itself into relatively simple order.

Either way, the room was empty.

He hadn't tied her up, Darryl. A mark in the gentleman's column there. Mike saw that he'd left her a big plastic water bottle on the nightstand to drink from, a galvanized bait bucket in the corner to pee in. All a girl needed.

To keep her leashed yet able to use the makeshift facilities if need arose, Darryl had tethered her to the bed by the ankle on eight feet of heavy-duty fish stringer—yet another item he'd have found in the canoe shed, along with the drill and the bait bucket.

Mike knew all of this because he could see the evidence Juliet Benson had left behind: the abandoned bindings; the bloody footprints zigzagging the bare wood floor; the bed shoved up against the wall beneath the open window; the sheet knotted securely to a spindle in the bed's foot rail, trailing over the windowsill, disappearing from view.

He barely knew what the Benson girl looked like, apart from the photo they'd shown on the news, yet he could imagine her clearly in his mind: her predicament, her solution, the evident results. Standing there, surveying the state of the room, he might as well have been reviewing security-camera footage of her escape. He could see it all in his mind, every step of the way.

Certainly she would have been able to hear the television downstairs, even through the padlocked door. Which meant that at some point she'd have been able to hear the snoring begin, the same way Mike could hear it now.

Mike wondered how long she'd waited before working up her courage. He imagined her testing, calling out for attention first, just to be sure no attention would be paid. Of course Darryl hadn't heard her, any more than he'd heard Mike honking the Power Wagon outside. And when no amount of hollering caused the snoring to stop—when at last she'd managed to satisfy herself that the coast was as clear as it was liable to get anytime soon—she'd gone to work.

The fish stringer was made of tough yellow nylon cord, with a steel ring on one end and a six-inch gill needle—about the diameter of a number-two pencil—on the other.

Darryl had secured one end of the cord to the girl and the other end to the bed, using a number of plastic zip ties. These Mike recognized from his own toolbox at home, left over from three months he'd spent doing installs for the cable company last spring.

The zip ties were a handy way to bundle up coaxial line. They were tough enough to batten a loose muffler on a 1992 two-door Buick Skylark indefinitely. They were good for all kinds of little jobs, really. Now that Mike thought of it, the zip ties were almost no different from the flex cuffs they'd used on captured Iraqi insurgents, once upon a time.

Mike had never seen anyone slip out of a pair of properly cinched flex cuffs, but Darryl had taken steps to ensure that Juliet Benson wouldn't be the first. He'd used half a dozen of the things to lash the steel ring to her ankle.

On the other end of the cord, Darryl had used several more ties to splint the stringer needle tightly alongside another spindle in the foot rail. He'd wound the stringer cord tightly around the spindle, top to bottom, crimping off the cord with one last tie at the end.

Had it been Mike's job to do, he might have fastened the cord to the iron bed frame instead of to the wooden foot rail, but that could have been hindsight on his part.

The practical fact was that this was a sturdy old bed, handmade from solid oak. Not like the new crap you could get for a price at the Furniture Barn. Kicking out one of these spindles with bare feet would have been a tall order for most anybody without a black belt in something, and Juliet Benson's spindle had been reinforced with 10-gauge steel and five-hundred-pound nylon. Bottom line: You wouldn't have expected her to be going anywhere.

But the girl was smart.

Smart enough to shove the mattress off the bed, lift the box spring, and find exactly what she needed: a spare floorboard someone had thought to saw down and use as a bed slat.

For Juliet Benson's purposes, a four-foot pry bar.

The slat now lay on the floor over by the night table, discarded near a parcel of thick dust where the bed had been. Looking at the bed in its new spot under the window, Mike could see the ragged wood splinters still caught in the ruined spindle holes, top and bottom, where she'd managed to pry out her binding post.

She'd taken the spindle with her to the cedar chest in the near corner, where she could sit down. Mike imagined her there, fixed in concentration, working the coils of stringer cord loose enough to expose the steel tip of the gill needle. It wouldn't have been easy. She would have had to stay patient. Very patient.

But she'd gotten the job done. And now she'd made herself a new tool: a sort of improvised awl mounted on a ramming handle.

Crouching next to the cedar chest, examining the abandoned spindle like some primitive artifact, Mike decided that it was about as well suited an implement as she could have come up with under the circumstances.

Then again, this was where the blood started. And Mike could see how that must have happened too.

The zip ties wouldn't have surrendered easily, and

she'd had five or six of them to go through. He saw
her pushing against the restraints with the steel prong
until her arms shook. He saw her slip and gouge herself, saw the tip of the gill needle digging furrows in
her skin. He saw her stifle an outcry as the furrows
welled up with blood. He saw her sitting there on the
cedar chest with her fists clenched, biting back tears.
Or at least he imagined it that way.

Then he imagined her pulling herself together, starting again. Working on each band one at a time.

How many times had she slipped before she was
through?

It didn't matter. The stringer, the bed spindle, and
the severed zip ties now lay in a pile on the floor
where she'd dropped them, a tangle of rope and
sprung manacles. The bloody smears and bare heel
prints charted her movements from there.

The window wasn't actually open, Mike discovered. Darryl had fixed that for good measure. Mike
could see the fresh screws toenailed into the bottom
corners of the window, fastening the sash to the
frame.

He also saw flakes of broken glass still caught in the
bed quilt, now discarded in a pile on the floor. Mike
imagined that she'd used the quilt as protection, or a
sound baffle, or both.

Leaning out through the vacant opening into the
cool, tangy night air, he could see wicked-looking
shards of broken windowpane glinting amid the jagged rock below, just beyond the dangling end of the
sheet.

She climbed down into that, he thought. *Barefoot.*
She wouldn't have had any other choice.

Mike went downstairs. As he crossed the room, the programming on television cut away to a commercial for Buck Morningside Bail Bonds. Familiar as they were this time of night, Mike had to shake his head at the stroke of timing.

Sometimes it seemed like the universe had a sarcastic sense of humor. Sometimes it seemed like the universe could be kind of an asshole.

He went over to the couch, nudged Darryl with the side of his foot, and said, "Dude. Wake up."

He might as well have been talking to Buck Morningside on the tube. Mike stepped around the coffee table and turned off the television so he could hear himself think. He came back and kicked Darryl in the leg. It was like kicking a side of beef. Mike kicked harder the second time. He raised his voice and said, "Wake up, man."

Darryl was as stubborn asleep as he was awake.

Screw this, Mike thought. He went upstairs, grabbed the bait bucket from the bedroom, brought it down with him. His knee had protested these stairs before, but Mike hardly felt it now. He took the bucket outside, filled it full of water from the hose bib around the side of the cabin. Two gallons, icy cold.

He brought the full bucket inside, said, "Rise and shine," and dumped the whole thing in Darryl's lap.

For a split second nothing happened.

Then, in curious slow motion, Darryl erupted into consciousness as though rising up from a great depth. He issued a strangled bellow, seemed almost to levitate from the cushions momentarily, and fell back, hands shooting out to either side like buttresses.

It was like watching a science experiment. Darryl

didn't even know who he was for a few seconds. He was soaked to the skin. For just those few seconds, the guy looked so confused and pathetic—shaking his head, blinking his eyes, croaking like a frog—that if circumstances had been different, the whole display might have been comical.

Then, all at once, Darryl's eyes sprang wide. His right hand began to scrabble around the sofa cushion beside him as if suddenly possessed of its own frenzied agenda.

Mike stepped forward into Darryl's field of vision. He pulled the .45 out of his waistband, held it upside down by the trigger guard between two fingers, and said, "Is this what you're looking for?"

At last Darryl found him with his eyes. His face registered nothing at first. Then came recognition, then renewed confusion, all in a span of two or three blinks. He coughed and said, "Mike?"

"No, Saint Peter," Mike said. He dropped the empty bucket to the floor with a hollow clang. "You died and went to heaven. I guess some paperwork got screwed up."

Darryl rubbed his eyes, sat up a little straighter on the couch. He coughed again, fully present now. Or at least fully awake. He spread his hands, looked himself over and said, "I believe it, you crazy fucker." He pinched his sodden T-shirt away from his chest. "I think you stopped my heart for a couple seconds."

"Yeah, sure," Mike said. "I'm the crazy fucker."

Casually, Darryl glanced at the gun in Mike's hand. Clearly no threat, but definitely his gun. And definitely not in the spot where he'd left it.

He looked at Mike. After a minute, he said, "And I was having the best dream too."

He was still drunk, Mike realized. A person might not have known it if they didn't know Darryl, but Mike knew Darryl. Hell, the guy had put away enough cheap whiskey in the last twenty-four hours to kill a teetotaler, and that wasn't even counting all the beer. Who knew what else? Of course he was still drunk.

"If I have to be awake for this horseshit," Mike told him, "then so do you."

Darryl blinked. Yawned. Said, "How'd you get all the way up here without a car, anyway?"

"I adapted and overcame."

"Oh," Darryl said.

"I'm not the only one either."

"Yeah?"

"Why don't you go upstairs and check on your new friend?" Mike glanced toward the loft. "I think she left a message for you."

Darryl craned his neck, following Mike's eyes up to the landing.

The moment he saw the padlocked door standing open, his spined stiffened. Almost before Mike realized he'd moved, Darryl was off the couch, across the room, taking the pine stairs up two a time.

Maybe he wasn't so drunk after all.

Mike tucked the gun back into his waistband, left Darryl up there with his discoveries, and went outside.

Eventually, Darryl came down to the lakeshore and joined him at the end of the narrow, weathered dock.

"Okay, I admit it," he said, his approaching footfalls vibrating through the planks ahead of his voice. "I did not see that coming."

Mike didn't say anything. He just kept sweeping the far shoreline with the three-million-candlepower spotlight he'd grabbed from the shed. From the dock, the beam was powerful enough to brighten the reeds and standing grass along the tree line like a roving circle of daylight.

"Girl's tougher than she looks," Darryl mused. He sounded more fascinated than upset. "Seemed like a real princess too. Guess you can't make assumptions."

I guess not, Mike thought. Using the spotlight, he'd been able to follow her trail from the broken glass under the bedroom window, like tracking a wounded deer. Based on the quality of the blood sign, she hadn't come through the glass unscathed.

He'd already formulated a pretty good idea of how Juliet Benson had completed the next phase of her escape. Now the spotlight beam confirmed his theory. Across the lake, he caught a flash of metal tucked away in the trees. Mike brought the spotlight back and identified the sudden shine for what it was: the hull of a canoe stashed in a stand of sumac.

The girl was tough, all right. And still being smart. Mike felt like he understood her strategy instinctively.

The lake was roughly peanut-shaped, narrow in the middle, rounded on either end. The blood trail told him that after climbing out the window and making it to solid ground, she hadn't dared reenter the cabin to look for her car keys.

But to take the lane out of here on foot, she would

have had to walk around the far end of the peanut, still barefoot, on rough cold driveway rock most of the way. And there were stretches along the south embankment—lake on one side, steep downhill drop on the other—where she'd have had nowhere to bail out if her captor happened to wake up and come after her.

Paddling straight across the water, on the other hand, cut her distance by more than half, saved at least a bit of wear and tear on her injured feet, and took her directly into the cover of the timber.

It would be slow going in the trees. Plenty of hidden rocks, holes, pinecones, broken branches, and thorny brambles waiting for her. But if she was careful and stayed patient, stuck to soft ground and pine straw as much as she could, and kept the rock lane in sight on her left, then she could make it all the way to the lake road—possibly even the state highway—without ever setting foot out in the open.

Mike was starting to admire the girl. Besides leaving a bottle of perfectly good drinking water behind, he found little fault in her thinking.

Still, a fifteen-foot aluminum canoe was a heavy, awkward thing. Hard to handle out of the water all alone. She could have dragged it across the rocks, but if she'd wanted to avoid making an unholy racket, she would have had to carry it over the ground for at least a hundred feet. Out of the shed, across the lane. At least to where she could push or drag it on the dewy grass the rest of the way. All the way to the sandy launch beside the dock.

All the time scared. Bleeding. And not quite the princess Darryl had taken her for. She might have been born with some money, but she hadn't been born soft, this girl.

Definitely tough enough in Mike's book.

He let up on the spotlight's trigger. The beam faded and then extinguished, draping the opposite bank in darkness again. Water lapped at the pilings under their feet. Mike stood at the edge of the dock, looking out over the inky, moon-dappled surface of the lake, and tried to think.

How long had she been gone?

Had he passed her on his way in without even knowing it?

"Okay," Darryl finally said. "I give up. What are we doing out here?"

Mike looked at him.

"We?" On impulse, he turned, raised the spotlight, and shone it full blast in Darryl's face. "What are *we* doing?"

Darryl raised a hand, standing pale as an over-exposed photograph in the ultrabright light. "Damn," he said. "Take it easy."

"You tell me," Mike said, holding the light steady. "What are we doing, man? I'll be damned if I can figure it out."

Darryl squinted his eyes, leaning his face away. He said, "Come on, turn it off."

Something overcame Mike then. An incredibly powerful urge. He surrendered to it with an ease that surprised him.

"Oh," he said. "Sorry."

He cut the light. While Darryl stood there, temporarily blinded, Mike punched the shit out of him. Just planted his back foot, pivoted with his hips, unwound his shoulders, and caught Darryl with a hard right hand across the jaw.

It was a gutter move, cheap and dirty, and Darryl didn't catch so much as a glimpse of it coming his way. The shot landed so pure that Mike felt the impact all the way to his elbow yet hardly felt it at all.

Darryl hit the dock with a heavy grunt, flat on his back, and laid there like he'd been tossed out of a helicopter. Mike put the light back in his face, leaned down, and shouted, "What are we doing, Darryl? Huh? You tell *me* what the hell we're doing out here."

He felt sick with nerves and adrenaline. In the five years he'd been home from the service, Mike honestly couldn't remember losing his temper over anything. The truth was, after six months in a combat zone, nothing ever seemed to matter enough to get bent out of shape about.

Now it was as if a floodgate had opened inside him. Standing over Darryl, Mike felt swept up in a hazy red tide.

"Stand up," he said, cutting the light again. "Stand up and tell me what we're doing out here."

Darryl didn't stand up. He only propped himself on an elbow. After a minute he leaned over the edge of the dock, spat blood into the water. In the light of the nearly full moon, with his five-day beard and disheveled hair, he looked like some kind of premature, half-changed wolfman with bloodstained chops.

"I said stand up," Mike repeated, knowing that if Darryl obliged him, even drunk, he'd have more than he could handle.

But he didn't care. He didn't care so much that, when Darryl didn't move, Mike reached down, grabbed him by his soaked shirt, and hauled him to his feet.

Darryl didn't resist. He only put out his palms. "Go easy," he said.

Mike hit him again before he could stop and think about it. This time it hurt like hell. He felt the big knuckle at the base of his ring finger give way. Fiery vines of pain climbed his hand and circled his wrist.

Darryl tripped on his own feet and went down again. He landed hard on his hip this time. The hollow thud of bone on wood echoed under the dock below them, and for a moment—just a moment— there it was.

That look. The look that told Mike things were about to get dangerous. As many times as he'd seen it, Mike had never been on the receiving end before now; as many times as he'd seen it directed toward others, he'd never seen it result in anything but blood loss.

Hot as he was, he had no trouble admitting it: That look scared him. He didn't want to lock horns with Darryl Potter. But enough was enough.

What happened next was the last thing Mike expected.

The impending mayhem in Darryl's eyes went away. It went away almost as quickly as it had appeared, fading out like the beam of Hal's big spotlight as the bulb cooled.

Darryl sat up. He touched his left cheekbone, looked at his fingers. No blood this time. He worked his jaw. "Ow," he said.

Mike sighed. All the fight ran out of him. He made an experimental fist, then shook out his jacked-up, aching hand. He could feel his fourth knuckle shoved off to one side, a loose, displaced knob under the skin.

"Goddammit," he said.

Darryl dabbed his mouth gingerly with the back of his hand. He spat more blood over the edge of the dock. Slowly, he opened his jaw wider and wider until it popped way back in the joint. He winced bitterly, glanced up, and said, "We finished with this part?"

It occurred to Mike that he could take out the .45 and shoot the son of a bitch.

He exhaled, extended a hand, helped him to his feet instead.

Darryl brushed off his ass with his palms. Mike turned toward the lake, settled his gaze on the water. He listened for sounds in the timber. All he could hear was the lap of the water against pilings beneath them, the seashell rush of his own blood in his ears.

Darryl appeared in his peripheral vision. They stood without speaking.

Eventually, Darryl said, "Guess Hal sold me out, huh?"

Mike turned and studied Darryl's profile. An oily patina of sour, boozy sweat made his skin look like room-temperature cheese. He said, "Did you think he wouldn't?"

Darryl shrugged. "I was kinda moving from A to B to C at that point."

"No kidding," Mike said. "Which part was A?"

Darryl didn't answer.

Mike turned and left him standing there. He walked back up the dock alone. He could think of about a hundred things he wanted to ask or say, but none of them really mattered. He knew what he had to do, or at least what he had to do next. Why waste time?

There was a good chance, he thought, that Juliet Benson had found her way to help by now.

On the other hand, it was just as possible that she was exhausted and bleeding in the woods somewhere. He hoped for the former, but he couldn't risk the latter. Wouldn't.

He'd reached the shoreline when, behind him, Darryl said, "Hey, Mike?"

He almost kept walking. But he stopped.

"You know I wasn't going to hurt her," Darryl said. "Right?"

Mike found himself lost for a reply.

He turned and faced Darryl from a distance. "I wasn't going to hurt her," Darryl said. "That was never the deal."

Mike thought about that. The next question was obvious. The answer didn't matter, but he wanted to know anyway. "Then what the hell *was* it?" he said. "What the hell was all this about?"

Darryl exhaled like a man putting down a burdensome load. Perhaps the point no longer seemed as clear to him as it had at the time. Or maybe he was only disappointed that Mike had to ask.

"Maybe it's just me," he said, "but it seems like the son of a bitch at least ought to know what it feels like before he gets to be done."

"Jesus," Mike said. His exasperation was complete and undivided. "Who should know what *what* feels like?"

"What it feels like," Darryl said, not bothering to address the *who* in the question, "to spend two days wondering if he'll ever get to speak to his little girl again."

He turned away and faced the water again.

"Lily Morse knows what the hell it feels like," he said. "Why shouldn't he?"

As Mike stood there watching him, a lone silhouette at the end of the dock, he thought of everything he knew to be true about Darryl Potter. His friend. Hell, these past couple of years probably the closest thing to family Mike had. He supposed it didn't add up to all that much, but he didn't know anyone better. They'd been through flames together.

Yet it was only then, in that moment, standing there at Hal's place, twenty feet of weather-beaten dock between the two of them, that Mike believed he finally understood the guy.

"I think it's just you," he said.

19

Toby Lunden kept thinking that this time two years ago he'd been turning down a 3M engineering scholarship to the University of Illinois based on his math SATs.

He'd never had any plans to go to college, in Illinois or anywhere else; school bored him stiff, and by that time he was already earning more dough in a year than his old man and his stepmom combined. The truth was he'd only taken the test in the first place to get his guidance counselor, Mr. Fairchild, the hell off his case.

Then the Super Bowl took care of that for him by February anyway, when Fairchild ended up into Toby for two grand and some change. When that scholarship letter had come in the mail, Toby tossed it in the trash and moved on.

Now he was starting to think maybe he regretted that decision. For once in his life—maybe the first time ever—Toby was starting to think that maybe he wasn't such a whiz kid after all.

"Well, well," Bryce said. The first thing he'd said in five minutes. "Well, well, well."

Toby sat behind the wheel and didn't dare say anything.

It was two in the morning. Other than a quick stop in Sauk Rapids for gas and Red Bull, they'd been on the road heading northwest ever since leaving St. Paul. Fifteen miles back they'd left the state highway; five miles back they'd left the county road; two miles back, they'd lost their phone signal in the heavy timber, hence losing their map, but Bryce had memorized the trip by then. Finally, a mile ago, they'd come upon the rocky lane that dove off into the woods.

Bryce made Toby kill the headlights, then the running lights. By the final quarter mile, Toby had been creeping along by nothing but the feel of crushed rock under his tires, the occasional bright glimpse of the moon through the canopy of trees over their heads. At last, they'd found the spot they'd been looking for.

And now they sat here, at the edge of a grassy clearing deep in the woods, Toby waiting for Bryce to say something else.

What he said was "You can turn the lights back on now."

Toby followed instructions numbly as Bryce undid his seat belt, grabbed Toby's phone, and climbed out of the truck. The Navigator's high beams flooded the vacant grass lot in front of them, where the lane bulbed into a little turnaround backstopped by a big lake-blue real estate sign. The sign said:

WELCOME TO MUSSEL SHORES!
YOUR VACATION LAND OASIS!!

10 ACRES
Private Water—Timber—Wildlife—Peace & Solitude
Call Myron at Lake Country Realty
(218) 555-5108

Bryce walked around the front of the truck, into the glare of the headlights, stopping somewhere near the middle of the turnaround. He stood there with his feet planted, arms crossed, rock dust swirling around him in the beams, as if he'd poofed into the spot like a magician. He stared at the sign so long without wavering that Toby imagined him setting it on fire with his eyes for his opening trick.

After a while, Bryce broke posture and walked up to the sign. He stooped down and lifted the lid of an all-weather brochure box attached to the bottom corner of the sign. Bryce pulled a brochure and stood in the lights. He looked at the brochure, then flipped it over and glanced at the back. Then he looked at Toby's phone in his other hand. He raised it up in the air. Held it this way and that.

Finally he lowered his arms and straightened his spine. Rolled his neck. Rolled his shoulders.

He walked back to the truck. Toby had another powerful urge to throw the thing in reverse and peel out of there, spraying rocks for cover all the way back up the lane, but of course he just sat and waited until Bryce climbed into his seat.

Bryce's good mood had dissolved. When he closed his door, and the dome light went out, the atmosphere inside the truck seemed to close in like a thundercloud.

Bryce sat quietly for a minute. He smelled different. *Hot* was the only way Toby could think to describe it. The guy actually smelled hot. Like an electric motor. A fuse burning. The lightning inside the thundercloud, waiting to strike.

"I gotta hand it to the old fucker," he finally said. "Hard right down to the core, wasn't he?"

Toby said, "You mean this isn't the place?" He heard how it sounded. Bryce had warned him about his mouth before.

But after driving all this way for nothing, he didn't care anymore. Money or no money. Thinking about that barkeeper back in St. Paul made him feel sick and small. It made him feel like a bad person. Jesus, he was only a numbers guy. How had he ended up here?

Bryce turned his head and looked at him. Toby tried to meet his eyes and stand his ground, but he couldn't. He tried to keep his heart from pounding in his throat, but he couldn't do that either.

He guessed he cared more than he wanted to.

"Look at us," Bryce said then. His tone was surprisingly easygoing all of a sudden. "Land of ten thousand lakes, and here we are, stuck looking for one."

"Yeah," Toby said. He tried to sound easygoing too. It didn't work. "Talk about odds, huh?"

"Hey, stupid question," Bryce said. "But you seem like a technology guy. I don't suppose there's a chance you carry a satellite unit on board. You know, like a backup? Just in case?"

Toby shook his head.

"Garmin? Magellan? TomTom? Anything along those lines?"

"Sorry," Toby said.

"It was a long shot," Bryce said. He placed Toby's useless phone gently on the padded console between them. "And if we looked all around, would we by any chance find a paper map on board the vehicle?"

Toby sighed.

"Possibly a road atlas?" Bryce said. "Something from the Rand McNally family of publications?"

Toby could feel himself shrinking in his seat. He forced himself to sit up straighter. "That's what the phone is for," he said.

"Ah." Bryce looked out the windshield at the realtor's sign standing broad and bright in the headlight beams. *Welcome to Mussel Shores!* After a minute, he looked around the inside of the car and said, "It's funny that we're sitting here in something called a Navigator. Isn't it?"

Toby said nothing.

Bryce looked at him and smiled. "Isn't that just classic?"

Something in his voice caused Toby to grope for a response out of reflex. But something else told him that it would be better if he kept his mouth closed.

"Drive me to a town," Bryce said.

20

A few months after he'd been home, when he could drive himself places and get around using a cane, Mike Barlowe went to visit Lily Morse at her house in West St. Paul. He hadn't known her son, Evan, as well as he'd known some of the other guys in the company, but he had a few stories he could tell her, and he thought she might like to hear them.

It had turned out to be one of the most unbearably depressing afternoons of Mike's entire woebegone life. Lily Morse could not have been kinder or more welcoming. She couldn't have seemed more appreciative of his visit. Her house couldn't have seemed emptier or quieter, and the whole time he was there, looking at the framed portraits of Evan Morse and his sister and his father on the mantel, Mike couldn't help feeling like a flagrant obscenity in their midst.

She had lost so much, Lily Morse. By contrast, Mike had never even known his own birth mother, who'd fled St. John's Hospital while his cord was still wet, and if she'd ever wondered what had become of him, he'd never heard word about it. But here was a woman who obviously would have given anything to have her son again, even for a minute, and it had felt like some kind of cruel joke to Mike that he should be the one sitting there with her instead.

Lily Morse had cooked him dinner and insisted that he take home leftovers. At the door, after she'd thanked him again for coming, after they'd said their goodbyes, she touched his face with the warm palm of her hand, looked him up and down, and said, "Honey, do you need anything?"

"Yeah," Mike had said, smiling. "A mom like you."

He'd meant it appreciatively, something to end the afternoon on a lighthearted note, but it came out sounding heavy and awkward.

Because he had no mother, and Lily Morse had no son, and neither one of them could do a damned thing about it.

Her eyes had welled up then, for the first time since he'd arrived, and she couldn't speak anymore after that. She squeezed his hands and let him go. Mike limped down her front steps and drove away and hadn't been in contact with her since.

He'd thought about Lance Corporal Morse often enough since that afternoon. At his lowest, Mike used to play a sort of self-pitying game with himself—wondering what Morse would have made of his life by now if their luck had been reversed. It would have been something, the way Mike imagined it. Something successful and good. The kind of life any guy who deserved a second chance would have made.

Mike wanted to be that guy himself. He truly did.

But for whatever reason, whatever deficiency in his character, he just didn't seem to have what it took.

He'd done a little roofing before joining the service, but the knee never healed like the doctors said it should, and you didn't see a lot of guys climbing ladders with canes. He knew law enforcement liked a military background, and he knew some guys who'd gone that route. But they didn't tend to let you carry guns for a living when you had a PTSD diagnosis on your medical discharge.

And that hadn't really mattered to Mike anyway. He'd already carried a gun for a living. He had no plans ever to do it again.

Post-traumatic stress disorder. If that's what they called insomnia, night terrors, mood swings, depression, and the inability to tolerate other human beings, then Mike guessed it was what he had. They had programs through the VA Center and for a while he tried going in, but it all seemed like a bunch of bullshit, so he stopped. Whiskey worked better than the pills they gave anyway, and after a couple of years the nightmares tapered off on their own. Life went on.

Little by little Mike started holding down jobs again. He picked up a decent gig for a time with a local outfit doing snow removal in the winter, riding around on lawn mowers in the summer. As the leg got stronger, he got on with Deakins framing houses and building decks. He learned how to drink enough to sleep through the night without dreaming—at least, not too often—but not so much that he missed work the next day. At least, not too often.

But he'd lost track of pretty much everybody he'd known before he enlisted by then. None of his old buddies understood him anymore, and Mike sure as hell didn't understand them. He'd met a few girls, but trying to manage a relationship with any one of them was more than he could take. He kept up with some of the guys from his unit through email, a few phone calls here and there, and he'd heard through the grapevine that Darryl Potter had gone a little high and right since returning stateside. He'd tried to reach out, but nothing much had come of it.

Eventually he got word from the Philippines—where the 4/8 had been sent to help pull villagers out of a mud slide—that Darryl had been served the Big Chicken Dinner he'd apparently been ordering for a while. Bad Conduct Discharge, in command parlance. Fighting and drugs primarily, according to what Mike was told.

Whatever the official charges came to, they'd amounted to the same thing in the end: no medals, no benefits, eighteen months in the brig. Take your coal-mining ass back to West Virginia.

The fish get big in Minnesota, Mike had written him in a letter. A proper letter, made out of paper, sent with a stamp through the United States mail. *You know you've got a place to stay if you ever need one.*

He'd heard nothing in reply.

Nothing, that was to say, until one hard gray sub-zero morning in the middle of January, when Darryl Potter showed up breathing clouds on Mike's snow-packed doorstep and said, "You could have told me it got so motherfucking cold up here."

Even then Mike had sensed he was opening the door to trouble. He could see it all over the guy, from the filth on his clothes to that faraway look in his eyes. He'd had no hat, Darryl. No gloves, no car, no story. Only his rucksack on his shoulder and the clothes on his back, standing at the end of a ragged trail of boot prints in the snow.

Christ, it had been good to see him.

They carried a canoe of their own from the shed down to the water and paddled across the narrow part of the lake. Mike sat up front with the spotlight. Darryl manned an oar in the stern. He was terrible at it and had to stop and rest before they were halfway across.

"You know we could just drive around," he said.

"We could," Mike agreed. "Except that's what *you're* going to do."

"How's that?"

"After you take me across," Mike said. He wanted to pick up the girl's trail as nearly as he could to where she'd landed, and he knew it would be easier to do that by following in her tracks than by working backward from the other side. But he didn't particularly feel like explaining himself to Darryl. "You're going to paddle back, take the truck, and wait for me at the lake road."

"Oh," Darryl said.

Mike scanned the tree line with the spotlight, re-establishing their bearing. He said, "Any other questions?"

"Think I'm clear, Sarge."

"Then paddle," Mike said.

As they splashed and wobbled their way to the middle of the lake, Mike thought of Darryl's .45 digging into the small of his back. He reached around, pulled the gun out of his waistband, and tossed it overboard.

The gun hit the water with a plop and sank into the dark.

Darryl said, "What was that?"

Mike shrugged. "Probably a fish."

There was silence behind him for a moment. Then Darryl said, "Hey, Mike?"

"Yep."

"For what it's worth, that fish wasn't loaded."

Mike sighed. He turned and looked at Darryl, sitting back there drenched in sweat, paddle resting on his knees. He shook his head. Couldn't think of a thing to say.

Darryl looked out at the water, somewhere in the vicinity of the spot where Mike had tossed in the gun. "I guess I jammed you up pretty good this time," he said. "Didn't I?"

"If I were you right now," Mike said, "I wouldn't be worried about me."

"I didn't mean to get you in on this." Darryl looked up from the water. "Probably hard to believe, huh?"

It *was* hard to believe. In fact, Mike didn't see how it could have been possible. And yet the fact that Darryl seemed to believe it somehow made perfect sense.

"Let me ask you something," Mike said.

"Okay."

"How does a trained United States Marine not know how to paddle a damn canoe?"

Silence for a beat. Then: "They kicked me out, remember?"

Mike put the spotlight down between his feet, hauled up the second oar from the bottom of the canoe. "Try to do what I do," he said, and started paddling.

In a minute they were gliding toward the opposite shore as if pulled in on a rope. Even with the hot throb in Mike's dislocated knuckle, the work of paddling calmed him. As he focused on his strokes, he felt in control for the first time all day. There was something soothing about being able to make the canoe go in the direction he wanted. The pain in his hand only made the result of his efforts more satisfying.

"Let me ask you something else," he said over his shoulder.

Darryl said, "Sure."

"How long have you been planning this?"

Nothing for a few seconds. Then: "*Plan* would be overstating it."

"Bullshit."

"Nope."

"You knew where they lived, man. That architect and his family."

Darryl didn't deny it. "Loose scenarios may have crossed my mind."

"Uh-huh."

"Can't say I actually *planned* to do anything 'til I did it."

As they neared the same cut in the cattails he believed Juliet Benson would have used, Mike transferred the paddle from one side to the other. "So, just out of curiosity," he said. "When you were coming up with this nonplan of yours. What the hell was your exit strategy?"

"*Strategy* would be overstating it."

"I'm getting that."

Darryl's voice changed pitch. He was looking out

over the water again. "Guess you could say there was a blaze-of-glory component involved."

Mike steered them through the reeds by the light of the moon. He thought of the .45 Darryl had claimed was unloaded. He tried to remember the weight of it in his hand. He couldn't decide whether he believed it had been empty or not.

But for the first time the idea came to him, with a chill on his neck and a feathery sensation in his chest, that "exit" hadn't been part of Darryl's thinking at all.

At least not the way Mike had meant.

He pulled up his oar and turned in the bow and looked at Darryl. Darryl worked on unsnarling his paddle from the thatch of cattails standing up all around them.

After a minute, Mike said, "And Toby's money? What was that for?"

Darryl cocked his head as though just now remembering that gym bag he'd stashed under the coffee table at the cabin.

"Well," he said, "the other thought was, I've never been to Canada."

"Jesus," Mike said, and he laughed. It felt good, even though nothing was funny in the least. "You really are a head case."

"Yeah, well," Darryl said. "Takes one to know one."

Mike put his oar in the water. He could touch the soft bottom with the paddle now. He poled them toward shore like a gondolier.

Behind him, Darry said, "But there's a difference between you and me, Mikey."

"Yeah," Mike agreed. "One of us knows how to drive this thing."

He felt a drag then, and the canoe seemed to hang up. He turned to see Darryl with both hands on his oar handle, gaze fixed on the starboard gunwale, forcing the paddle down into the muck three feet below them.

"You told me this thing one time," Darryl said. "You said the worst dreams you had after you got home were the ones looking down your rifle at somebody." He raised his eyes. "Always woke up squeezing the trigger, you told me. Remember?"

"I remember," Mike said.

Darryl nodded and looked off. "What I never told you, Mike?"

Mike waited.

"I had that dream too." Darryl shrugged. "Only for me it wasn't a nightmare."

Mike said nothing.

"And it never has gone away," Darryl said. "Know what I'm saying?"

For just a moment, Mike didn't see the Darryl Potter in the canoe with him. Instead, he saw the beat-up Marine leaning over him in the back of a Humvee. In his mind, Mike saw a white smile in a battle-grimed face, and he recognized that face for what it truly had been: the face of a soul at ease. A man in his element, doing a job he'd been cut out to do. Happy.

If he honestly thought about it, Mike couldn't say that he'd ever seen Darryl look so content with himself anywhere else. And he believed he understood now, all these years down the road, what he'd somehow never understood about Darryl before today:

Darryl Potter hadn't caught his discharge working mud slides in the Philippines.

He'd gotten it the day the 4/8 shipped home from Iraq. The Marine Corps had taken away his medals and his benefits, but that came only later. And it wasn't what any of this business with Darryl was about. Not the drugs or the booze. Not the bar brawls. Not the nights in the brig or in plain old jail. Not a gym bag full of Toby Lunden's cash. And not Juliet Benson either. Not really.

Darryl Potter didn't need any medals. What he needed was an enemy.

When Mike stayed quiet, Darryl repeated his question. "Know what I'm saying, Mike?"

This time, when Mike looked at him, he had a powerful feeling that it was going to be one of the last times he looked at Darry in a while.

"Not a clue," he finally said.

Darryl chuckled softly. "Hell," he said. "Me either."

21

Juliet Benson had made it about two klicks into the woods by the time Mike caught up with her. A series of smart decisions had delivered her most of the way to that point, but it had taken only one bad one to do her in, and it struck him with a pang of genuine discouragement that she'd needed his help after all. He felt connected to the girl by then, irrational as it was, and he'd been pulling for her.

Mike started at the stand of sumac where she'd stashed the canoe. It looked like someone had been stabbed to death in the bottom of the thing, the sun-dulled aluminum smeared dramatically in crimson. But the blood tracks dried up at the trail of broken underbrush leading away into the timber, and Mike concluded, with renewed admiration, that she'd found something she could use to wrap her feet.

Whatever she'd used had soaked through a couple hundred meters into the woods, where he began picking up dollops of blood again in the spotlight beam. Before long, the blood signs dried up once more. Mike imagined mud and leaf litter from the forest floor gradually kneading into clammy poultices underfoot, caking her soles like accidental slippers.

At one point, at the edge of a shallow ravine choked with deadfall, where a drainage culvert tunneled under the rock lane and emptied into the timber, he'd lost her trail completely for about an hour. At first he assumed that she'd emerged from the timber and had taken to the lane after all—at least long enough to hop the ravine and be on her way.

But there was no sign of her on either side. After forty minutes of searching the ground, it occurred to him that she could be hiding under his nose, and he used the spotlight to check the inside of the culvert pipe itself. He found nothing but an empty cylinder choked with cobwebs and sludge. It was as if she'd been airlifted out of there.

Then, a hundred paces down the line, he finally found the spot where she'd crossed the washout. And there, within moments of crossing himself, he found the spot where she'd made her mistake.

Why? That was what confounded Mike at first. That she had chosen, in her compromised physical state, to navigate the wicked terrain of the ravine— instead of risking half a minute's worth of exposure in open ground—was one thing.

But so far she'd kept the moonlit lane on her left for nearly an entire winding kilometer. She'd had it right there, always within sight through the trees, a white ribbon guiding her out of this place. She'd done it just the way Mike would have told her to do it. Just the way he'd have done it himself, if he'd been her.

So why the hell did Juliet Benson decide, here, to turn *away* from the lane and follow the bank of the washout deeper into the woods instead?

She wasn't stupid. She wasn't reckless. She wasn't

tripping along by the seat of her pants. She had a plan, based on every piece of evidence Mike had observed so far, and it seemed like a good one. Up until this very spot she'd been sticking to it.

That was when it came to him, and the answer was so obvious that Mike felt stupid for having to ponder the question at all.

What could have made Juliet Benson deviate from her plan for no good reason he could identify? The same thing that caused a perfectly good Marine to lose focus when tracer rounds suddenly turned a pitch-black sky into screaming neon spaghetti overhead, that was what.

Fear.

Something had scared her, simple as that. Something unexpected had turned her away from the road, disrupted her mission, driven her off route. This time Mike didn't have to think very hard to guess what that thing had been.

You, he thought. His stomach sank at the clarity of the logic. *She was running from you.*

From the edge of the ravine, Mike imagined looking through Juliet Benson's eyes. He imagined the sight of the Power Wagon coming up the lane, headlights strobing across the trees. He could almost hear the rocks crunching under the tires in the distance, the Doppler echo as the truck passed over the empty culvert pipe and rolled on toward the cabin at the end of the road.

Of course she'd been scared.

The girl was tough, all right, but she had to be running on fumes by now. She was hurt, surely cold, probably dehydrated. Possibly hungry. Who knew if

Darryl had given her anything to eat all day? The sight of a strange new vehicle arriving at Rockhaven would have cleared all bets from the board.

Who else might be coming, as far as she knew? Who knew how much farther she could get before they came after her?

At least she could use the ravine as a landmark. She could hide herself down amid the deadfall if it came to that. And the ravine had to lead somewhere. Away from traffic, first and foremost.

Half a click later, the ravine petered out into a gully, then a trench, then a crease, and finally disappeared into a low sprawling bowl of marshy ground.

Mike found her hiding under the root snarl of a fallen pine tree, not more than fifty paces back in the timber, a good bit farther removed from safety than she'd been when she'd started. Though to say that he found her would have been assigning himself more credit than he probably deserved.

The truth was, she'd heard him coming first. She'd seen the spotlight and watched him pass by. She'd watched him come back again, and when he neared her hiding spot, she screamed, "Stay away!"

The shrill bark of her voice in the stillness startled the breath out of him. Mike jumped half out of his skin. He almost dropped the spotlight. If she'd been a land mine he'd have been blown to high heaven. Or somewhere.

"I've got a knife," she called out. Voice trembling. "I've got a big-ass knife, and if you come near me I'll cut you wide open." Louder: "Don't you come near me!"

Mike stopped in his tracks, heart pounding in his

neck. The moonlight barely penetrated the timber here, and the darkness felt like a physical presence all around him. He stood for a minute and caught his breath.

"I'll kill you if I can," she yelled, a disembodied warning in the gloom. "Do you hear me?"

He triggered the spotlight and swung the beam slowly toward the sound of her voice. In a moment he saw her, a mud-streaked face not twenty paces away, crouched behind the roots like a cornered animal. Her hair hung limp on her scalp, sticking to her face in damp tangles. Her eyes shone in the light, and she squinted against the beam.

She hadn't been bluffing, Mike saw. She did have a knife. She held it out in front of her, white-knuckling the wooden handle with both hands. The long, thin blade trembled in the air, and Mike identified the weapon immediately by its shape: a six-inch fillet knife. She would have found it in the canoe shed with all the rest of the fishing tackle. Probably in the same place Darryl had found the stringer and the bait bucket he'd used to accessorize her room.

Mike let up on the trigger. The spotlight beam faded slowly as the bulb cooled. Darkness again.

"I'm warning you," she said. "Stay away."

But all the bark had gone from her voice. He could hear that she was on the verge of crying.

"Juliet," he said. As softly as he could and still make himself heard. "My name is Mike. I'm here to take you home."

Silence.

"Juliet?" He listened. "It's safe now. Okay? I'm going to get you out of here."

He heard a ragged breath in the darkness. "Who are you?"

"I'm Mike," he told her. He thought about lying to calm her down, telling her he was with the police or something. But she wasn't stupid, only terrified, and it wouldn't do much for the trust-building effort if she sensed he was lying to her. *Hearts and minds,* he thought, and kept it simple. "I'm a friend."

"Are you from the white pickup?"

"That's right," he said, sounding like something straight out of that sci-fi theater show his roommate at the VA hospital used to watch on television. *My name is Mike, and I come from the white pickup.* "I know you're hurt. But you don't need to be scared anymore. Okay?"

For a minute he couldn't hear anything but the sound of her breathing. Shallow and quick. Mike resisted hitting the spotlight to check on her. He forced himself to stand there and wait until she said, "Mike?"

"I'm right here." He listened a moment. "Can I come over there?"

When she didn't respond, he took her silence as permission. Mike took a few careful steps toward the fallen pine. When that seemed to go okay, he took a few steps more, and when he reached her, he knelt down. Out of knife range, he hoped. His knee creaked like a rusty hinge. His busted knuckle throbbed. His back hurt. *Jesus,* he thought. *I'm falling apart.*

"Hi," he said. "Listen, I'm going to turn this light on again. I won't shine it right at you or anything. I just want us to be able to see. Is that okay?"

"You don't have to talk like that," she said. "I'm not a basket case."

"Sorry," he said. "Okay."

"And I will totally still cut you."

"Loud and clear," Mike said.

He pointed the spotlight away from them and locked the trigger with the switch on the handle. He laid the light down on the ground beside him so that the beam pointed straight up in the air, illuminating the tops of the pines.

"There," he said. "Now we're just like a used car lot." She didn't laugh, but that was okay. It wasn't that funny.

He finally got a better look at her. She was shivering, filthy from head to toe. She wore what she must have worn to campus yesterday afternoon, a sort of thin jersey sweater with a hood. No doubt warm enough for afternoon classes, not so well suited for a night in the woods. He saw that she'd used the knife to cut off her own sleeves at the shoulders. She'd done her best to fashion the material into a pair of makeshift moccasins.

Her bare arms were covered in scrapes and scratches. In the shadows cast by the spotlight beam, he could see the lean contours of her shoulders and gathered that she took care of herself. He wasn't surprised. The sweater looked to be some kind of a light-beige color under all the dirt stains. Her feet were black, sodden with blood and mud, bristling with leaves and pine needles.

Mike reached for the spotlight and angled the beam toward her right foot. She'd turned her ankle badly at some point near the end of her trail. She'd already peeled the fabric down past her heel in order to have

a look for herself, and what she'd found could not
have been encouraging.

Her right ankle was easily twice the size of her left,
swollen so tightly that the skin shone in the light.
Amid the pulpy discoloration, Mike could see weep-
ing gouges in her flesh from the stringer needle, along
with angry ligature marks from the zip ties that had
bound her. It was the same ankle Darryl had tethered
to the spindle bed back at the cabin.

This, he realized, was the reason she'd gone to
ground. She'd stepped wrong, sprained the ankle se-
verely, possibly broken it. She'd gotten as far as she
could on it but could go no farther.

"Can I see this?" he said, nodding toward the ankle.
She didn't say no.

Mike propped the beam against a root and reached
out slowly. She stiffened at his approach, renewed her
grip on the knife handle. Over the soaked denim of
her jeans, he cupped her calf with one hand, lifting
gently. He took the base of her heel lightly in the
other. She flinched and cried out at the slightest pres-
sure. Her skin felt hot and bloated under his fingers.

"Sorry," he said. He kept hold of her calf to keep
the foot elevated but took the offending hand away.
"Sorry, sorry."

"I stepped in a hole," she said, biting her lip, voice
shaking with frustration. "It just folded over and I
felt it pop."

"Can you walk on it at all?"

She shook her head tightly. The tip of the knife
wobbled in front of her.

"That's okay," Mike said. "No worries." He pulled
over a half-rotted oak limb, eased her leg straight,

settled her calf down on the spongy wood. "Are you hurt anywhere else?"

"I cut my foot on some glass," she said. "Bad, I think."

Mike nodded. She hadn't said which foot, but by the look of her wraps he guessed her left. Both feet were so filthy he couldn't be sure. He pointed, and she nodded again, confirming his worry: she had two bad wheels, not only the one.

"All that mud is good," he told her. Something positive. "It stopped the bleeding."

"Lucky me." The knife tip lowered a few inches.

"How much pain?"

"Not as much as before."

"That's good too."

"They're so cold I can't really feel much."

Mike leaned back on his heels and tried to sort out their options.

A ride would be swell. It occurred to him that if he hadn't chucked the .45 in the lake, and if Darryl had rounds for it rattling around in a pants pocket—as Mike felt reasonably certain he probably did—they could have worked out some kind of signal Darryl would have been able to hear from the lake road.

Then again, Darryl arriving in the truck to give them a lift probably wouldn't have done much to strengthen the delicate relationship still forming between Juliet Benson and him.

Anyway. By Mike's general calculations, at this point they were closer to the lake than the lake road. Or the lane in, for that matter.

If his bearings were correct, and Mike had always had a reliable compass in his head, the shortest way back to the cabin was due east, through the woods. Based on the distance he'd traveled to the ravine and the distance he'd followed it, he estimated the third side of the triangle to be about half a klick's hike more or less straight to Juliet's canoe.

"How did you find me?" she said.

As the sound of her voice reclaimed his attention, Mike noticed something that did not overwhelm him with optimism: the beam of the spotlight. If it had been pumping out three-million candlepower when he'd started, a couple-odd-million candles had flickered out by now. Locked on full blast the way he had it, the beam was actually dimming before his eyes.

He reached out and released the trigger switch. Darkness pulled around them like a lead blanket.

Louder, she said, "How did you find me?"

"I followed you," Mike told her. He almost said *tracked* but edited himself. *Tracked,* he reasoned, would have sounded far too much like *hunted* for anyone's comfort. "You left me just what I needed. You did good."

"I mean how did you *find* me," she said. "How did you know where to look?"

"I'm pretty good with—"

"How did you know where to look for me in the first place?" Her voice regained its edge as she spoke. "Who are you?"

Mike thought about how to answer.

Truthfully, he decided. At least as truthfully as he dared.

"I use this place sometimes," he said. "The man who owns it is a friend of mine."

"A friend?"

For the first time in two hours, Mike realized that he'd stopped checking his watch. After all this, he'd completely forgotten to call Hal as he'd promised he would. The terms of their deal had long expired by now. Nothing to be done about that at this point. Onward.

"He lets me come here when I ask him," Mike said. "That's how I found you."

As his eyes readjusted to the darkness, he could make out Juliet Benson's shape amid the pine roots. She seemed to have made herself smaller. When she spoke, he almost couldn't hear her.

"The guy who brought me here," she said. "Do you know him too?"

Mike decided to step away from the truth for the sake of expediency. "No," he said.

"He has a gun," she said. Almost a whisper.

"You don't have to worry about him anymore," Mike told her. "Trust me, you're safe now. I promise."

He must have sounded convincing, because she didn't ask him how he could promise her such a thing. For a long time she was quiet. Mike waited until she was ready to speak again.

"Do they . . ." she started, then stopped and took a breath. "Does anybody else know I'm gone?"

"You're not gone. You're right here. So am I now. And I'm going to get you back where you belong."

"My parents—"

"It's okay," he said. "Listen, you're all over the news. The cops are looking for you too. Your folks are going to be a couple of very happy people as soon as we get you out of here."

"The police are looking for me?"

"Turning Minnesota upside down. Believe it."

"They're coming here?"

Probably any old time now, Mike thought. He thought of Darryl, waiting in the truck at the lake road. Nothing to be done about that either. "Soon," he said.

"You called them?"

Jesus, she had a lot of questions for a girl hiding under an uproooted tree with sleeves for shoes. His knee was starting to throb from crouching there with her.

He shifted his weight and said, "There aren't any phones out here. And I can't get a cell signal until we're about three miles down the road. Let's get you back to the cabin, fix you up, and haul our chilly asses out of here." He picked up the spotlight. "The minute we hit a signal, we'll call the whole world and tell everyone you're safe." He reached forward carefully, offering her his hand. "Sound like a plan?"

She didn't flinch when he reached out to her this time. And she didn't take long to think about it. She nodded her head.

"Okay," he said, and leaned forward. "Grab on to my neck. I'll help you stand up."

Almost without hesitating, Juliet Benson reached out her arms. When she draped them over his shoulders, he could feel the goose bumps all over her cold bare skin. He could also feel the edge of a very sharp fishing knife resting lightly against his earlobe.

"Hey, Juliet?" he said.

She nodded against his neck. Her damp hair smelled like rainwater.

"Don't let your hand slip, okay?"

After a pause, he felt the blade of the knife turn away from his ear. The hand with the knife in it stayed where it was.

Fair enough.

"Upsy daisy," he said.

22

They found a twenty-four-hour gas-and-shop off the state highway north of Brainerd. Attached to the station was a small, well-lighted diner called Okerlund's, which started serving breakfast at the inexplicable hour of 3:00 a.m.

Sitting in a booth by the window, Toby watched a Crow Wing County sheriff's deputy chat up the waitress behind the register as he paid for his coffee and eggs. He felt like he wanted to crawl underneath the table, having a cop right there under the same roof with them, standing so close Toby probably could have blown a paper straw wrapper and hit the guy. But Bryce's mood only seemed to improve.

The deputy was short and overweight and shaped like a bowling pin, with hammy cheeks and a mustache like the kind they gave out at deputy school. When he finished at the counter, he hitched up his gun belt and weeble-wobbled for the door, nodding as he passed their booth. Through the window they watched him shove into his prowler, back out of his parking space, and drive away.

"Crow Wing County," Bryce mused, after the

deputy had rolled out of sight. "How much ground would you guess that covers?"

Toby stared at his plate: hash browns and two sausage patties sitting in twin puddles of grease. Food had smelled good when they came in, but now he didn't feel like eating anything. "How much ground does what cover?"

"Crow Wing County."

"I have no idea," Toby said.

Bryce sipped his coffee. "Well. Good a place to start as any, right? As long as we're up here?"

"Whatever you say."

"Let's do this," Bryce said. "Fire up your space phone and find me the website for the Crow Wing County Assessor."

Without looking up, Toby shoved his phone across the table. After a moment of silence, Bryce pushed it back gently. Toby looked at the phone, sitting by his hand where it had started.

He looked at Bryce.

"You'll feel better if you're able to contribute," Bryce said. "I want us to feel like partners."

Toby sighed, shoved his plate aside with his elbow, and called up the browser on the phone. In a minute he found the site Bryce wanted.

"Nicely done," Bryce said. "Now. Are the tax valuations online?"

At the top of the page, there was a link that said *Find Property*. Toby tapped the link, and a search page came up. "Guess so," he said.

"Look at us, with the teamwork," Bryce said. "See what they've got under Macklin."

"Can't," Toby said.

"No?"

"You can search by address or parcel number," Toby told him. "Can't search by name."

Bryce nodded. "A sound policy, privacy-wise."

Toby didn't want to be involved in this anymore. But he couldn't help asking, "What makes you think the place is even in Crow Wing County?"

"That would be what we in the fugitive-recovery business refer to as a hunch," Bryce said.

"What makes you think there's a place at all?"

"Let's try to stay optimistic."

You stay optimistic, Toby thought.

"Lake Country Realty," Bryce said. "Is that here in Brainerd?"

"You're asking me?"

Bryce nodded toward the phone.

Toby didn't bother arguing. He went back to the browser, ran a keyword search, found the answer. "Main office is in Baxter," he said. He linked to a map and had the GPS show their location. "About two miles from here, looks like."

Bryce sat with his coffee and didn't say anything for a minute. Finally he reached behind his hip, pulled out his wallet, and handed Toby a twenty-dollar bill.

"Here's what I want you to do," he said. "Go up front and buy us a Minnesota road map and a red ink pen. And one of those yellow highlighters, if they have them. Actually, it doesn't matter what color. Any kind of highlighter will do fine."

Whatever. Toby took the twenty. "What are you going to do?"

"Finish my coffee," Bryce said.

Toby slid out and stood up, thinking, *You do that, you creepy bastard.*

He was happy to be allowed to leave the booth by himself. He was going to be even happier walking out the front door alone. He was going to be straight-up ecstatic peeling out of the parking lot in the Navigator while this lunatic his uncle had sent him watched out the window, wondering how he could have been so stupid. Wondering how he could have managed to misjudge Toby Lunden the Numbers Guy. Toby hoped the asshole enjoyed his coffee.

"Be right back," he said.

As he turned to go, Bryce said, "Hey, do me a favor."

Toby waited.

"Leave the phone," Bryce said.

Toby put the phone on the table. Whatever. He'd buy a new phone. An even better one. With a different number. Maybe a different area code. Someplace warmer.

"And the truck keys," Bryce said.

At that, Toby glanced up too quickly. Over the rim of his coffee mug, Bryce gave him a wink.

Shit. "The keys?" Toby said. He stood there as his heart sank slowly, settling down somewhere in the silt at the bottom of his stomach.

Bryce sipped his coffee. "Something wrong?"

Toby didn't know what to say. After feeling for the past few hours like he'd been shuffling along through some kind of long, bad dream, everything seemed to tighten into high-def clarity all at once. Now was the time, Toby thought. Wasn't it? If he was going to do it—ever in his life—now was the time for Toby Lunden the Numbers Guy to take a stand.

He looked away.

Bryce sipped his coffee.

Toby dug out his keys. Put them on the table next to the phone. He'd walked maybe half a dozen steps away from the booth when he heard Bryce call out behind him, "Thanks, partner."

23

Mike carried her all the way out on his back.

It was tough going at first, but coming out of the marsh he found a deer path that cut through the woods on a line more or less back to Rockhaven. He took to the path and the ground evened out beneath them. If not for the dark and the cold, and the smell of mud and pine trees, and the ache in his overstressed knee—not to mention the sting of a well-cared-for Rapala fillet knife making shallow hash marks on the side of his neck every time he stumbled or misjudged his footing—he might have been a high school jock giving his cheerleader girlfriend a piggyback ride down the midway at the county fair.

At one point they had to leave the deer path, which gradually meandered in the wrong direction. Shortly after that, they lost the spotlight's battery altogether. But Mike could already see the western shore of the lake through the trees by then.

He expected to see police flashers as well. In his mind he'd imagined returning to the same kind of scene at Rockhaven that he'd left behind in St. Paul.

But no. They emerged from the woods to find a solitary cabin across a peaceful lake in a sleepy moonlit clearing, not far up the shoreline from the grove of staghorn sumac still faithfully concealing Juliet's blood-smeared canoe.

He felt her arms tighten around his neck. "Where's your truck?" she said.

These were the first words either one of them had spoken since striking out from the marsh, and Mike had fallen out of conversation mode.

He was utterly gassed. His back and neck and shoulders screamed with the strain of carrying her, and his knee felt like someone had gone to work on it with a hammer. He hadn't wanted a Vicodin—or a handful—so badly in as long as he could remember. For the past couple hundred meters he'd been day-dreaming about the last gulp of Old Crow Darryl had left behind in the cabin, and now that the cabin was in sight, he found himself physically salivating.

"My what?" he said. It was the best he could come up with.

"Your truck. You said you came in the white pickup. Where is it?"

Across the lake, he could see her little Subaru sitting dark and deserted in front of the cabin. All the lights still burned in the cabin's ground-floor windows as he'd left them.

Mike thought of Darryl waiting for him on the lake road. It had been at least two hours since they'd split up. A big part of him wondered if Darryl had waited around at all. It was approximately the same part of him that hoped Darryl hadn't.

"It's around back," he lied, too exhausted to lift the truth at this point. "Where you climbed out the window. We can't see it from here."

It wasn't a very good lie, but it seemed to be enough for her. He felt the extra tension leak out of her arms as they released their tourniquet grip on his neck. She was at the end of her rope, just like he was. She wanted to believe things.

"I need to let you down," he said. "Hook your arm over my shoulder. I'll help you walk the rest."

They hobbled out of the timber together like a pair of plane-crash survivors. Slowly they made their way along the shoreline to the canoe. Mike spied a log near their spot that would do for a bench. He helped her sit, then went to work hauling the canoe out of the brush, down to the water's edge. He dropped the dead spotlight into the canoe and took out the single oar. When he was ready, he went back to Juliet.

Before he could say a word, she shook her head firmly, gripping her arms.

"What's wrong?" he said.

"I don't want to go back there."

Aw, no, Mike thought. *Not this now. Please.*

"It's okay," he said. "It's safe, I promise."

She sensed she was being pushed and hugged her arms tighter.

"Juliet," he said. "Listen."

"Nope." She shook her head again. "Definitely not going back there."

Mike released a long, weary breath. He felt like he weighed hundreds of pounds, and all of them were sore.

With effort, he crouched down in front of her, assuming more or less the same position he'd taken back at the fallen pine tree. He patted her on the sides of her legs. He rubbed some warmth, or at least some friction, into her cold bare shoulders with his cold grimy hands.

She didn't protest. After carrying her all that way with her hot breath on his neck, touching her in such a familiar way hardly seemed like a breach of personal space. In fact, it was starting to feel to Mike like they'd known each other longer than they had.

"Hey," he said. "I wouldn't want to go back there either."

"I didn't think I was going to be leaving that place at all," she said. Her voice caught a tremble, but she took a breath and shook it out. "Do you know what that feels like?"

"I have some idea," Mike said. "And that's the God's honest truth. If you want, I'll tell you about it. When we're on the road out of here."

She didn't seem to hear him. "I'm sure as shit not going back."

"Juliet. I get it," Mike said. "But listen to me. You're hurt, and right across this water there's all the first-aid stuff we need. I can disinfect those cuts and wrap your ankle nice and tight, get you warm and dry. Patch you up."

"I'm not going to die," she said.

"No," he agreed. "Not tonight, you're not. But. . . ."

"Where is he?"

"Where is who?"

"You know who I mean," she said. "You said I don't have to worry about him anymore. How do you know that?"

Mike realized he'd worked himself into a corner. What could he possibly tell her in this situation?

Don't worry about it, the guy's a buddy of mine. I know I said I didn't know him, but actually we go way back. He went a little nuts there for a minute, but I'm pretty sure he's okay now.

He didn't want to keep lying to her, but he didn't want to be sitting here in the mud when the cops came roaring up the lane either. All Mike wanted was to get the hell across the lake, get a drink, boost her Subaru, and get them out of Rockhaven.

The lie that would best help him achieve this objective had already popped into his mind. He used it with a guilty conscience, if not with much hesitation.

"He's dead," he told her. "Okay? That's how I know."

Juliet Benson stared at him. But her shoulders loosened. She said, "He's dead?"

"Yes."

"You . . . you killed him?"

"He had a gun, just like you said." It sounded preposterous to Mike's own ears, but it was working. "I did what I had to do."

Her hands drifted into her lap. The knife dangled loosely in her fingers. She looked out across the water, toward the cabin. She looked at Mike. She said, "He's still there?"

"You won't have to see him," Mike said, the impromptu fiction unfolding without conscious effort on his part. Had he already planned it out on some level, knowing they'd come to this conversation eventually? "Why do you think I took the truck around back?"

Juliet went limp. He had to reach out and steady her before she tipped facefirst off her log.

When she'd regained her composure, found her equilibrium again, he peeled a grubby clump of hair away from her eyes and said, "Easy does it."

She looked right at him and said, "Who *are* you?"

At least he didn't have to lie to answer that one. "I'm a very tired guy," he said.

She surprised him then. She reached out and grabbed his hand.

Mike gave her hand a squeeze. "You okay?"

She nodded. "I'm ready."

He helped her down to the water and into the canoe. When she was settled in the bow, he climbed in after her, grabbed the oar, and pushed them off the bank. In the gloom, he could still see the cut through the cattails, and he poled them through. In no time they were gliding in open water.

"Barlowe Lake Ferry at your service," he said between paddle strokes. He sounded like a cornball, but he didn't care. He was feeling good now. "Reasonable rates, and we almost never capsize."

Her chin appeared over her shoulder. "Barlowe?"

"My last name," he told her. "Mike Barlowe."

Her chin swiveled away, and he was looking at the back of her head again. She said, "Very glad to meet you, Mr. Barlowe."

The general mood had taken quite a turn in the past few minutes. For both of them. "Pleasure having you aboard, Miss Benson," he said.

They'd just reached the narrow middle of the peanut-shaped lake when the mood abruptly changed again.

Behind them, in the distance, there came a faint sound through the timber. As the sound grew louder,

Juliet Benson shifted her whole body sideways in the bow seat and cocked her head, listening.

But Mike had already identified the sound they were hearing. It was, unmistakably, the sound of a vehicle coming up the lane, and he felt a strange combination of tension and release. This was the sound he'd been waiting for since he realized that he'd forgotten to call Hal back home at the Elbow. This, or the whop of helicopter blades.

He had just time enough to wonder why he didn't hear sirens when the approaching vehicle emerged into view and took the long curve around the far end of the lake.

Mike felt his heart sink at the sight of the Power Wagon barreling toward the cabin. Already on alert, Juliet Benson went straight as a board, sitting up so quickly that the canoe bobbed.

Mike stopped paddling. For a free-floating moment they watched the truck together: his missing white pickup, not missing anymore. Not parked behind the cabin but gleaming like a beacon as it followed the lane, trailing exhaust and rock dust in the moonlight.

"You goddamn rotten fucker," he heard her say, and all at once the canoe yawed violently starboard. When Mike looked to the bow, it was empty.

Instinctively, he swept the paddle wide through the water, righting his balance, even as he heard the splash off his port. It sounded like someone had heaved a steamer trunk overboard.

Next he heard a high, garbled cry. More splashing. Coughing. Sputtering.

He spotted her four or five feet out, flailing at the water, gasping for breath. The way she was struggling, she seemed to have no sense of her own orientation, and Mike knew exactly why.

The lake temperature at this time of year couldn't have been much more than fifty degrees; the shock of jumping over your head into water that cold could make you forget your own name, let alone how to coordinate your limbs. Juliet Benson had just given herself a billion-odd-gallon dose of the same medicine Mike had given Darryl earlier, dumping that bucket of water in his lap.

"Christ," he said, and got himself together. With one careful draw of the paddle, he angled the bow of the canoe so that he could slide near without plowing into her. "Juliet! Calm down. Grab the paddle."

She didn't seem to hear him. Mike braced himself in the canoe and reached out to grab her by the arm, trying to prepare himself for the quite likely possibility that he was about to end up in the lake with her.

He got her by the meat of her biceps, under her armpit. He propped his free hand on the gunwale, spread his legs as wide as he could manage, and pulled her toward the hull.

He felt a hot bite across the back of his wrist. A shock of pain went shivering up his arm. Mike sucked in a breath, letting her go and pulling his hand away from her out of reflex. He saw watery rivulets of blood already streaming from a gash across the outer knob of his wrist bone.

She cut me, he thought dimly. Despite the shock of the cold lake water, the girl had somehow managed to hang on to the knife. He almost couldn't believe it.

And now she was swimming. Back toward the tree

line, in the direction they'd come. Away from the cabin.

"Juliet!" he called out. "Hey!"

She didn't stop to see what he wanted. On the cabin-side shore, Darryl parked and got out of the truck, turning toward the lake. His silhouette assumed a quizzical posture.

Perfect, Mike thought, and started paddling after Juliet.

She was a good swimmer. But she was also exhausted, and the water was cold. And he doubted she could kick very well with her bad ankle. Even buoyed by adrenaline, after twenty meters she was running out of gas in a hurry, and Mike grew concerned. All this trying to swim away, he yearned to explain, was actually robbing her of body heat instead of generating it, her heart pumping blood from her core to her extremities, to be quickly cooled by the April lake water.

He took a wide arc and piloted the canoe a meter or so in front of her, across her path. "Juliet, come on," he said. "This is nuts."

He half-expected her to go underwater and try to swim beneath him, but she changed course instead, now moving parallel to shore. She wasn't thinking anymore. Only fleeing. Another bad sign.

Mike sighed and paddled along with her. "Come on," he said. "Knock it off."

"Screw you!" she called back. She swallowed a mouthful of lake water and came up sputtering and coughing again. "Stay away from me."

"Let me help you into the boat before you drown," he said.

"You goddamn liar!"

"Fine, I lied to you," he said. "But I can explain."

"Go die. Liar." She was accomplishing little more than treading water by now. But she wasn't giving up yet.

Mike steered the canoe in front of her again.

Again, she changed directions. Back the other way.

It was unbelievably frustrating. He brought the cumbersome rig about and paddled to catch up. They went on like this for an impossibly long time, Juliet trying to find her way past him, Mike turning her away with the hull of the canoe as if herding a wounded otter. He tried to imagine what they must look like from dry land.

At last she began to founder. Her strength was gone, and in a blink their absurd choreography transformed into a critical situation. She was in trouble.

"Juliet, goddammit," he said. He reached out with the oar and said, "Grab it. Please."

Still she resisted, sinking below the water for seconds at a time, gagging as she surfaced.

He was getting ready to dive in for her, hoping like hell he had the strength himself to get the two of them to shore, when she succumbed at last. Juliet grabbed the oar above the paddle with one hand, holding on for all she was worth. *Still* holding the damned knife in her other hand. It was a wonder she hadn't cut her own nose off by now.

Mike leaned back and pulled, hauling her toward the canoe and the canoe toward her. When they met in the middle, she let go of the oar and grabbed on to the gunwale. Her fingers were all but useless, and her grip slipped immediately.

Mike caught her wrist. At the same time, in desperation, she flung the knife into the canoe with a clatter and grabbed the gunwale with her other hand.

Mike took care to place the oar down beside him; it wouldn't do to drop it overboard and watch it float away. Without feeling his busted knuckle or the bone-deep cut on his wrist, Mike reached over her, plunged his hand into the icy water, and got a grip on her by the back of her jeans.

With the help of some miracle and no doubt the most hellacious wedgie Juliet Benson had ever sustained, he managed to haul her up out of the water and over the gunwale without flipping the whole canoe upside down on top of them.

She collapsed in a pile. Her sprained ankle struck the bow-side bench with such a sickening thunk that Mike flinched at the sound of it.

Juliet didn't seem to notice. She laid there in the bottom of the canoe, coughing and panting for breath, the lake water from her clothes and hair making new puddles out of her own blood, long dried on the aluminum beneath her. She was beyond spent.

Mike sat, doubled over, catching his own wind. It took a couple of minutes.

Meanwhile, Juliet Benson stopped moving. At first he was worried that she'd lost consciousness.

Then, slowly, he saw a pale hand work its way out from under her body. While Mike watched, she reached out as far as she could. Reclaimed the knife. Brought it back close.

Mike shook his head. Unbelievable.

He picked up the oar and paddled them the rest of the way home.

*   *   *

He carried her to the cabin in his arms as if she were a feverish child. As he was getting her settled on the couch, both of them dripping water all over everything, Darryl came in, carrying an armload of firewood. He said, "Some timing, huh?"

Mike looked at him. "What happened to waiting for me at the lake road?"

"I ran out of cigarettes."

"Gee. You must have been terrified."

"Dude, you were taking forever." Darryl walked past them, dumped the firewood on the hearth, and knelt down to slide open the fireplace screen.

"My bad," Mike said, disarming the girl carefully. At this point, half conscious at best, she didn't seem to notice the knife leaving her grip.

He grabbed a wool blanket from the back of the nearest armchair and wrapped her up in it. He found an old T-shirt in Darryl's rucksack and tied the fabric tight around his sliced wrist with his free hand and his teeth. When he saw Darryl watching, he raised his eyebrows.

"That's okay," Darryl said. "You can keep it."

24

By two in the morning, Maya estimated that volunteers on the ground outnumbered sworn personnel by a ratio of three or four to one. They worked in groups, combing the timber in overlapping swaths between the freeway and the riverbank.

It was cold and the ground was soggy from the rains. After an hour, Maya tried telling herself that the conditions—unpleasant as they became in no time at all—were still preferable to heat and bugs. Had Juliet Benson been abducted in the middle of August instead of early April, they'd be dealing with overnight temps in the eighties, steam-bath humidity, and mosquitoes the size of Black Hawk helicopters.

It worked for a while, but eventually she ran up against the truth: She was in the worst shape of her life. There had been a time when Maya hit the gym faithfully after work, no matter how late the hour, but it had been too much gin and not enough stairstepper these past couple of years; slogging off path through the woods, trying to hold her place in line, proved far more demanding than churning out script at her desk. She wasn't prepared for it.

It didn't help that the overall vibe from the supervising officers did not exactly pulse with optimism. Judging by what she overheard, catching occasional low snippets of conversation between cops, many of them seemed to have settled on the notion that the whole thing was little more than a snipe hunt in progress.

After all, the dogs had yet to find so much as a whiff of scent to follow, even with Juliet Benson's clothing items for aid. If she was in the creek—possibly even carried to the river by now—they weren't going to find her until she washed up or until someone broke out the scuba gear, whichever came first.

Either way, what kind of kidnapper would have taken time to stuff the girl's coat and shoes—along with her cell phone, conveniently—into a drainpipe? Just off a major freeway? And for what possible reason if not as a decoy, a way to keep everybody busy playing grab-ass in the trees for a while?

After three hours, seeing her lime-green clown shoes radiate in the darkness below the cinched elastic of her yellow sweatpants, Maya began to feel like a character in an off-kilter cartoon. Her overtired brain started up its own batty Dr. Seuss narration in the back of her head: *The searchers kept searching. They kept searching for more. They searched and they searched 'til their search feet were sore.*

So far she'd personally found half a dozen discarded snack wrappers, the random beer can, a child's pink sock, what looked like a used rubber, countless deer turds, and no sign whatsoever of Wade Benson's missing daughter.

She'd tripped a hundred times and had fallen to her hands and knees twice. Her palms were scraped raw.

The knees of her sweatpants had turned into wet, muddy circles. Her search feet were sore.

She ran across Buck Morningside and his crew several times along the way. Eliott Martin pretended he'd never seen her before, and who knew? Maybe he didn't realize that he had. Maya watched the young producer stumble along with his clipboard through the underbrush and wondered where he saw himself five years from now. She wondered where he'd seen himself this morning.

At one point, Morningside himself sidled up alongside her, touched the brim of his hat, and said, "You changed clothes, darlin'."

"Oh, these?" she said.

"Word around the campfire is you went and quit your job too." He nudged her with an elbow. "Was it something I said?"

"Don't flatter yourself."

"Hell, I'm too old for flattery. Here's an idea: Why don't you come work PR for me?"

Maya might have laughed if she'd had the energy. "Thanks anyway," she said. "But I'm sure Twin Cities Public Television has a capable publicity department." Thinking: *They'd better.*

"Who said anything about *public* television?" Morningside looked both ways in front of them as if checking for traffic. "Between you and me, I'd already had lines in the water with that Spike channel on cable. Couple others too. Let's say we've had nibbles. I'd guess this oughta turn some of 'em into bites."

"Sounds like an exciting time for you."

"Don't it, though?" He handed her a business card.

Maya shone her volunteer-issue flashlight on it. The card said *Morningside Media Corp.* in embossed lettering and featured a studio head shot of Morningside himself, Stetson, mustache, and all. "Just had these printed. Like 'em?"

Maya clicked off the flashlight. "They're something."

"I could order some with your name on 'em." He touched his brim again. "Give it some thought."

Before she could answer, he'd peeled away, leaving her to marvel at the notion that this patch of woods might well stand forever in her memory as the setting where Maya Lamb's career in television ended and where Buck Morningside's began.

Every so often, her phone rang in the front pocket of her hoodie, as it had been doing since she'd piled all her regular clothes into the back of the news van. Each time, she pulled the phone out and looked at the screen, hoping for word from Roger Barnhill; each time, she found the same name waiting for her.

Rose Ann calling.

Maya had switched off the ringer after a while, leaving the phone to buzz in her pocket like an irritated dragonfly.

Finally, at about half past three in the morning, while Maya and her group broke for coffee and a rest break at the picnic shelters, her phone buzzed again. A short zap against her belly button. Not a call this time but an incoming text message, also from Rose Ann. The message said:

Fine, screw you then. See if I lose any more sleep at my age.

Five minutes later, the phone resumed its regular pattern.

Maya finally gave in. "Hey, Rose Ann," she said. "Sorry. I had my phone off."

"Bullshit," Rose Ann said. There came a heavy silence, then: "So. I hear you've gone off and joined the natives, is that right?"

"Something like that," Maya said.

Rose Ann humphed. "Find the girl yet?"

"Not yet."

Another pause. "Are you *smoking*?"

Maya felt like she'd been caught by a parent. She ground out the butt she'd just finished under the heel of her sandal and said, "They're Deon's."

"What the hell am I going to do with you?" Maya heard sheets rustling and imagined Rose Ann sitting up in bed, putting on her glasses. "Actually, check that. What the hell are you going to do with yourself? You're too young to retire, unless you hit the lottery and didn't mention it. Did you hit the lottery?"

"No," Maya said. "I didn't hit the lottery."

"So what, then? By all means, do tell."

"I don't know," Maya said, and it was the truth. "I've got some money saved. I can take a few months to figure it out."

"That's your plan? Take a few months and 'figure it out'?"

"Maybe I'll write a book."

"Oh, God save your soul."

"If nothing else, Buck Morningside offered me a job." Maya couldn't resist. "Have you seen anything on this *American Manhunter* show they're doing over at TPT?"

"No," Rose Ann said. "I can't say that I have."

"Well. It's an option."

"It'd serve you right too."

Rose Ann sounded honestly peeved. Maya didn't know what else to say. "I'm sorry, Rose Ann. I guess I haven't handled my departure with a whole lot of class, have I?"

"What departure? As far as I'm concerned, you just started your vacation early."

"Rose Ann—"

"You don't get off the hook that easy. I'm not finished with you."

Maya started to tell her that, with all due respect, she didn't necessarily have any choice in the matter. But then she realized she was only talking tough to a bunch of dead air. Rose Ann had already hung up the phone.

The group mustered for duty again over by the footbridge to the lower side of the creek. Maya rubbed her hands and stretched her aching back and joined the others. As the young state trooper assigned to their detail started giving instructions, her pocket buzzed again.

Maya grabbed out the phone and said, "Rose Ann, I love you, but I'm not talking about this anymore tonight. I'll be in touch. After I've slept for about a week."

"Miss Lamb," a male voice said in her ear. "This is Roger Barnhill."

Maya straightened, groping automatically for her pen and notebook. She thought, *Quit that,* stepped away from the group, and said, "Detective. What's the news?"

"We traced that tag number you gave me," Barnhill said.

Af first Maya didn't know what he was talking about. Then it came to her: the white pickup, back on Front Avenue. She'd forgotten all about it.

"Oh. Right," she said. "And?"

"The truck is registered to a neighborhood business owner named Harold Macklin," Barnhill said. He sounded very, very tired. "Macklin is in critical care at United Hospital in St. Paul with a skull fracture. And related issues."

Maya didn't understand. "What happened to him?"

"We're trying to sort that out," Barnhill said. "In the meantime I'd like to hear more about that vehicle you saw. Where are you now?"

"Still in the park," she said. "The picnic shelters. Where are you?"

"Command," Barnhill said. "Parking lot of the mall. When can you be here?"

Maya watched the search group moving off from the footbridge, heading into the trees along the west bank of the river, spreading out into a line as it moved.

"On my way now," she said.

A couple of miles south of Nisswa, they found a road-side bait shop with a sign out front that read:

Early Crappie/Stream Trout Season Hours
4:30 a.m.–Dusk or So
M–Su

"You've got to hand it to these lake people," Bryce said, as they pulled into the gravel lot and parked. "They do get up early in the morning."

"Uh-huh," Toby said. He killed the engine and shut off the headlights. It was 4:05, according to the read-out on the stereo. He leaned his head back. Closed his eyes.

"Aw," Bryce said. "You're mad. I can tell."

Toby said nothing.

"Let's look at the map some more while we wait," Bryce said. "Keep our eyes on the prize. My prediction, by sunup we'll both be about eighteen grand richer. And heroes to boot. That'll chase those frowns away."

Heroes, Toby thought grimly. What the hell planet did this nutcase call home?

He heard thin paper crinkling as Bryce unfolded the map, which he'd marked up with the pen and the highlighter back at the diner in Brainerd. Through his eyelids, Toby sensed the overhead dome light come on.

He opened his eyes. Bryce folded the map back down into sections and smoothed what was left on the console between them. He studied it a minute, humming to himself. Then he pointed to a spot and said, "I'm guessing somewhere in here." He pointed to another spot. "Or here." He paused, tilted his head, moved his finger in a loose circle. "Or maybe right around in this area here. What do you think that is, all told? Ten miles square?"

Toby didn't know how many miles square it was. He didn't know how to make sense of what he was looking at. On paper, Bryce had filled up this section of Minnesota with circles and radiating lines, highlighting routes this way and that until the whole thing looked like a bunch of cave drawings.

"Sure," he said. *Whatever.*

"Yep." Bryce nodded. "That's what I was thinking."

"So what?" Toby said. "Dude, you're only guessing around anyway."

Bryce raised a finger. "Educated guessing, kid. There's a difference."

"Doesn't look like much of a difference to me."

"That's because you're not educated yet," Bryce said. "It's not your fault. Stick with me."

I'd rather kill myself, Toby thought.

Of course, it was a ridiculous thing to think, him

still sitting there behind the wheel of the Navigator, miles and miles from home, waiting for some bait shop to open on the side of the road in the middle of the night. Still driving this freak everywhere he said to go, imagining he had the sack to do something about it. But he didn't, and both of them knew it.

And Toby had been lying anyway. Bryce seemed to know exactly what he was doing. Which, frankly, seemed about as scary to Toby as anything else he'd seen out of the guy so far.

"First thing we have to do is try to think like a bartender from St. Paul," Bryce said. "We own the bar, but, let's face it, the place ain't much. We are not a rich guy. We manage to get up here, what, two, three times a year?"

"I don't know how to think like a bartender from St. Paul," Toby said.

"I know you don't," Bryce said. "That's what I'm trying to help you learn. So pay attention, okay?"

I don't want to learn how to think like a bartender from St. Paul, Toby thought. For the second time, he asked, "If the guy lied about the address, how do you know he has a place up here at all?"

"He knew the bogus address, didn't he?"

Toby hated that he saw the guy's logic.

"That's the key, really," Bryce said. "Think about it with me: If I get up here only a couple three times a year, but I can throw this bogus address off the top of my head? Under duress? It's got to be a place I've seen enough times to remember." He pointed to the X he'd marked on the map in red pen. Like they were pirates. "Here's Mussel Shores. Nearest town here.

Main highway here, paved county road here. Follow?"

The longer Toby looked at the map with Bryce's guidance, the more all the markings started to make sense. It was just a probability graph, sort of. The places where the lines overlapped were the same spots Bryce had pointed out before. It was sort of impressive, actually.

"So if I'm up here at my lake place that I get to use only two or three times a year," Bryce said, "how am I most likely spending my time?"

Toby knew the answer, but he didn't want to give Bryce the satisfaction.

"Oh, come on," Bryce said. "Play along. It's fun."

Toby sighed. "Probably fishing."

"Probably fishing. Which means I probably need a place to buy bait and tackle." Bryce gestured toward the windshield. "Here we have a bait shop." He went back to the map, pointing around at the various areas he'd indicated previously, tracing routes with his fingers. "Could be I've driven past glorious Mussel Shores on my way to this very bait shop."

"Could be there's a million other bait shops around here."

"Probably not a million."

"Lots."

"Might as well start with this one though, huh?" Bryce reached up and turned off the dome light. Map class was over. "Anyway, it doesn't matter if this is the right bait shop or if it isn't. I'll bet whoever runs this particular bait shop knows a thing or two about who owns what in these parts. If we ask him nice, who knows what he might be able to tell us?"

You mean like you asked the last guy? Toby thought. He looked at Bryce and said, "This is all a game to you, isn't it?"

"I wouldn't say game," Bryce said. "But it is a challenge. I like challenges."

"Yeah? How you planning to explain that bartender from St. Paul?" Toby felt himself growing bolder all of a sudden. He liked the feeling. "Bet that'll be a challenge."

"What's to explain?" Bryce said. "We find that girl, he'll be the one with some explaining to do."

"Guess he'll have a hard time doing that though, huh?"

"How's that?"

Toby looked away, out his window. The light outside the bait shop threw long shadows that disappeared into the darkness.

"All right," Bryce said. "You obviously have something you want to get off your chest. Why don't you go ahead and lay it on me?"

"You didn't have to do him like that," Toby muttered.

"Sorry? Didn't hear you."

Toby raised his voice. "I said you didn't have to do it."

"Do what?"

"You know what."

Bryce was silent a moment.

"Ah," he finally said. "Is that what's been hanging you up? Seriously?"

Toby's newfound confidence slipped away. He kept his trap shut.

"You think, what? I *killed* the guy?" Bryce said it like he'd just heard a joke. "Come on, kid. What do you think I am? Some kind of psychopath?"

"You said it, not me."

Bryce laughed. "Well, hell, partner. You can rest easy. We haven't started leaving corpses behind us yet."

"I heard the shot, man."

"Yeah, I heard it too," Bryce said. "I was the one getting shot at."

Toby looked at him. "You're telling me the guy isn't dead."

"Hell of a headache, probably. Dead? Come on."

Toby didn't know whether to believe him or not. He didn't know if he was relieved or not. He didn't know what to think or what to feel. In a way he only felt more confused than ever. He said, "Then what the hell, man?"

"What the hell what?"

"What the hell are we supposed to do when the guy tells the cops about us?"

"So you think I *should* have killed him?"

"No! Jesus. I mean . . ."

"Easy. I'm just messing with you." Bryce reached out and clapped him on the knee. Toby jumped at his touch. "Believe me, our bartender from St. Paul isn't going to be telling the cops anything about you. And he sure as hell isn't going to be telling the cops anything about me."

"How do you know that?"

"Because I supplied him with appropriate motivation, that's how."

"Motivation?"

"In addition to being a handsome devil," Bryce said, "I'm also an effective communicator."

"Dude, what does that even mean?"

"It means you can relax," Bryce said. "I'm the ideas guy, remember?"

Toby felt like his brain was cooking.

"You have questions," Bryce said.

"Jesus, man. Yeah, I have questions." He didn't know where to start. "How do we explain . . . I mean, what do we tell the . . . dude, we're gonna get—"

"Kid, let me tell you a story," Bryce said. "I think it'll help put all this into perspective. Okay?"

Toby closed his mouth.

"I used to be an Airborne Ranger," Bryce said. "By the look on your face I guess you didn't know that."

"No," Toby said. "I didn't know that."

"Well," Bryce said. "When I was with the Rangers, we did a little business in Honduras and Costa Rica that'd cure your eyesight if you knew about it." He propped an elbow on his door. "After I was out of the Rangers, I spent sixteen weeks on my own in Thailand at this camp in the mountains. Learned some hand-to-hand shit that ain't what you'd call ring-legal even in Thailand. The only other westerner I met there ended up with spinal fluid leaking out his nose. You with me so far?"

Toby didn't say anything. He heard the leather upholstery squeak as Bryce shifted position.

"Then one pretty fall day a couple years ago," Bryce said, "up in the northwoods, I hit a moose on my bike doing about ninety. Nothing but clear road ahead of me, then all at once out of nowhere, boom.

Spent a month in the hospital, came out with a slightly different profile than I had when I went in. The moose didn't make it, sadly."

In the semidarkness, that profile of his looked like buckled pavement. *Poor moose,* Toby couldn't help thinking.

Bryce said, "Do you know what I learned from those experiences?"

Toby took off his glasses and rubbed his face with his hands. "You learned that life doesn't always go as planned," he said. "I get it."

"No," Bryce said. "No, I knew that already. What I learned is that even though life is unpredictable, things generally seem to work out in my favor." He shrugged. "I'd rather be with me than against me, I guess is what I'm saying."

Toby put his glasses back on and lowered his hands.

"So," Bryce said. "How about it?"

"How about what?"

"Are you with me or against me?"

And just like that, Toby realized he'd wandered onto thin ice again. Bryce hadn't changed his tone in the least, but Toby could almost hear the cracks forming under his feet.

At that moment, before he could gather himself, more lights came on outside the bait shop, spilling across the gravel lot.

"Tell you what," Bryce said. He reached across the console, pulled the keys from the ignition. He grabbed Toby's mobile out of its cradle on the dash. "Why don't you take a little time and think about it. I'll be right back."

The bait shop's paint-flaked front door shimmied,

then screeched open. An old guy in a flannel jacket stepped out on the stoop and gave them a wave. *Come on in.*

"And, hey. Don't worry," Bryce said, opening his door. "I won't shoot this one either, if I can help it."

26

Mike needed to get Juliet Benson out of her cold, wet clothes, but that was a can of worms he wasn't sure how to open. The dunk in the lake had capped off a long night in the cold woods, and considering the stress her system had already sustained, he knew that she was probably suffering at least a mild case of hypothermia. But she was conscious and more or less lucid, at least capable of answering questions, and by the time he got the fire roaring along under its own power, she'd ceased her uncontrolled shivering.

By the time he brought down a quilt from upstairs to add to the blanket he'd already wrapped her in, the girl had fallen asleep on the couch where she sat.

He wasn't surprised. Mike had seen enough different kinds of fatigue in his time to imagine that not even Juliet Benson's formidable self-preservation insincts could keep her online now that she'd stopped moving. In front of a crackling fire, no less. Either that or she'd slipped into a coma.

But she seemed to be fine. Mike was no physician, but he knew a good pulse when he felt one. Her breathing was regular. When he eased a pillow under her head, she actually began snoring lightly. He felt he could leave her alone for a bit.

Mike went out onto the porch, where Darryl sat with his back to the cabin, smoking a cigarette. The first hint of morning twilight had seeped into the sky over the trees across the lake. Dawn would be along soon. A fresh new day for everybody.

Without turning, Darryl said, "Give it to me straight, Doc. How's our girl?"

"Resting comfortably," Mike said. *But we're not out of the woods yet,* he thought.

"Good," Darryl said.

Mike limped down the steps and put the gym bag containing Toby Lunden's cash on the top riser, next to Darryl's leg. He dropped Darryl's rucksack next to the gym bag. Darryl looked at both, then looked at Mike.

"I figure the cops would be here by now if Hal had called them," Mike said. "I guess he likes you more than I thought."

"Huh," Darryl said.

"Which means nobody's looking for the truck yet." Mike tossed the keys on top of the gym bag. "It's got a brand-new starter."

Darryl's eyes followed the jingle of the keys, stopping where they landed.

"Canada's that way," Mike said, pointing. "You'll be across the border in time for breakfast if you don't stop and sightsee. But you'd better get going."

Darryl leaned forward and sat that way for a bit, elbows on his knees, cigarette trailing smoke between his fingers. He said, "What about you?"

"What about me?"

"What are you going to do?"

"Take care of the girl," Mike said. "There's a hospital in Brainerd. I can drive her in the Sube. Things should take care of themselves from there."

"Think so?"

"As soon as you get the hell out of here and let me do it."

Darryl took a drag from his cigarette. The glow of the ember cast his face in orange light and dark shadows. His left cheekbone was bruised and swollen where Mike had tagged him.

"And what do you think the cops are gonna say when she tells 'em you went ahead and let me go?" Darryl asked. "Thanks for all the help, Mr. Citizen?"

"Let who go?" Mike said. "You overpowered me and took off in the truck."

"Did I?"

"It's hard to admit, believe me."

"Why'd I do that again?"

"Because you're an asshole," Mike said.

Darryl chuckled softly. "Guess they'll believe that, huh?"

"Can't think of a reason why they wouldn't."

Darryl finished his cigarette. Instead of tossing it off the porch, he ground it out on the top riser and put the butt in his pocket. No littering at Rockhaven.

"Probably have to come up with something better than that when you tell Hal how you lost his truck, though."

"Yeah, well," Mike said. He nodded toward the

gym bag. "I took out a couple grand. That ought to get something he can drive around. At least until I can do better."

"You know, I doubt he likes me all *that* much," Darryl said. "I figure I left 'em plenty busy. The cops."

Mike didn't know what that meant. He didn't want to know. He said, "Either way, sounds like you're good to go."

Darryl sat in silence. Then he said, "Mike?"

"Still standing here."

"When I came up to Minnesota." Darryl straightened on the stoop. "I never mentioned it, but I was dodging a little business back home. I guess you probably figured that, huh?"

Mike nodded. "That's more or less the impression I got, yeah."

"I never mentioned it, and you never once asked. Did you?"

"Not that I remember."

"I remember," Darryl said. "You didn't."

"Okay."

"How come?"

Mike hadn't much thought about it before. "I guess I figured if it was any of my business, you'd tell me about it," he said.

Darryl grabbed the truck keys. He stood, slung his rucksack over one shoulder, and picked up the gym bag. He came down the steps, stopped in front of Mike, and stood there. Mike tried to look him in the face, but Darryl wouldn't meet his eyes.

Instead, he put a rough hand on the side of Mike's

neck. Pressed his clammy forehead against Mike's own. He smelled like he'd been buried and dug up again.

"You're the only goddamn friend I ever had," he said. "If you didn't know."

Mike didn't speak. They just stood together, breathing each other's air, until Darryl said, "You still hit like a fourteen-year-old girl."

"Jesus, you're good at wasting time."

Darryl squeezed his neck once and broke the clinch. He pressed something into Mike's palm, then left him standing there.

Darryl walked to the truck and opened the driver's side door. He flung the gym bag inside, tossed his rucksack in after it. At the last moment he turned and said, "Sometime I'll make this up to you, Mikey. You can believe that."

Mike took a good look at him, knowing deep down that this would be the last time he ever saw Darryl Potter. Even after everything the dumb grunt had put him through, the thought made his heart a little heavier.

"Make it up to me now," he said.

Without another word, Darryl climbed into the truck, pulled the door shut behind him, and started the engine.

Mike stood and watched him back away from the cabin, turn around in the grass, and take off down the lane. He watched the Power Wagon trailing dust around the curve of the lake. He watched until brake lights pulsed red and disappeared behind the tree line. He stood there until the grumble of the big old V8 faded away.

When it was quiet on the lake again, Mike opened his palm and looked down at what Darryl had left for him, having already guessed what he'd find: a set of Subaru keys.

He dropped them in his pocket and went inside.

27

Maya found Roger Barnhill standing with a group of suits and uniforms near a K-9 unit in the Camden Center parking lot. He looked over as she approached, then returned to what he was doing. She waited on the periphery for a moment, then said, "Detective?"

This time Barnhill recognized her. He leaned back slightly, looking her up and down. He finally said, "You changed something. I can't put my finger on it."

Maya smirked. "At least you haven't lost your sense of humor."

The detective broke away and they walked to a spot nearby where they could speak without interruption. There weren't many such spots available. Barnhill said, "Thanks for getting up here so quickly."

Maya nodded. "What about this white pickup?"

Barnhill regarded her for a moment without answering. He said, "You look like you could use a cup of coffee and a place to sit down."

"I'm fine," she said. "Have you heard anything more about Macklin's condition?"

"If you're fine, then you're doing better than I am," Barnhill said. "Me, I could use a cup of coffee and a place to sit down."

Maya didn't have to study the man very long to take him at his word. And she'd been lying anyway. *Fine* was not, in fact, among the words she'd have used to characterize herself honestly.

"Lead the way," she said.

On a normal day, the Joy Luck Restaurant in Camden Center wouldn't begin serving customers until eleven o'clock in the morning. On this day, the owners had opened their doors to law enforcement and volunteers, serving free coffee and hot tea, along with eggs to order, fried pork, duck sausage, and a choice of soups: wonton or hot and sour. They sold the food at half their regular menu prices, which were reasonable to begin with.

Maya and Barnhill took a booth up front and ordered coffee. They weren't alone in the place, but there wasn't a crowd, and the majority of their fellow patrons appeared to be cops. While the detective scribbled notes, Maya told him everything she could about what she'd seen of the white Dodge Power Wagon that had blocked their news truck hours ago, which amounted to almost nothing beyond what she'd glimpsed of the driver himself.

"He was wearing a hat and sunglasses," she said. "That was what struck me funny."

"The hat struck you funny?"

"Not anything specific about the hat," she said. "Just, you know. Shades at night, ball cap pulled down low. Like a celebrity at an airport."

"Like he didn't want to be recognized."

"Maybe," Maya said. Thinking: *How could I have*

been so close? How could I have been so close twice?
"At the time I thought it seemed strange. How he was sitting there, the way he took off when we honked at him. Anyway, strange enough that I wrote down his plate and handed it to you."

Barnhill appeared visibly frustrated. Bordering on angry, Maya thought, though she didn't know the detective well enough to make that determination. She said, "What is it?"

"What is what?"

"About that truck," she said. "It's connected to Juliet too. Isn't it?"

"Not beyond what you're telling me, as far as we know. If that constitutes a connection."

"Then you've got something else."

"We've got lots of things we didn't have last time you and I communicated," Barnhill said. "But nothing that tells me where I can find Juliet Benson."

"Then I guess that explains it," she said.

"Explains what?"

"Why you're sitting there looking like you want to crumple that coffee mug like it's a Dixie cup."

Barnhill lowered his head. He pondered the mug between his hands, then said, "You passed me the tag number on that pickup around nine p.m. last night. Is that about right?"

"Around there," she said.

"Harold Macklin closed his bar, for reasons we haven't yet determined, a little after ten p.m. He was discovered unresponsive on the floor of his place by one of his employees, who happens to be an ex-wife, just after midnight. Evidence on site suggests a robbery—emptied register, what have you—but the ex-wife says Macklin never closes early and that he'd been acting out of the ordinary for most of the evening up to that point. Which is what eventually brought her back to check on him."

The reporter in Maya saw the problem with the detective's timeline even as he laid it out. It might have taken the sheriff's office an hour to trace a license plate under the circumstances, but it wouldn't have taken three. Not if that tag number had been given much priority as a lead. It hadn't.

She didn't mention it. "I guess it hasn't been a joy luck kind of night," she said.

"No." Barnhill shook his head slowly. "Not very joy lucky so far at all."

Maya put her elbows on the table and rested her head on her hands.

Barnhill watched her, sipping his coffee. "Would it be okay if I asked you a personal question?"

"Sure."

"When's the last time you slept?"

She hadn't thought about it until the detective asked. Counting the two or three hours she'd taken to sleep off Rose Ann's birthday party, she'd put in nearly a twenty-four-hour day by now.

"That's what I thought." Barnhill finished his coffee and collected his things. "I'm on my way over to United Hospital to check on Harold Macklin first-hand. Talk to the ex-wife. Why don't you let me drop you off at your station on the way? I assume that's where you left your car?"

"It is," Maya said. "And thank you. But I need to get back to my group."

"Looks to me like you'd do better with some rest," Barnhill said. "If you don't mind my opinion."

Maya found that she did mind, in fact. Partly because it rubbed her the wrong way to be told what was good for her, and partly because the offer seemed so tempting. The warmth of the restaurant and the comfort of the booth had sapped the strength out of her, the way a deep winter night drained a worn-out car battery. The thought of her apartment—a hot shower, dry pajamas, bed—was almost too much to withstand.

"I appreciate it," she said. "But I'd rather keep going."

Barnhill rubbed his eyes. "Fair enough."

As he slid out of the booth and stood to go, Maya lifted her head and said, "Detective?" When he turned back, she glanced at his vacant spot across the table. "Don't you want to see what yours says?"

Barnhill took a moment to consider the fortune cookies their server had brought out with their coffee. Two golden-brown crescents centered on white porcelain saucers, one fortune for each of them.

He said, "Don't you?"

Maya hadn't touched hers either. "I think I'd rather not know," she said.

Barnhill nodded. "That was my thought."

28

It took only ten minutes before Bryce emerged from the bait shop, walked back to the Navigator, and climbed in. He shut the door behind him, leaned over, and slid the keys into the ignition.

Toby didn't want to ask. "Well?"

Bryce smiled and returned Toby's phone. "The moment you've been waiting for. Go ahead and make the call."

Toby looked at the phone in his hand. "Call who?"

"Your uncle," Bryce said, fastening his seat belt. "Who else?"

29

At the southern border of the park, between the Camden Bridge and the Soo Line railway trestle, sat an industrial plywood distribution complex with a freight yard along the westbound tracks. The Webber–Camden Homeowners Association had set up a volunteer shuttle service from the freight yard back up to the command post at Camden Center. Meanwhile, all the network affiliates had set up for their daybreak live shots.

It was nearly five in the morning by the time Maya's group trudged into the mix. The sky had lightened in the east. Birds had begun chirping in the trees. Reporters cherry-picked incoming searchers for interviews, looking for last-minute color for their stand-ups.

Maya steered clear of anything resembling a camera or a microphone, especially anything bearing a News7 call sign, and in doing so ran nearly headfirst into one of her colleagues in disguise.

Justin Murdock apologized without really looking at her. Then he looked at her and said, "Holy shit. Maya?"

She almost didn't recognize him either. Justin was

decked from the ground up in what looked, at first glance, like safari gear: hiking boots, khaki trousers hanging with cargo pockets, a pullover made of some kind of tech fabric. On top of all that, he wore a stiff new Domke photography vest that must have cost an arm and a leg.

"That's me," she said. "Holy Shit Maya."

Justin looked her up and down. She braced for the inevitable questions: *What happened to you? Is it true you quit the station? Are you okay?* But he only smirked and said, "Nice outfit."

"Thanks," she said. "You too." With the rucksack strapped over his shoulder, he looked like he was preparing to report live from a hot zone in Afghanistan. She'd have laughed if she'd had the energy. "Who are you supposed to be, anyway? Indiana Jones?"

"Ha ha," he said. "Rose Ann gave me the backpack gig full-time this morning. Welcome to the future, News7."

Well, well, Maya thought. *There goes the neighborhood.*

It had been bound to happen sometime. In his rucksack, Justin Murdock would be carrying his own digital video camera, digital audio recorder, high-powered laptop computer, satellite phone, and probably enough spare batteries to sink a jon boat—everything he needed to shoot, write, edit, and file his own stories from the field, without ever setting foot near a truck or a newsroom.

So-called "backpack journalism" had been slow in coming to News7, in part because Rose Ann Carmody thought like Maya: Very few reporters were good at everything, and giving some kid out of

J-school all the technology he needed to pretend otherwise was a good recipe for sloppy reporting.

It was also a hot trend, and sooner or later Rose Ann had to give in to what their network competitors had already embraced. Justin—who had done this kind of work in his previous market, had done it fairly well, and had been lobbying for the job ever since he'd arrived here—was a logical choice.

Still, Maya couldn't help imagining Rose Ann sending her a personal message in cargo pants: *How do you like giving up your big story now, Miss Maybe I'll Write a Book?*

"Congratulations," she told him. "It's a hell of a pilot piece."

"I guess I owe you one there." He seemed to recognize the way that sounded and added, "Hey, you kicked ass on this thing. Everybody knows that. I'll nail it for you."

"You'd better," Maya said. "Who's on the live shot?"

"Kimberly."

Now, there's a team, Maya thought, remembering the awkward scene between Justin and Kimberly Cross at Rose Ann's birthday party. But she left it alone. That party seemed like ancient history anyway.

"Hey, let me interview you." Justin perked up. "Right here, coming out of the park. What is it, seven hours since anyone saw you on camera? It'll be perfect."

Maya looked at him.

"What do you say?"

She discovered that she had the energy to laugh after all.

*   *   *

Maya Lamb became a reporter again on her way to the command shuttle, seven hours since anyone last saw her on camera, five hours after she'd stopped being a reporter in the first place.

But not a reporter, exactly—Maya didn't exactly know what it was that she became. *Possessed* came to mind.

It started the moment she spotted the crew from Twin Cities Public Television. They were packing their gear into the back of a black Chevy Suburban the size of a river barge, which was parked around the side of a low Quonset building. Maya glimpsed the Suburban on her way across the freight yard to the main entrance, where a handful of Webber–Camden minivans sat with their doors open, loading in a steady stream of bedraggled volunteers.

She saw the Suburban, and she saw the TPT crew. She even saw the scruffy director in the peacoat and Chuck Taylors, milling around with a cup of free coffee while everyone else did the lifting. But she didn't see the star of the show anywhere in their midst.

Then she spotted a familiar bolt of sheepskin: Buck Morningside, standing alone by the chain-link security fence, talking on a cell phone.

That struck her as odd. Every network affiliate in the Cities was preparing to go live from this freight yard; the Buck Morningside she knew should have been right there in the thick of it, mugging for the cameras. Yet the American Manhunter and his Northstar Justice League appeared to be packing up shop instead.

She angled toward him almost without thinking. Morningside saw her coming, finished up his call, and vacated his spot. He touched the brim of his Stetson as he met her going the other direction.

"Until next time, darlin'," he said. "Pleasure as always."

He'd turned his back on the KARE 11 crew set up by the entrance. Maya fell in step beside him. "Leaving so soon?"

"Been a hell of a long night," he said. "I know when I'm licked."

"Bullshit."

Morningside slipped her a sidelong glance. His mustache quirked. If he'd been a cat, he'd have had canary feathers caught in his whiskers.

"You've got something," she said. She couldn't believe it, couldn't imagine how it was possible, and at the same time absolutely knew in her gut it was true. It was all over his smug, folksy face. "Don't you? You've actually got something."

"Sure wish I did."

"Hubert, tell me that was one of your cop buddies you were talking to on your phone just now."

"Oh, hell, darlin'. These cops got all the job they can handle as it is. Last thing I came down here to do is get in anybody's way."

Then he winked at her.

Something about that stopped Maya in her tracks.

"'Course, if you're really interested," Morningside said over his shoulder, "you know that job offer's still good. No dress code either."

The cheese-eating son of a bitch winked at me, she thought. Winked and kept walking.

Maya finally snapped. She looked all around. She turned in a full circle where she stood, scanning for somebody in a uniform. Anybody. What would she tell them when she found them? Buck Morningside was leaving the premises? She'd have to figure it out as she went.

Just then she caught sight of Eliott Martin in the near distance, hurrying from another direction toward the Suburban, carrying his clipboard under his arm like a football.

Maya intercepted him at a hard angle. "You!" she said, pointing a finger. "I want to talk to you."

The young producer's eyes went wide. He veered off to avoid her.

"Oh, no, you don't," she said. "Come here."

"I can't talk now," Martin said. "I have to go."

"What are you up to?"

"Me?"

"I'm on to you," Maya said. "Do you hear me? Tell me where you're going."

Martin looked genuinely afraid of her. He adjusted his glasses and tried to steer clear, but Maya cut him off every time he changed directions. "I have to go," he kept saying.

"Listen to me, you little shit weasel," Maya said. "You're out of your league."

"I don't—"

"You ever hear of interfering with a police investigation? Obstruction of justice? You can go to jail for that, Eliott. Do you want to go to jail?" He tried to slide past her. She jumped in front of him. "Come on. You're a PBS affiliate. Do you want really want blood on your hands? Think it through."

Eliott Martin clammed up and kept his eyes locked straight ahead of him. He seemed to be on the verge of panic. Maya sensed a tremor in his resolve and knew she'd gained the upper hand.

Then, just when she thought she had him, the kid yelped and put a move on her. He juked one way, spun the other, and then fled away toward the Suburban, pumping his arms.

At the Suburban, Buck Morningside leaned against the open rear door as the crew finished loading in their gear. He stood with arms folded, Stetson propped back on his head, watching the scene with amusement. He gave Eliott Martin a thumbs-up in encouragement.

"I'm going to get you, Eliott!" Maya called after him. "Do you hear me? I'm going to take you apart a piece at a time!"

Martin kept on running toward safety. Morningside waved at her.

Maya turned and hustled away in the opposite direction, across the loading yard. After scrambling her way upstream through another bunch of volunteers returning from one of the other groups, she raised up on her tiptoes and found Justin Murdock, who was not gathering news from the woolliest reaches of Minnesota but rather chatting up the little blond morning reporter from Channel 9, well within view of Kimberly Cross and the nearby News7 broadcast truck.

Kimberly scowled and pretended to be looking in another direction. The Channel 9 reporter recoiled visibly when she saw Maya bearing down on them.

"Come on, Indy," Maya said. She grabbed Justin

by the back collar of his photographer's vest, turned, and pulled him along after her.

"Hey!" he said. "Take it easy. What's the—"

"Your car," she said. "Where is it?"

"My what?"

"Your *car*," Maya said. "The thing you used to drive yourself here. Focus now."

"My car's over there," Justin said. He pointed in the general direction of the main entrance, where Buck Morningside's smoke-windowed Suburban now sat idling in line behind two minivans, a car, and three SUVs, all filled with passengers, waiting to turn out onto Soo Avenue. "Why? What's going on?"

"Hang on to your backpack," she said, and started running.

VACATION LAND

30

Mike unwrapped Juliet Benson's savaged feet and washed them in a plastic dish tub filled with warm soapy water. He gently cleaned away the pine needles and grit. At one point he heard her suck air through her teeth and found her awake, still wrapped to her chin in the blankets, watching him work in the warm light of the fire.

He tried to be as soft-handed as he could. She said nothing, and he said nothing in reply. When the water turned black with mud and blood, he rested her feet on a towel, dumped the tub over the porch railing, came back inside, and started over fresh. He had to change the water three times before he was through.

She'd been right about the cut on her left foot. It was bad. Long and plenty deep, swollen wide open, running crossways from the base of her pinky toe to the curve of her instep. But it looked to be a clean slice, and it had stopped bleeding freely.

Mike went to the bathroom and came back with an armload of stuff from the closet where Hal kept all the med supplies: bandages, gauze pads, ointment, tape, iodine swabs, half a bottle of Tylenol 3. He ran a tub of clean water, tore open a fistful of swabs, and swizzled them around in the tub. The iodine turned the water a clear amber color that made Mike think of the last bit of whiskey left in the bottle on the coffee table.

"This probably won't feel great," he said. "But I'll be quick and then we'll be done. Okay?"

She nodded her head.

"Ready?"

She nodded again, and he lowered her feet into the tub. She flinched but didn't make a peep. She took in deep breaths through the nose and let them out through her mouth, handling herself like a pro as he cupped his hands and sloshed the disinfectant solution up over her calves and ankles.

"So," he asked as he worked, meaning to distract her from the sting. "Where'd you learn to paddle a canoe, anyway?"

It sounded completely stupid, and she went so long without responding that he assumed she wouldn't respond at all. Not that he could blame her. So much for small talk.

"Camp Chickadee," she finally said.

"What's that, like a summer camp?"

"Up in the north woods," she said. "Every summer until the year I turned sixteen."

Mike grinned. "They must have been a hardcore bunch," he said. "Those Chickadees."

"Power Girls."

"What?"

"Camp Chickadee Power Girls," she said. "That's what they called us. I still have all the guide booklets."

"Guide booklets?"

"'Camp Chickadee Power Girls' Guide to Canoe-ing,'" she said. "'Camp Chickadee Power Girls' Guide to Knots.' 'Camp Chickadee Power Girls' Guide to Being Lost.'" She paused in thought. "No 'Camp Chickadee Power Girls' Guide to Being Tied to a Bed,' though."

"No," Mike said, lifting her feet out of the tub, set-ting them down gently on another clean towel. "No, I don't expect there was."

They fell silent again for a little while. He dabbed her feet and legs carefully with the ends of the towel. When her skin was dry, he smeared ointment on a bandage pad and taped it over the big cut, then wrapped her feet in rolled gauze.

"Almost out of here," he told her. "Are you still cold?"

She shook her head.

"Good. I think Regina's got some dry clothes in a drawer somewhere around here. When I'm done I'll clear out so you can change."

"Who's Regina?"

"Ex-wife of the guy I was telling you about. Guy who owns this place."

"You mean that really wasn't him?"

Mike shook his head. No need to ask who she was talking about. "No. I didn't lie about that part."

"But you do know him."

"Yeah. I know him."

"He's a friend of yours."

Mike nodded. *We went to war together,* he almost said, but he held back. What did he want? To impress her? Sympathy?

She said, "Why did he do this to me?"

Mike didn't know what to tell her. God knew the girl deserved some kind of explanation, but how far back would he have to go to find one that made any sense?

"It's something to do with my father," she said. Not a question this time.

He nodded again.

"What's his name?"

"Darryl," Mike told her. "His name is Darryl."

"Did Darryl know Becky Morse? Is that it?"

Mike considered telling her the simplest version of the truth: that they'd served with Becky Morse's brother, that Darryl believed Juliet's father hadn't been held sufficiently accountable for Evan Morse's death, and that somehow in Darryl's tangled-up mind he'd decided that it was his job to even the score a bit. But he realized that telling her all of that wouldn't really answer her question, so he kept it even simpler.

"He knew the family," he said.

Juliet was quiet a moment. "Did you know the family?"

"A little."

"Do you hate my father too?"

Mike looked at her. Even as a half-drowned wreck, she was still a very pretty girl. And not just pretty. There was something about her. She looked back at him openly, calmly, waiting for his answer.

"No," he said. "I don't hate anybody."

"Not like Darryl."

"I don't think Darryl hates your dad either," he told her. "Not really."

"Then why did he do this?"

Mike finished taping off the gauze, then took up the

elastic compression bandage and wrapped her bad ankle. Snug, but not tight enough to cut off her circulation.

"You're not answering," she said.

Because there isn't an answer, he thought, but she deserved one anyway.

"The guy who owns this place," he finally said. "His name is Hal. A good man. Runs a bar down in St. Paul." Mike fastened off the compression bandage with the aluminum clips, crimping them in place with his fingers. "Two weeks a year, Regina takes over so Hal can come up here. Every year, the old goat comes back looking like a new man. I asked him one time, what was his secret? Want to know what he told me?"

Juliet shifted positions on the couch. "What did he tell you?"

"Everything makes sense up here," Mike said. "That's what he told me. He grew up fishing with his granddad on this lake, and every time he comes back, he says, it reminds him who he is. Where he came from, where he wants to go. What matters." He took her feet off his lap and settled them on the floor. All clean and bandaged. Ready to go. "He told me that no matter how tired he is, no matter how low he goes, no matter how shitty or screwed up life ever seems to get, for him it's nothing a couple weeks in the lake country can't fix."

"That sounds nice," she said.

"It does," Mike agreed. He stood up. "Want to know what I think?"

She raised her eyes and waited.

"I think some people find a place like that," he said. "And Darryl ain't ever going to be one of 'em."

Juliet Benson seemed to study him closely. Mike looked at her, then looked away. What a hell of a pretty girl.

"What about you?" she said.

"What about me what?"

"Do you have a place like that?"

Mike thought about it honestly. It took longer than he would have liked to come up with a truthful answer. "I have a place I can borrow," he said. "But it isn't mine."

She waited for him to say more, but he didn't know what more to say. So he left her on the couch while he went to get clothes. He found some of Regina's things in the bottom drawer of the dresser in the bedroom at the top of the stairs: wool socks, a sweatshirt, a pair of flannel lounging pants with a drawstring. The clothes smelled a little musty, and they weren't exactly high on style, but they would do.

He went across the landing to the other bedroom, which was still in scrambled disarray, and grabbed the unopened water bottle from the night table. He went back downstairs and laid the folded clothes in a stack at the end of the couch. He handed Juliet the water bottle, grabbed the Tylenol, and shook three caplets into her palm.

"Use as directed for pain and inflammation," he told her. He shook out a few more for himself and picked up the last of the whiskey to wash them down. Something stopped him, and he stood there a minute, pondering the image of the black crow on the bottle in his hand. He finally put the bottle down on the table where he'd found it and swallowed the caplets dry.

"Mike?" she said.

He looked at her.

"I'm sorry I cut you," she said.

Mike looked at Darryl's T-shirt cinched around his wrist. The material had soaked through on top. A small blob of red, no bigger than a dime.

"You let me off easy," he told her.

She took the Tylenol. Drank some water.

He said, "Ready to hit the road?"

She nodded.

Mike stooped, collected up the scattered first-aid supplies, and went off to the bathroom so she could have some privacy.

"Hey, numbers guy," Bryce said, looking through his binoculars. "You don't happen to remember the license plate the cops put out on that girl's car, do you?"

"Nope," Toby said. He laid his head back and looked at the ceiling.

They'd been parked for fifteen minutes in the middle of another narrow rock lane, deep in another bunch of thick woods, a few yards from the spot where the trees opened up and the lane continued on into another clearing. This road didn't end in a real estate sign.

They sat there doing the same thing they'd been doing when all of this started back in St. Paul: no headlights, no engine, Toby behind the wheel, Bryce surveilling the little cabin on the far side of the lake. The sky grew pale with the light of dawn.

"Yeah, me either," Bryce said. "How about the make and model?"

"Subaru Outback."

"Green, right?"

"That's what they said."

"Damn, I'm good." Bryce lowered the binoculars and gathered himself. "All right, I'm satisfied. Let's move."

Toby raised his head off the seat back. "Move? Move where?"

"Jesus, kid," Bryce said. He grabbed the keys and the phone. "It's like you're not even trying."

Toby looked at him in disbelief. "We're not going in there."

"We're not?"

"Dude. We found the place."

"We sure did."

"And we called my uncle."

"Called your uncle. Check."

"So now we wait, right?"

Bryce tilted his head. "Wait for what?"

"For my uncle," Toby said, increasingly alarmed. "And the cops. Like, backup. Right?"

"Backup," Bryce said. "Your uncle's two hours away. And you know *he's* not bringing any cops. How long were you planning on waiting, exactly?"

"Dude, until they get here," Toby said.

"Oh," Bryce said. "And what do you think Potter might be doing to that poor girl in there while we're sitting out here waiting around?"

"How should I know?"

"Exactly," Bryce said.

Like you care about the girl, Toby thought.

"What about your money? You remember your money, don't you?" Bryce snapped his fingers as though trying to jog Toby's recollection. "The whole reason you needed my help in the first place? The reason we've had the opportunity to spend all this quality time with one another?"

"I remember it."

"I guess you're planning on letting a bunch of dumb cops put it in an evidence bag, now? Is that the new plan, partner?"

"Are you serious?"

"Why wouldn't I be serious?"

"Dude, it's eleven grand."

"And?"

"And whatever. It's nothing. Take the stupid reward yourself if you want eleven grand so bad."

Bryce leaned back in his seat. He seemed to need a moment to regroup.

"Okay, couple things," he said. "First, stop calling me dude. You sound like a moron."

Toby looked out his window. Nothing there to see but trees. Probably like eleven thousand freaking trees.

"Second," Bryce said. "Look at me when I'm talking to you."

Toby looked at him.

"It could be a dollar for all I care," Bryce said. "It could be a cheese sandwich. Hear what I'm saying?"

Toby heard him.

"Nod if we understand each other."

Toby didn't understand at all. But he nodded anyway.

Silence.

Bryce pulled his door handle, eased the door open, and slipped out of the truck. Toby heard rocks crunch under the guy's boot soles as Bryce turned back and leaned in, bracing an arm on the door frame over his head. "Follow me and stay close," he said. "And, you know. Try not to slam your side when you get out. Right?"

"He could have guns," Toby said. A last-ditch effort. "Potter. He could have hand grenades for all we know. I told you before, the guy's crazy."

Bryce hung his head like someone had snipped a string in his neck. He stayed like that for a minute. Toby sat where he was and waited. When Bryce finally looked up, he was grinning.

"Dude," he said, inflecting the word in a way that didn't seem entirely necessary. "Were you not even listening to that story about me I told you before?"

31

Upon reflection, Mike Barlowe figured it was just about par for the course that after everything—after all he'd been through in the past fifteen hours—his day would end the same way it had started: with Toby Lunden coming through the door.

He'd spent maybe ten minutes in the bathroom. If that. Only enough time to take a leak, scrub his hands, clean and bandage his wrist, put all of Hal's first-aid stuff back the way he'd found it, take a brief look at the red-eyed, raggedy-assed individual in the mirror, and give Juliet Benson a chance to put on the clothes he'd left for her.

He was about to lean out the door, call to check on her progress before he went waltzing in on her, when she cried out from the front room: a high, startled-sounding hoot, followed by pounding footsteps. Before he could react, Mike heard another cry. A male voice this time. More thudding.

He bolted out of the bathroom into the main room without thinking, as fast as his stiff knee would carry him, and what he saw dumbfounded him: Juliet sprawled on the floor by the couch, looking wild-eyed; Toby Lunden standing over her, prancing in place, shaking his open hand in the air. Somehow, without understanding what the hell was going on, Mike got the picture that she'd bitten him. She'd yelled, Toby had tried to cover her mouth, and she'd bitten him.

"Toby?" he said, and had just time enough to see the kid's eyes dart to one side, hear Juliet call his name in warning, and sense movement behind him. All his internal alarms went off, and in that split second Mike recognized the position he'd put himself in. *Shit,* he thought.

"Say good night," the voice behind him said.

Before Mike could turn, something hard and heavy slammed into his head. He was a three-million-candlepower spotlight flaring white, then fading to dark. He was an empty gun floating to the bottom of a cold black lake. Then he was nothing at all.

32

They were almost to Little Falls before Maya could get Roger Barnhill to pick up his phone. "I'm here," he said. "What is it?"

"Listen, I know how this is going to sound," Maya said, "but I think Morningside may know where to find Juliet Benson."

"Who?"

"Buck Morningside." Met with silence, she recalled one of the first things Detective Barnhill had said to her in Jerry Spilker's office at the jail. *I'm new to this county.* She said, "From all the billboards. The jackass running around your search site with a TV crew, dressed like Marshall McCloud?"

"Oh, him," Detective Barnhill sounded distracted. "I was informed about him, yes. What about Mr. Morningside?"

"I think he's found something. I don't know how or what, but I think he's found something."

"What makes you think that?"

"A hunch," she said. What else could she tell him? That the man had winked at her?

"A hunch," Barnhill repeated.

"Reporters get them occasionally." Maya didn't

mean to go on the defensive, but she'd been trying to reach him for an hour and a half, and her impatience got the better of her. "Detectives too, I hear."

"I'm sorry," Barnhill said. "I don't mean to sound skeptical, but—"

"Last time I shared one of *my* hunches," she reminded him, "I heard you found a pickup truck registered to some guy in the hospital."

From behind the wheel, Justin Murdock raised his eyebrows. Maya knew this last comment went over the line, and in the dead silence that followed she could imagine the detective bristling on his end. She didn't want to break his balls. She only wanted him to listen to her. "Sorry, that was shitty," she said. "But I think I'm right about this."

Barnhill sighed in her ear. "All right," he said. "What's going on?"

"All I know is that Buck Morningside left your park an hour and a half ago doing his best impression of a guy who didn't want to get caught talking to anybody with a news camera," she told him. "If you're new around here, you might not realize how out of character that is, but believe me, it's out of character. When I talked to him, he was acting like he'd just come back from screwing the next-door neighbor's wife, and now he and Twin Cities Public Television are tearing ass up Highway 10 like they're late for a party somewhere."

"Twin Cities Public Television."

"They're filming some idiot reality show," she said. "*American Manhunter: Northstar Justice*. If you can believe that horseshit."

"I was informed of that, too."

"So then you know they're busy shooting their big Juliet Benson episode."

Barnhill seemed to have a bunch of things demanding his attention, and local television programming did not top his list of concerns. Nor did this phone conversation. Still, he said, "How do you know where they're going?"

"I don't. That's my point."

"I mean how do you know where they are? You said Highway 10. How do you know their location?"

"Because I'm right behind them," Maya said.

"You're *following* them? Right now?"

"In a Toyota Yaris, if you can picture it." She rolled her eyes at Justin, who smirked and held up his middle finger. "It's like riding around in a milk carton."

"Miss Lamb, I'm not sure what you think you're doing," Barnhill said. "Whatever it is, I'm advising you to stop."

"I'm not breaking any laws," Maya said. "And we've driven a hundred miles already. I'm not going anywhere. And you're still not taking me very seriously, are you?"

She heard Barnhill take a deep breath. "Where are you specifically?"

"Morrison County. South of Little Falls."

"Are you still in verbal contact with Morningside?"

"No," Maya said, and at that moment—after all this time cooped up in Justin Murdock's uncomfortable toy car, watching the rear bumper of the Suburban in front of them, needing to pee like crazy, and yet still struggling to keep from falling asleep in the passenger seat—Maya wanted to slap her own forehead. She said, "Hang on a minute. I'll call you right back."

"Miss La—"

Maya hung up on the detective and plunged one hand into the front pocket of her hoodie. She felt all around. Watching her instead of the road, Justin said, "Was that the sheriff's investigator?"

"That was him."

"What did he say?"

"Tell you in a minute."

"This is still my story, you know. You gave it up."

"Just keep driving," she said. "Don't lose them."

She rummaged past the drugstore lighter and Deon's nearly empty pack of cigarettes, finally closing her fingers on the thing she was looking for. Until this minute she'd forgotten all about it. She was so tired her brain must have stopped working. Maya pulled out the business card Buck Morningside had given her and dialed the number embossed on it.

He answered after three rings. "That you back there, darlin'? I wondered."

"Right behind you," she said.

"Hell, you coulda rode with us. This rig seats nine up here. Who's your friend?"

"My friend?"

"Driving that little old thing behind us."

"That would be News7's Justin Murdock," she said. Mistaking the sound of his name for an introduction in progress, Justin eagerly reached out for the phone. She batted his hand away. "This is his story now."

"Trainin' your replacement, are you?"

"Something like that."

Morningside chuckled. "That was a trick question. Can't replace you, darlin', but what the hell. The more the merrier, I say."

Cut the crap, Hubert, she almost said, but held herself in check. "I'll admit it, I'm impressed," she told him. "I just got off the phone with the lead investigator on this thing. You've got 'em paying attention, Morningside, let me be the first to hand it to you."

"Well, that's all right. I got a feeling they'll be paying real close attention soon enough."

"So where are we going?" Maya asked.

"Follow right along. We'll all see when we get there."

"Oh, come on. I can't stand the suspense."

Morningside didn't take the bait. He was enjoying himself, she could tell.

"Fine, be that way," she said. "At least tell me one thing. One manhunter to another."

"Shoot."

"A hundred cops out beating the bushes, and somehow you're the one with the hot lead," Maya said. "What's your trick?"

"Oh, now, I know you can do better than that. I already told you I'm too old for flattery."

"Fair enough. But I'm still dying to know."

"Well, let me put it to you this way," Morningside said. "While all them cops were running around beating bushes? Me, I had my two best guys finding out where Potter and Barlowe do their drinking."

Maya processed the information on the fly. Michael Barlowe: the owner of the Buick Skylark police had tracked to the shabby little house in St. Paul. Darryl

Potter, his roommate. She said, "Your best guys, huh?"

"Well. My best guy and my half-blind nephew. Point is, cops think like cops. My guys think like guys. No real trick to it."

"Just like that, huh?"

"You'd be surprised what all a regular old neighborhood bartender can tell you," Morningside said. "If you know how to ask."

Maya had opened her mouth to ply him for more when the connection snapped into place. A sick thrill crept into her belly. It felt like victory and defeat combined.

She said, "Did you just say bartender?"

"That's what I said, darlin'."

"You mean like the bartender they've got over at United Hospital?"

"What's that, now?"

Maya felt her blood heating up. "You mean that bartender from the North End with his head busted? Is that the kind of regular old neighborhood bartender you're talking about?"

For once, Buck Morningside lacked an immediate reply.

"What did you do, Morningside? Have a couple of your goons go to work on the poor bastard? Is that what you mean by knowing how to ask?"

There was a long silence. Morningside came back sounding noticeably less pleased with himself. "I'm pretty sure I wouldn't know anything about any of that."

To her amazement, Maya believed him. "I am so all over your ass," she said. *"Darlin'."*

Before he could reply, Maya hung up on him, called Barnhill again, and told him everything she'd just heard. Morningside had been right about one thing: The detective was paying very close attention now.

"I'll notify the state patrol offices in St. Cloud and Brainerd," he said. "I want you to keep your phone ready so that we can keep track of your position. We'll send you some company and see what this piece of work has to tell us."

"He's a piece of something."

"Just tell me if you copied everything I said."

"Oh, I copy," she said. "Is there anything new on Barlowe and Potter?"

"Sorry?"

"Morningside talked about finding where Barlowe and Potter did their drinking. I'd say that makes them official, wouldn't you?"

Between the strange look Justin Murdock gave her and the momentary silence on Barnhill's end of the line, Maya got the distinct impression that she'd missed something.

Barnhill said, "Are you telling me you didn't see your own station's news report this morning?"

"I've been in a car."

"So you have," Barnhill said. "All right. Quickly. So that you understand who we're looking for, and so that you can keep it in mind from here forward. Are you listening?"

"Listening and waiting."

"Lily Morse called our hotline five minutes after receiving her morning newspaper," Barnhill said. "Not long after you and I spoke at the restaurant."

Maya's breathing quickened. "Lily Morse called you?"

"We brought her in. Issued warrants on Potter and Barlowe as soon as we'd talked to her."

"You've named *suspects*?"

"This is what I'm trying to explain, if you'll listen to me."

"I'm listening."

"Barlowe and Potter are Marine Corps buddies. Both saw combat in Iraq. One of them's a stress case, the other was kicked out over misconduct. Neither one of them has a regular job, and Potter has a criminal record. We're still backgrounding these two, but I don't like what we know so far."

It felt surreal to hear all this. Maya couldn't get past the irony. For the past six hours she'd wandering around inside this story, actively participating in it, and apparently she knew less about what was happening than if she'd simply gone home and watched the news.

But that wasn't what disturbed her. "You said these guys saw combat?"

"Heavy combat, from what I understand."

"Where and when?"

"Ramadi in '05, according to Lily Morse."

"Lily Morse gave you this information?"

"That's right."

Maya squeezed her eyes closed. She felt dizzy and realized she was holding her breath.

"Please don't tell me," she said, "what I think you're going to tell me."

"Barlowe and Potter served with Lily Morse's son. Becky Morse's older brother."

"Evan," Maya said.

"That's right." Barnhill paused. "Are we on the same page now?"

"Yes."

"Keep your phone ready. And stay clear of these yahoos. I'll be in touch with further instructions."

After the detective hung up, Maya sat numbly in her seat, staring at her lap.

Then she straightened and slapped Justin Murdock around the shoulders. He flinched and swerved the car, and she stopped before he lost control and killed them both.

"Holy shit, why are you hitting me?" he said.

"Why didn't you tell me about Potter and Barlowe?"

"You didn't ask!"

"All this time we've been driving, you couldn't have filled me in on the new stuff? Professional courtesy? *Personal* courtesy?"

"You were asleep!"

"Bullshit I was."

"For like an hour," Justin said, sounding thoroughly exasperated. "I figured you needed some rest. Damn."

So maybe she'd nodded off a couple of times, Maya thought angrily. Five, ten minutes, tops.

Then why, now that she thought about it, couldn't she remember them getting off I-94?

Jesus, she thought. *I must be losing my mind.* She looked at Justin. He was shaking his head slowly, eyes on the road.

"I'm sorry I hit you," she said.

"And I thought Kimberly was nuts."

Maya looked out the windshield, noticing for the first time that Morningide's Suburban appeared to be trying to put some distance between them. Justin was doing his best to keep pace. The little car's engine whined as if in pain. She leaned over and checked the speedometer. They were doing almost 90 miles an hour. That was when she noticed the needle of the fuel gauge hovering just below the halfway mark.

"If we lose these assholes because we have to stop for gas," she said, "I swear to God, I don't know what's going to become of me."

Justin checked the gauge, glanced at her briefly, and put his eyes back on the road. "Don't worry about it," he said. "I can drive this thing from here to Winnipeg on half a tank."

Maya sat back in her seat. She took in a deep breath through the nose, held it for a five count, and let it out slowly through her mouth. "I'm glad to hear that," she said.

Justin kept his eyes in front of him. After a moment, he smirked. "How do you like my milk carton now?"

33

While Bryce cleared the rest of the house, searching the place upstairs and down for any sign of Darryl Potter, Toby stayed put with the girl and wondered what he was supposed to do.

She hadn't made a sound since they'd first come in the door. She just sat on the floor where she'd tumbled off the couch, propping herself up on one hand. She kept staring at Barlowe, still lying where he'd dropped like a sack of potatoes ten feet away. The back of his hair looked dark and sticky where Bryce had clubbed him unconscious with the butt of his gun.

"Hey, I'm really sorry," Toby said. The girl's silence was making him nervous. "I didn't mean to scare you, I didn't want you to give us away, that's all."

She turned and glared at him with such penetrating hostility that Toby wished he hadn't opened his mouth. He tried to start over. "You're Juliet, right?"

She looked him up and down. "Who the hell are you guys?"

"We're here to rescue you."

She rolled her eyes and pointed at Barlowe. "*He* was rescuing me."

Bryce came back then, and Toby had never been so glad to see him. Compared to Juliet Benson, the guy seemed downright companionable.

"Juliet," Bryce said. "I want you to calm down. Can you do that for me?"

She turned her glare on him. "He needs medical attention," she said, still pointing at Barlowe.

"Help is on the way," Bryce told her. "In the meantime, I want you to listen to me carefully and do everything I say. All right?"

"Who are you?"

Bryce put his hands on his hips and surveyed the room, then the girl. "How much do you weigh?"

"*Excuse* me?"

"An indelicate question. I apologize." Bryce propped his hands on his hips and judged her for himself. Then he grabbed the nearly empty bottle of whiskey from the low table and disappeared with it.

Toby stood there like a fence post as the girl pulled herself back up to the couch. Her feet were all bandaged, and she looked like hell. The place was a wreck. What had happened up here? When had Barlowe showed up? Toby liked the guy, and he hated seeing him on the floor like that. But what was he doing here? *How* was he here? And where was Potter?

Toby heard cupboard doors bang. Silverware rattled. In a minute, Bryce returned with a drinking glass in one hand, stirring a generous shot of whiskey with a spoon.

"Try this," he said.

She looked at him like he was certifiable. "You've got to be kidding."

"You'll feel better."

"What is that?"

"Medicine," Bryce said.

"I'm not drinking that."

Bryce tilted his head. "No?"

"Not on your life."

Bryce shrugged. He turned and handed the glass to Toby. Then he went over to Barlowe, reached inside his jacket, pulled out his gun again, and pointed it straight down at Barlowe's head.

"If you drink it," he told her. "You'll feel better."

The girl's eyes went wide. "Wait!"

Toby felt his heart jumping against his ribs like a terrified monkey. The fire in the fireplace seemed to burn hotter all of a sudden. The floor seemed to bend under his feet. Everything slid off kilter.

Bryce caught his eye, then nodded toward the girl.

Toby didn't know what else to do. He went over and handed her the glass. She looked at him with pleading eyes. Toby didn't know what to tell her. He didn't know what was happening. The girl gave up on him, looked back at Bryce.

"Num num," Bryce said. "Bottoms up."

She sat without moving.

Toby jumped when Bryce thumbed back the hammer on the gun. It sounded like twigs crackling in the fire.

The girl took out the spoon and gulped the whiskey. She coughed and shuddered as it went down.

"There you go," Bryce said, reholstering the gun under his arm. "Now. Let's get you comfortable."

*   *   *

They got the girl settled in the back bedroom. All the spunk had gone out of her, and she could barely walk on her hurt feet without help. When Toby eased her onto the bed, she promptly rolled over and curled up, facing the wall. He draped an afghan over her and followed Bryce down the hall.

"Dude," he said. "What was all that?"

Bryce stopped over Barlowe, leaned down to make sure he was still breathing, then checked his pockets. He pulled out a wrinkled wad of folded hundred dollar bills and said, "Well, well." He counted the money, then pressed it into Toby's hand. "Here's two thousand. I guess that leaves nine more. Sound about right to you, numbers guy?"

As Bryce moved on, Toby looked at the bills in his hand. They felt grubby. Touching them made his skin crawl. He almost flung the whole wad away from him.

Then he looked over at Barlowe and realized—now that he held the money—that he didn't feel quite so bad for the guy anymore. He shoved the cash into his own back pocket, where it belonged.

"So I figure we've got about an hour before the boss shows up," Bryce said. He checked his watch. "Give or take. Should be plenty of time to find out where the rest of your dough went. Meanwhile, I think we can agree, the last thing we need is a reliable third-party witness."

Toby walked after him. "What did you give her?"

"Just a little sedative." Bryce jerked a thumb toward Barlowe. "Found it in this clown's medicine cabinet yesterday morning. You know, I only lifted the stuff for personal recreation, but I guess it came in handy. See what I mean about things working out?"

Toby didn't see what he meant about things working out. He didn't see how this made the situation anything but worse. "Dude, you drugged her."

"Who drugged her?"

"Fine, whatever," Toby said, misunderstanding. "*We* drugged her."

"Who says we did anything like that?"

"*She* will!"

Bryce shook his head. "If that girl remembers anything after the nap she's about to take, I'll be very surprised."

He took off his coat, folded it over the back of the couch, and sat down in the scuffed leather chair. Looking at him in his T-shirt and shoulder holster, Toby realized that it was the first time he'd ever seen the guy's bare arms. They looked like bundles of logging cable wrapped wrist to sleeve in tribal tattoos.

Toby said, "What if she does remember?"

"That's the beauty," Bryce said. "Even if she does, she doesn't. No cop in the world is going to be able to accept her account over ours now. Not after everything this poor kid's been through. And not with that shit in her system."

Toby couldn't find a way to argue with the guy. He had all the angles covered.

"The more her story differs from ours," Bryce said, "the less they'll be able to believe her. You and me, we haven't been drugged. See what I'm saying?"

"I don't know," Toby said.

"There's only two people on earth who can tell our

story, kid," Bryce said. "It ain't that bartender back in town. And it sure ain't this clown on the floor with your dough in his pocket." He spread his hands. "Only you and me, partner."

At last Toby got it. Not just what Bryce was saying now, about partners, but what Toby had been wondering for hours, only hadn't had the nerve to ask:

If Bryce had all the angles covered then what did he need a partner for anyway?

The answer was so simple it almost seemed stupid: Bryce didn't need a partner.

He only needed a corroborator.

They were a lot alike that way, Toby realized.

"So what do we do now?" he said.

Bryce settled back in the chair. "Why don't you go keep an eye on the girl," he said. "I should be fine out here."

34

Maya scrutinized herself in the visor mirror while Justin talked to Rose Ann on his phone.

It was hardly any wonder that people had been gaping at her all night long. She almost didn't recognize herself. Her face was pale and her lipstick was gone. Her mascara had settled in dark half-moons beneath her bloodshot eyes, giving her a hollow, spooked-out look. Her hair was a limp, tangled mess. The unsettling image that came to her was the camera photo Barnhill had showed her, hours ago, of Juliet Benson staring up from the trunk of a car.

Justin handed her the phone and said, "She wants to talk to you."

Maya flipped up the visor and shook her head.

Justin shrugged. Into the phone, he said, "She says to tell you she's not here." He held the phone a few inches away from his ear. Maya could hear Rose Ann's miniaturized voice cursing a blue streak over the speaker.

They rode mostly in silence after that, following the Suburban off the highway onto a paved country road. The sun had come up. The landscape had changed to woods and meadows. Ropes of mist hung over the trees. Maya waited for her own phone to ring.

After a little while, she got the sense that Justin wanted to say something. It took him a few more miles to work up to it.

"Hey, I don't know if you knew this," he said. "I went to Missouri too."

Maya did know that. And Justin knew that she knew it. They'd talked about it at the Fox and Hound one night after work, Justin's first week at News7, before he'd finally given up trying to talk Maya into the sack and had moved on to Kimberly Cross. She said, "Is that right?"

"I came through a couple years after you."

More than a couple, she thought, but she gave him credit for manners. "I'll be darned," she said. "Small business, I guess."

"I guess so," Justin said. "I had Slater for 452."

"Yeah? He's still there?" Maya knew full well that Gerald Slater was still teaching. He'd been her senior adviser, and they traded letters at Christmastime.

She thought again of the day they'd discussed the Vietnam photo in Slater's class. She wondered if Justin Murdock's class had done the same.

"He's still there," Justin said. "Still talks about you too."

"Oh?"

"He does a couple days on those Hemlock Hill stories of yours."

This, Maya had not known.

Justin said, "What was the name of that town?"

"Clark Falls," she said.

"That's it." He nodded to himself. "You know, when I first came here, I was actually nervous to meet you."

"Come on."

"Seriously," he said. "Came in sort of crushing, to be honest."

Maya didn't know what to say.

Tentatively, Justin said, "Can I ask you something?"

"Ask away."

Justin watched the road as they followed the Suburban around a slow bend through a grove of pines. They lost sight of the truck for a moment. He picked up his speed again as the road straightened out. Little by little, they made up the distance, and Justin finally asked his question.

"What happened to you?" He glanced at her as he said it. "Sorry, that came out wrong. I only mean . . ."

Maya nodded. "I know what you mean."

"No offense," Justin said quickly. "I guess I was just . . . you know. Wondering."

"If it's contagious?"

"No, that's not what I meant." He paused. "Or maybe it was. Sort of. I don't know."

"It's okay," she told him. "I'm not offended."

"You always seemed sort of . . . unbeatable, I guess." He shook his head. "That's not fair, I know. I haven't been here that long, we don't even really know each other. I'm just saying."

Maya thought about how to answer him in a way that would mean anything. It was the question she hadn't answered for herself yet, and she didn't know how to answer it for Justin Murdock. In the end she took the easy way out and told him the honest truth.

"I don't know," she said. "It happpened while I wasn't looking, for whatever that's worth."

Justin's expression told her that it wasn't worth all

that much. At least not much that he could personally use. And Maya understood that too. She wouldn't have been able to use it either when she'd been sitting where Justin was sitting.

Her phone rang. Maya glanced at the screen, accepted the call, and said, "I was starting to think you forgot about us."

"I've been talking to Macklin's ex-wife," Detective Barnhill said. "And a couple auto mechanics who work across the street from Macklin's bar. We think we know where you're going."

35

In the dream, Mike sighted down his rifle from the edge of a rooftop, unable to see the ground below. A hot wind blew in from the desert, obscuring his view. As he squeezed the trigger, a shape emerged from the haze. The rifle punched his shoulder, the round cracked through the air, the target stumbled and went down in a pile. At that moment, the sandstorm parted and he saw the face of the enemy. It was his own.

Mike's eyes fluttered open. He squinted against the glare of daylight streaming in through the cabin's east windows. His head felt cracked; each heavy throb in his skull made his vision bend. As he tried to sit up, a rush of vertigo swept his balance out from under him, and he had to brace himself with his hands against the floor and wait for the room to stop turning.

A cool morning breeze drifted in through the screen door; Mike breathed the fresh air slowly in through his nose until his equilibrium returned. When he could move, he leaned against the couch and touched the back of his head. His fingers came away sticky with half-clotted blood.

Bryce the Fugitive Recovery Specialist sat in the leather chair a few feet away, boots up on the coffee table, reading a back edition of *The Lake Country Herald*. He lowered a corner of the paper and looked at Mike over the edge.

"Morning," he said. "I was starting to think maybe your head wasn't as hard as I thought."

Mike closed his eyes, but the vertigo returned, so he opened them again. Bryce had taken his feet down and set about folding his newspaper. He tossed the paper on top of the stack and leaned forward, elbows on his knees.

"You know," he said, "I had this funny feeling you and I might cross paths again."

Mike tried to swallow. His throat felt like a dry creek bed. He said, "Where's the girl?"

"Why don't you let me handle the questions? You've had a blow to the head." Bryce reclined in the chair, then sighed. "Wouldn't it have been easier on everybody if you'd just told me where I could find your buddy Darryl in the first place?"

Mike touched his scalp wound again. He felt a hell of a lump there, risen up in a bed of blood-matted hair like a pulpy orange with a split rind.

"Let's work backward," Bryce said. "Where's the rest of the money?"

Without thinking, Mike reached for his back pocket. Empty.

"I know you're probably thinking, this guy must be crazy to go to all this trouble over eleven thousand bucks," Bryce said. "Am I right?"

Mike tried to pull himself together. He had to start thinking straight. He was in a jam here, and he needed a plan.

"Just so we understand each other," Bryce went on,

"let me tell you the same thing I told the kid. It ain't the money." He shrugged. "But if I don't *get* the money? Then I have to live the rest of my life with the idea that, somewhere out there, there's a couple dumb-ass, low-rent, broke-dick leatherneck pussies walking around, believing they got one over on me. And that would disrupt my worldview. You know?"

Whatever Mike was going to do, he couldn't do it from the floor. He hauled himself up and sat on the edge of the couch. His stomach lurched, and his vision smeared, and he was afraid he might vomit.

He hung on until the moment passed. When the couch stopped seesawing under him, he said, "How did you find the place?"

"There he goes with the questions again." Bryce shook his head slowly. "You jarheads are stubborn, I'll give you that. I just hope you're not as stubborn as your buddy Macklin back at that shithole bar you like so much. Now *he* was hardheaded."

Mike understood why Hal hadn't called the police the way he'd promised.

Bryce said, "Do I have your attention now?"

"You have my attention."

"Wow. If looks could kill, right? Lucky for me they can't, I guess."

"Lucky," Mike said.

"Let's try again. Where's the money?"

"I wouldn't know."

"It's not your department, I get it. Who would I talk to? Let's see." Bryce pantomimed a man in thought. "Oh, right. Back to the first question. Where's Darryl?" He put his elbows on the armrests of the chair, fingers laced. "I don't know, maybe I'm jumping to conclusions, but I just can't help thinking that both questions have the same answer."

The gun, Mike thought, looking at the hardware hanging in Bryce's shoulder holster. *If you want any kind of chance, you've got to get that gun away from him.*

As if reading Mike's mind, Bryce reached under his arm and pulled the gun out of its seat. A big automatic. Nickel finish, black grip. He rested the weapon flat on his knee, finger indexed along the slide, muzzle pointing in Mike's direction.

"Thing is, we haven't got a lot of time left at this point," Bryce said. "So let's not make this harder than it needs to be. I'll ask you one more time, and then it's gonna get real easy. For one of us, anyway. Where's Darryl?"

Mike had his eyes on the gun when he heard the rusty squeak of the screen door opening, followed by the wooden slap of the door dropping closed against the frame. He heard footfalls on the hardwood and looked up. The answer to Bryce's question stood just inside the cabin, backlit by the morning sun.

At first Mike thought he was hallucinating. He hadn't heard the sound of the Power Wagon coming up the lane. Hadn't heard the porch boards creaking outside. Other than the sound of his own heart beating, and the occasional pop of an ember in the dying fire, he hadn't heard anything at all. It was as if Darryl had simply appeared.

"Well, well, well," Bryce said. He smiled. "What's your name?"

Darryl ignored him. To Mike, he said, "The hell you still doing here, anyway?"

Mike couldn't believe the stupid idiot had come back. "I was about to ask you the same thing."

Darryl shrugged. "Turns out that hospital in Brainerd never saw any dumbshit grunt come in with a cut-up hand and a cut-up girl."

Bryce said, "Ahem." He stood from his chair.

Darryl looked back and forth between Mike on the couch and Bryce the Fugitive Recovery Specialist. "I'm interrupting something," he said.

Once again, Bryce had been right.

By the time Toby returned to the back bedroom, the girl was already down for the count. She was still on the bed where he'd left her, still curled up facing the wall. Her shoulders rose and fell in a slow, steady rhythm. Toby took the old rocker in the corner and sat with her.

He didn't realize he'd conked out too until a loud noise woke him up so suddenly that he practically threw himself out of the chair. Daylight brightened the curtains over the bedroom window. How long had he been asleep?

Toby had no idea. All he knew was that it sounded like the cabin was falling in. He scrambled to his feet, feeling such great thuds and tremors through the floorboards that he could almost imagine something prehistoric coming out of the woods. Toby pressed his ear against the closed bedroom door and tried to listen, but he couldn't hear anything besides a crashing racket.

What the hell was going on out there? A big part of Toby didn't want to know. But he didn't want to stay

trapped here in the bedroom like a rat in a box either.
He looked at the girl. She hadn't moved a muscle.
Toby had no idea how she could still be sleeping
through this.

He left her and crept down the hall. The commotion grew louder, and when he finally peeked around
the corner, what he saw made his mouth go dry.

Mike Barlowe was sitting on the floor, rocking back
and forth, clutching his right leg like it was trying to
stand up without him. The leather couch was tipped
over on its back, chairs overturned this way and that.
There were blankets and newspapers and garbage
strewn everywhere. The coffee table was a splintered
pile of busted-up wood.

Toby saw that they'd finally accomplished their
mission: They'd found Darryl Potter.

While Mike Barlowe writhed on the floor in obvious agony, Potter and Bryce circled each other in the
rubble like a pair of wolves. From where he crouched,
out of sight behind the corner of the sideboard, Toby
found himself thinking about that thing he and his
gamer buddies used to play in junior high: *Who'd win
in a fight between King Kong and Godzilla?* Not in
the movies, but, like, in a real fight.

Who'd win: Wolverine vs. Predator? Iron Man vs.
RoboCop? Christopher Walken vs. Harvey Keitel?
The list of matchups had gone on like that forever,
and all these years later Toby found himself with a
ringside seat to a sick one, an epic, live and just getting started:

Bryce vs. Darryl Potter.

Who'd win?

Toby watched Bryce shrug out of his empty shoulder holster and toss it aside. He watched Darryl kneel down by the hearth and stand up again, holding a knobby stick of firewood in his fist like a club. He watched them circle, weave, and go straight at each other, and he decided then and there: He didn't want to know.

Screw this. Just totally screw it. This wasn't a video game. It wasn't a movie from one of his buddies' dad's DVD collections. This was Uncle Buck's fault, sending Toby a psycho like Bryce on what should have been a damn milk run. So Uncle Buck could deal with it. And Bryce could tell his own damn story.

Crawling on his hands and knees, Toby scooted out into the open, just far enough to grab Bryce's leather jacket from where it had flown off the back of the couch and landed in a pile on the floor. Then he scooted back for cover again as fast as he could scoot. He dug around in Bryce's pockets until he found the keys to the Navigator.

Toby stopped by the bedroom on his way out. The girl was still sleeping like the dead.

Unbelievable.

Screw it. It wasn't like he could carry her out of there. He was a numbers guy.

He hustled through the kitchen, through the mud porch, and banged out the back door into the cool morning sun. Toby ran in a crouch around the front of the cabin and then sprinted up the lane. Past the shed. Around the curve of the lake. He didn't stop until he reached the spot where they'd left the Navigator in the trees.

Parked directly behind the Navigator, blocking Toby's exit, was an old white pickup, its warm engine still ticking under the hood. Keys still hanging in the ignition.

Lungs burning, legs like rubber, Toby climbed into the truck and cranked the motor. It started right up. He backed it up, ran it off to one side of the lane, and cut the engine again.

Just as he was about to climb out, Toby looked over and saw a gym bag sitting on the passenger seat. He paused. Thought: *No way.*

He reached over, unzipped the bag. Sure enough, inside he found a great big pile of loose, crumpled bills: His restaurant guy's money.

He almost couldn't believe it. Luck had turned his way at last. And Toby Lunden felt he damn well deserved it. He snatched the bag and took it with him.

Toby ran to the Navigator, throwing the pickup keys into the woods on the way. He climbed in behind the wheel, fired it up, and pulled forward until he had room to turn around. He took one backward glance at the peaceful-looking cabin across the misty, peaceful-looking lake, then did what he should have done hours and hours ago:

He mashed on the gas and got the hell out of there.

36

They tailed Morningside and his crew down a road through the woods until finally they saw brake lights, and the Suburban slowed down in front of them. After cruising along for a hundred feet or so, the SUV took an abrupt right-hand turn through the overgrowth, onto a narrow rock lane. As they approached the same spot, Maya saw the broad side of an old, beat-up sign at the mouth of the lane, and she could just make out the faded lettering: *Rockhaven.*

"Oh, you're kidding," she said. She looked out the windshield, down the empty road ahead, then twisted and looked up the empty road behind them. "Where the hell is everybody?"

Justin leaned forward over the wheel, joining her in looking out the windows. "Maybe they already went in?"

Maya didn't think so. According to Detective Barnhill, both the Crow Wing County Sheriff's Department and the state patrol district office in Brainerd had been notified of Harold Macklin's lake house, and units had been dispatched to the site. This road should have been lined with cops, not deserted in both directions.

She grabbed her mobile and dialed Barnhill's number. No signal.

"Go go go," she told Justin, urging him on with hand gestures as the Suburban suddenly disappeared behind a curtain of trees.

"Should we wait?" he said.

"Are you kidding?" Maya undid her seat belt and lunged into the backseat, hauling Justin's gear bag up front with her. "Ain't nobody else here but us Mizzou alums."

"What are you doing?"

"Shooting while you drive." Maya pulled his station-issue camera, an expensive Sony DV camcorder, out of the bag. "We're going to get every last move these assholes make on tape. And I swear to God, if Juliet Benson really is here? And if something bad happens to her because Cowboy Bob up there decided to get cute? You and me, we're going to barbecue the son of a bitch." Maya pulled the lens cap and flipped open the camera's side-view screen. "Gerry Slater can teach *your* stuff next semester. How about that, Indiana? You in?"

"Oh, I'm in," Justin said, stepping on the gas. The Yaris fishtailed on loose rock as he hauled the wheel to the right and careened into the lane. He goosed the car past the entrance sign and around the next curve, following the lane into the woods. They fell in behind the Suburban just as the SUV's brake lights pulsed and disappeared around the next bend.

Maya fired up the camera and centered the Suburban in her frame, bracing her elbows against her own midsection for as much stability as she could maintain.

"Maya Lamb and Justin Murdock," she said for the audio pickup, her view of the world in front of them now reduced to the four-inch color LCD panel of the cameras's display screen. "April eighth, seven-nineteen a.m., following Buck Morningside and members of Twin Cities Public Television production staff." She zoomed in on the Suburban's rear license plate and quoted the tag number just in case it didn't read on tape. "Minnesota five one dash five zero three."

They followed along, winding this way and that through the timber. At one point the lane dipped low through a tunnel of trees, then rose up along a shallow embankment, taking a gradual left-hand course around yet another blind turn. Maya started to say, *Keep us in tighter,* but Justin was already ahead of her. He punched the gas, hit the curve, and reeled the Suburban back within sight.

They'd almost made up the distance when all at once, without warning, the Suburban swerved left, then bore hard right, disappearing completely off the edge of Maya's screen.

She jumped and looked out her side window, panning with the camera. She saw the Suburban jouncing violently down the embankment, into the timber, and thought, *What in the world?*

She had just enough time to reframe the scene in her viewfinder before the Suburban came to a dead stop, crunching head-on into the trunk of a stout burr oak tree. The Suburban's hood popped up like a tent. Bursts of glass shimmered in the rays of sunlight slicing in through bare branches. A blast of steam geysered up from the engine compartment.

At the same moment she witnessed all this, Maya heard Justin shout out in alarm. The Yaris pitched suddenly, throwing her against her door. Maya knocked her head against the window with enough force that she saw spangles in her vision.

But she held on to the camera.

As Maya dragged her foggy gaze back to center, she had the sensation of watching everything that happened in the next dreamlike half second on two different planes of vision at once: one through the windshield, and one through the camera's display screen, each view representing half of the whole picture in front of her.

As if in slow motion, she saw a second gleaming black SUV barreling toward them, speeding out the same way they were going in. She saw the wide, spectacled eyes of the other driver. She saw him swerve to his right as they swerved to their left, each vehicle remaining directly in the other's path. She saw a Minnesota license plate growing larger. An oncoming grille filled up the camera's LCD panel with chrome. Then time sped up again, and a thundering quake shook apart the world.

The way they were positioned, Bryce couldn't watch Mike on the couch and Darryl in the doorway at the same time. Darryl took advantage by sliding to his left, toward the fireplace, into Bryce's blind spot. This maneuver left Bryce with a choice.

He chose to regard Darryl as the greater threat.

The moment Bryce turned his attention, raising his weapon smoothly, Mike made his move. He dove forward off the couch, aiming for Bryce's exposed rib cage, just underneath his gun arm.

It was an awkward, lumbering effort, and he certainly wasn't at his best, but none of that mattered. He had only a few feet of ground to cover, and his goal was simple: disrupt the asshole's aim.

But the guy had eyes all the way around his head, apparently. And he had Mike's number all the way. And he was fast.

As soon as Mike came off the couch, Bryce took a step backward, at the same time snapping off two quick shots that sent Darryl diving for cover. The first round struck the fireplace façade in a burst of stone chips; the second went higher, shattering the gills of the mounted walleye, knocking the trophy off its peg.

In the same fluid motion, before Mike could correct his balance, Bryce took a gliding step to one side and came around hard, delivering a downward stomp to the side of Mike's bad knee.

The pain was like a detonation. Mike heard a crunch and felt the knee give way, hinging in the wrong direction, and his mind went blank. He went down like a bag of sand. When he opened his eyes, he was looking straight up the pipe of the gun. Somewhere above that, Bryce was smiling.

Then Darryl was all over him. He came airborne over the couch, body extended, hitting Bryce high and hard. Bryce stumbled back, overpowered. The gun flew out of his hand and skidded across the floor. Darryl wrapped his arms and rode him down like a rodeo steer.

Even as he was driven backward, Bryce somehow shifted his balance, twisted his body, and used Darryl's momentum to his own advantage. They landed together in the center of the coffee table. The table splintered and flattened under their weight.

Bryce was already moving again. Rolling onto his back, bringing his arm down in a hammering backhand, going for Darryl's windpipe. Darryl saw it coming and rolled the other way just in time to avoid the strike. Bryce's fist pounded the spill of newspapers where Darryl had been with enough force to rattle the floor.

Then they were on their feet again, moving, sizing each other up, while Mike sat on his ass, blinking away rage and frustration.

His knee felt like a broken rattle. Getting blown up the first time hadn't hurt like this. He heard a sound to his right and looked over, glimpsed the back of a familiar windbreaker disappearing down the bedroom hall. *Toby,* he thought. *I'm going to find you, you bug-eyed little coward.*

But he had other things to find first.

While Bryce and Darryl charged each other, Mike dragged himself around on the floor, sweeping through beer cans and newspapers with one hand, looking for Bryce's gun.

Nothing. He kept searching, all along the base of the overturned couch, underneath Bryce's overturned chair, dragging himself on his elbows like a useless invalid.

At one point, he glanced up. What he saw made him freeze in wonder.

Mike had seen Darryl Potter fight more times than he cared to remember. For a while—at least up until that assault charge cooled his heels last year—one of

Darryl's favorite pastimes had been to find some sports bar on a night when they'd be running the MMA cage fights on pay-per-view. Darryl liked to wait for the testosterone junkies to get worked up into a lather watching the event, then put himself within orbit of the baddest-looking wannabe in the joint. And then start mouthing off.

Mike had seen Darryl fight fair, and he'd seen him fight dirty. He'd seen him fight sober and drunk. He'd seen him fight hurt. He'd even seen him fight in the throes of a ripe case of food poisoning.

The only thing he'd never seen Darryl do was lose.

Bryce the Fugitive Recovery Specialist was handing Darryl's ass to him, and he appeared to be having a fine time doing it. In the twenty seconds Mike sat there watching, Darryl went down and got back up three different times. Each time a little slower. Each time a little bloodier. Each time looking less like an opponent and more like a practice bag.

Bryce used his fists, knees, elbows, and shins; he was so fast and so accurate that it was spooky to watch. Everything Darryl tried was met with a block and a return strike—usually a combination of them— all delivered with speed, force, and precision.

They'd been at each other less than two minutes. Bryce didn't have a mark on him. Meanwhile, Darryl looked like he'd fallen down a flight of concrete stairs. He couldn't last much longer.

And he seemed to know it. While Mike watched from the floor, Darryl let out a roar, lowered his center of gravity, and drove his shoulder into Bryce's ribs.

Bryce rolled with the impact, dipped, twisted. He

pulled Darryl over the top of his shoulders and slammed him down.

Before Darryl could move, Bryce scrabbled atop him like a spider. He locked up Darryl's legs with his own. He delivered three vicious jabs to the middle of Darryl's face, then a right cross, followed by a left. Then he reared back and spread his arms wide, like brutal wings, and chopped down from either side at the same time.

By that last blow, Darryl had already gone limp as a rag. Mike felt his heart in his throat. He needed to get over there. He needed to get over there now.

But he was ten feet away. Practically helpless. Even as he tried to crawl on one knee, dragging his ruined leg behind him, he watched Bryce lift Darryl's lolling head off the floor with his hands. He watched him twist with his whole body. He heard a sound like a bundle of sticks cracking. And he knew that Darryl was gone.

Just like that.

Two minutes, tops.

Bryce stood up. Rolled his shoulders.

Mike dropped his head and let it hang. He felt as though he were floating. He felt numb all the way through. He didn't know where he was for a minute. He didn't know what had happened or how he'd gotten here.

Then, somewhere in the haze, he noticed something.

Two feet from his hand. Hiding under a torn, tented back issue of *The Lake Country Herald*.

Juliet Benson's fishing knife.

Mike reached out for it as if moving through a

dream. He felt the knife's wooden handle under his palm. He drew his hand back, folding the long blade against the inside of his forearm even as he heard footfalls on the floorboards, saw black boots approaching from the corner of his eye.

A fire started in his scalp as Bryce reached down and pulled him up by the hair. Mike struggled to get his good leg under him, suns of pain imploding in his knee. He grabbed on to Bryce's shoulder for balance with his free hand, feeling the Kevlar under Bryce's T-shirt. His mind had gone clear and calm. His only thought: *He's wearing a vest.*

"I hope you realize," Bryce said, lightly winded, "that it didn't have to go like this."

Mike finally made it upright. He hopped on one leg until he'd steadied his balance. They were about the same height, which made it almost too easy to look Bryce in the eyes.

"It didn't," Mike said. "You're right."

"Too bad," Bryce said. He pulled Mike's head back, laying his throat bare. "Nice knowing you. Sort of."

As Bryce drew back his free arm, flattening his fist into a wedge, Mike brought his other hand up fast. He shoved the knife into the side of the bounty hunter's neck.

Mike watched the guy's eyes go wide. He watched confusion bloom on his screwed-up wreck of a face. He thought, *I'm so sorry, Hal. You were right. I should have listened.* He didn't stop pushing until the knife reached its hilt. When it did, he wrenched the handle.

Bryce the Fugitive Recovery Specialist looked as if he'd forgotten what it felt like to be surprised. He gagged and grabbed at Mike's hand. Mike let go of the knife handle and shoved Bryce away, two hands in his chest, as hard as he could manage on one leg without falling down.

Bryce reeled back. For a moment he stumbled like a drunk in an alley, holding his hands out for balance, trying to untangle his own feet. Then he tripped on a broken table leg and sat down hard on the floor.

Mike watched all this with almost no feeling. Not satisfaction, not sorrow. Certainly not victory. All he could think was that Hal had trusted him. And he'd let the man down. And now look at this place.

Bryce made a gulping sound, working his mouth like a fish. Mike looked away. Only then did he finally spot Bryce's gun, lying where it had skidded to rest against the baseboard beneath the east windows.

Mike hopped over on one leg, gritting his teeth through the pain. He braced himself against the windowsill, stooped, and picked up the gun. Brought it back with him.

Bryce was pawing at the side of his neck. He finally found the knife handle. Gripped it with both hands.

"I wouldn't do that," Mike said.

Bryce didn't listen. Still gagging, he pulled the knife out, then sat there, wheezing. Nothing happened for a beat. Then a red gout blurted out of his neck and splatted on the floor.

Bright red. Arterial blood, Mike knew by looking. He'd seen it enough times to remember.

When he'd come home from the service, Mike Barlowe made himself only one promise: that for the rest of his life he would never again do, for any reason whatsoever, what he was about to do now.

He hobbled over to Bryce. Pressed the muzzle of the gun against the top of his head. Thumbed back the hammer. He took one look at Darryl's lifeless body, then slid his finger over the trigger.

"Mike!" a voice shouted behind him. "Don't!"

Mike looked over his shoulder. Juliet Benson stood in the doorway to the bedroom hall, eyes big as hubcaps. She had both hands on her head, gripping her hair. When she saw she'd gotten his attention, she untangled her fingers and lowered her hands. Held her palms out.

"Please don't do that," she said. "Please."

Mike looked at Darryl.

He looked at Bryce, who had slumped off to one side. The bounty hunter's shoulder was covered in a blanket of blood. There was still more where that came from, pumping from the wound in his neck with every beat of his heart, a pool of it spreading all over Hal's floor.

But his eyes had gone flat, and he'd stopped gurgling. There wouldn't be more coming out of his neck for long.

Mike looked at Juliet.

"Please," she said.

She almost sounded drunk. What the hell was wrong with her? Did she even know what she was saying?

"Please don't," she repeated.

Mike's good leg gave out. He sagged into the only chair still upright. He didn't move.

Then, as if operating under someone else's control, he disengaged the hammer of the gun. Reengaged the safety lever. Let the gun drop out of his hand. The gun hit the floor with a thud he could feel through the soles of his shoes.

He looked at Darryl's motionless body. He looked at Bryce, still working his mouth in silence, bleeding out on the floor.

He looked up at Juliet in the doorway. She'd covered her mouth with her hands.

Somewhere in the distance, Mike finally heard sirens.

37

Later, when they asked her what she could remember of the crash, Maya wouldn't be able to offer much beyond the images she'd captured on digital tape, up to and including the crash itself.

After that point, things got hazy. She could remember opening her eyes and looking at spatters of red on a white canvas. She remembered seeing Justin Murdock's face and thinking that Kimberly Cross's fiancé must have finally caught up with him. She could remember the point when things came into focus and she realized that the white canvas was her airbag, and the red was her blood, and that Justin wasn't moving in the seat beside her.

They'd had to cut them out of the Yaris—much the same way the techs at the station had to cut the DV cassette out of Justin's demolished camcorder—but Maya didn't remember any of that. She only knew because people told her afterward.

She had a few other flashes here and there. A memory of looking up from the stretcher, an image of pine tops against blue morning sky. There were voices in the background. Pulsing lights and radio chatter. Running feet. At one point she remembered looking over and seeing the scruffy director from Twin Cities Public Television, blood streaming down both sides of his mouth from a nasty gash across the bridge of his nose, wandering around with a camera on his shoulder, taking the story into his own hands. She remembered thinking, *I'm going to be on the news.* Other than that, it was mostly dead air.

MEASURING TIRED

They transferred Hal to the VA Medical Center late Thursday, awake and complaining. The way it worked out, he and Mike ended up half a dozen rooms apart on the second floor, which made it easy for Regina to shuttle back and forth between them.

Friday morning, after they'd stitched him up, fitted him with crutches and a three-panel knee splint the size of a hard-shell rifle case, and while Mike waited for the ortho to come in and schedule him for surgery, a guy in a suit appeared in the doorway. The guy chatted a few minutes with the county deputy posted in the hall, then came into the room.

Mike didn't recognize him. He looked too slick to be another cop. He stood at the end of the bed and nodded crisply. "Mr. Barlowe. How are you feeling?"

"Unwell," Mike said. "Can I help you?"

"I certainly hope so," the guy in the suit said. "If you can't, it will limit my ability to help you."

"Who are you?"

"My name is Morton Clay." He placed his brief-case flat on the roll-around table and released the latches one at a time. "I'm Wade Benson's personal attorney."

Mike thought, *Here we go.* He'd rather have talked to another cop.

"Pending your consent," Clay said, "I am also your attorney."

"Say what now?"

"I'm here to act as your legal counsel, Mr. Barlowe. I thought we should begin by meeting each other. And there are items we should discuss sooner rather than later." Clay tilted his head. "Is now inconvenient?"

"Listen, I'm not sure what this is," Mike said. "But if you want to talk to me about what happened, I need my advocate here."

Clay nodded. "The VA has already referred you to someone, then?"

"That's right."

"You'll want me instead. No disrespect intended. Your advocate—do you have his information?"

"Her information," Mike said, "and yes. Where did you come from again?"

"I'm here at the request of the Benson family. At the request of Juliet Benson, specifically."

"You're shitting me."

"Miss Benson has asked that I represent your interests going forward. If that's agreeable to you."

I'll be damned, Mike thought. "Thanks," he said. "But I don't think I can afford you."

"A fact that needn't concern us." Clay opened the briefcase. "Felony conspiracy, aiding and abetting, accessory after the fact. These are the things that need concern us at the moment. Now." He looked at Mike grimly. "If you've lied to the police in any way, this is the time to tell me. If you knew about, or participated in, the events of these past two days in any way, or to any degree that differs from your accounting of said events up to this point, this is the time to tell me."

"I didn't," Mike said. "And I haven't."

Not that it mattered. The people who were dead were still dead. Mike had done what he'd done. He wished he'd done differently. He thought that he'd wish he'd done differently for all the rest of his days. But he couldn't go back and do it again.

"Then congratulations," Morton Clay said.

"On what?"

"You may just turn out to be one of the lucky few whom the truth actually does set free." The Benson family attorney took a brown folder and a stack of papers from the briefcase. "Let's take about an hour for now. We'll meet again after you've been discharged. Does that sound reasonable to you?"

Around noon, just as Morton Clay was leaving, Regina came in. Mike sat on the bed with his brace up and his head spinning. Regina jerked a thumb over her shoulder and said, "Who's Mr. Fancy Pants?"

"My high-powered lawyer, apparently." At Regina's look, Mike shook his head and said, "Tell you about it later. How's Hal?"

"He has a message for you."

"Yeah?"

Regina came over and took Mike's face in her hands and planted a fat smooch on his forehead. She was a roving cloud of sweet-smelling perfume. "He says to tell you that you have to pay for your sandwiches from now on."

Mike smiled. It caught him by surprise and felt good. "I guess he's going to be okay, then."

Regina took his hands and squeezed and said, "He

also said to tell you how sorry he is." Her eyes filled up with mother-hen mercy and she squeezed his hands tighter. "About Darryl."

Mike looked at her. Her eyes gave her away almost immediately. "Hal said that, huh?"

"Well," she said. "I'm saying it for him."

Mike nodded. "Tell him I said thank you."

Regina smiled and nodded back. Then her lip started quivering, and she let go of his hands. Mike looked out the window. He heard hoopy bracelets clatter together as Hal's third ex wiped her eyes.

After a minute, she stood up and said, "Here we are sitting around, talking about sandwiches, and you're probably starving. What would you like me to bring you from the cafeteria?"

Late Monday morning, her fourth full day in the hospital, Maya woke up from a nap to find Rose Ann Carmody sitting in the chair by the bed, typing on a laptop.

Maya thumbed the incline button on the control and raised herself up a little, servomotors humming quietly beneath her. When she released the button and the humming stopped, Rose Ann looked up and said, "It's alive."

Maya tried a smile. Her mouth felt gummy. "Hi, Rose Ann."

Rose Ann appraised her over the top of her reading glasses. "Well, I'll hand it to you," she said. "When you decide to insert yourself into a story, you don't stop halfway, do you?"

I guess not, Maya started to say, but she was so dry

that her voice barely worked. She looked around in the folds of her blankets for the nurse call button.

Rose Ann put her laptop aside. "What do you need?"

Maya gave up. She relaxed her head against the pillow. "Some ice chips?"

Rose Ann stood from her chair and said, "Don't get used to this." She grabbed an empty foam cup from the roll-around table and disappeared.

Ten minutes later, Rose Ann returned with a new cup in each hand: ice chips with a tiny plastic spoon in one, steaming coffee in the other. She handed the ice to Maya. "There you are."

Over the weekend, in between nurses and residents, Maya had entertained any number of visitors. Detective Barnhill. Her surgeon. A few colleagues from the station. A few reporters from other stations, as well as from the newspapers. A short call from her dad back in Wichita, who arrived in Minnesota by Winnebago RV early Saturday morning.

Sunday evening, around seven, she'd even been visited by Wade Benson and his family—including Juliet, who came in on a crutch but otherwise looked amazingly well, considering. She'd hugged Maya's father and kissed his cheek, and they'd all stayed about half an hour. It had been so nice to see them that Maya had been sorry to see them go.

But this was the first she'd heard from her news director. Maya thanked her for the ice. "Does this mean you're not still mad at me?"

"Of course I'm still mad at you," Rose Ann said. "Are you in pain?"

Maya shook her head.

Rose Ann frowned at her.

Maya nodded her head.

"Shall I get the nurse?"

Maya looked at the clock on the wall by the television. A few minutes of eleven. "No," she said. "They'll be around with drugs soon."

As Rose Ann sat down with her coffee, Maya crunched a few ice chips in her teeth. The cold slush felt sublime against her throat. She said, "How's Justin?"

"Better than you," Rose Ann said. "I just came from his room. They'll release him this afternoon."

"Good to hear."

"He said you can expect a visit on his way out. Fair warning."

"Even better."

Rose Ann smirked. "You realize that you nearly disfigured a perfectly good-looking backpack reporter."

"He was the one driving," Maya said.

"I suppose that's true." Rose Ann shook her head. "You're both lucky."

Maya couldn't argue. Even at moderate speed, a fair fight between a Lincoln Navigator and a Toyota subcompact wasn't much of a fight at all. Morningside's nephew, Maya heard, had walked into police custody with hardly a scratch on him, while a medevac chopper from the Northern Memorial/HCMC Air Care base in Brainerd had transported Maya and Justin Murdock back to Minneapolis. Justin had come through with a concussion, stitches, broken ribs, and a punctured lung. Maya had woken up in a recovery room with pins in both ankles, missing her right pinky toe and her spleen.

As of this morning, she hurt all over. But she was still here. And here she would stay, the doctors assured her, for at least three more days, counting her lucky stars.

Funny the way those stars had aligned. More than once it had occurred to Maya that she was recuperating in the same hospital where Becky Morse had died.

"Well, at least we didn't lose you," Rose Ann said when Maya mentioned that fact. She sipped her coffee, then tilted her head. "Did you think I was kidding when I said that I wasn't finished with you yet?"

Maya sighed. "Rose Ann, I'm in no condition to discuss my future at News7. Or lack thereof."

"I'm not talking about your blasted future at News7. Or your lack thereof."

When she met Rose Ann's eyes, Maya saw a seasoned perspective. An intuitive grasp on the meaningful angle here. The way the sun came in through the window, Maya could almost see her own reflection in Rose Ann's half lenses. Or at least she liked to imagine that she could.

With a little effort and a sharp jab in her side, she raised her cup of ice chips and said, "Well. To happy endings, I guess."

Rose Ann winked and touched her cup to Maya's. "I was going to say big fat book deals," she said. "But whatever makes you feel better."

Wednesday came around. With it, an anniversary:
   One full week since Juliet Benson's abduction.

All that day long—cooped up in bed, too spaced on pain meds to read or concentrate on television, by now nearly bored out of her skull—Maya found herself glancing at the clock, trying to place where she'd been the same time a week ago.

Her surgeon came by to check on her incision around 8:30 a.m.; a week ago, Maya had been looking out a window with Juliet Benson in Linden Hills.

Detective Barnhill stopped by around noon. She and Deon were back at the station, eating vending machine cookies in an editing bay.

The nurse brought drugs at 4:00 p.m., just as Maya and Deon arrived at the county facility in Plymouth. Miles Oltman, her assignment editor, came around with a pot of flowers in the middle of the six o'clock news; Maya was looking at an abandoned Buick Skylark on Third Avenue.

Sometime after that, she fell into a dreamless sleep, and when she awoke, the room was dark. Her dad's chair was empty. Downtown Minneapolis twinkled outside her window.

And she had a visitor.

Maya blinked her eyes. The clock on the wall said 8:23 p.m. Last week, at this very moment, she and Deon had been stuck in traffic, trying to get over to St. Paul. Here and now, in room 517 of the Hennepin County Medical Center, visiting hours were nearly over for the day.

"Darlin'," the figure in the doorway said.

How long had he been standing there? Maya hit the buttons. Motors hummed in the bed as Buck Morningside came into the room. He took off his Stetson and held it in his hand.

"Hubert," she said thickly.

When she reached for her water, Morningside said, "Lay back, now." He tossed his hat on the chair, picked up the water bottle from the roll-around cart, and handed it to her. "That's a girl."

In the dim light from the window, Maya could see white tape across the bridge of the bondsman's nose. Both his eyes were black, and he had stitches over one eyebrow. He was balding on top, she noticed, and it occurred to her that she'd never seen him out of character before. All in all, the one-and-only Buck Morningside looked remarkably humanesque. Maya wasn't sure she liked it.

"Heard you lost a damn toe," Morningside said.

Maya shrugged. "Only a small one."

"Hell of a cute one though, I bet."

There. She'd used up all her banter. Maya nodded at a fat manila envelope Morningside held in one hand. Even in the dimness, she could see her own name written on the envelope in heavy black ink. "What's that supposed to be?"

Morningside looked down. He seemed to consider the envelope in his hand as though unsure of where he'd found it.

"Well, now, this last week, I been thinkin'," he finally said. "Going over things, I guess you'd say. Some of 'em . . . well. Some I guess I'd do differently. Hindsight-wise." He shook his head. "But we only do 'em once, don't we?"

Maya sipped her water. "Usually the way it goes," she said.

Morningside handed her the envelope. "Had a couple of my gals put this together. Ain't much, but I thought you might find a use. Interesting to read, any-how."

She took the envelope. It was dense and heavy. Before she could ask about it, Morningside spoke again.

"Now, this one here," he said, a sly look crossing his bruised eyes, "I already had."

Maya watched him reach inside his coat and pull out a second manila envelope. This one was much thinner than the first. Crisp along the edges. There was nothing written on it.

He placed the second envelope on the bed beside her leg.

"What are these?" Maya said.

Morningside picked up his hat. He patted her leg gently through the covers on his way out. "Feel better, now," he said.

That night—after Ernie Lamb returned from the cafeteria downstairs, tucked his poor maimed daughter in, and departed for the Best Western three blocks from the hospital—Maya sat up in bed, going through the contents of the envelopes Buck Morningside had delivered.

She started with the fat one bearing her name. Inside, she found an alarmingly in-depth dossier on one of the state senators she'd interviewed early last week for her highway-safety story.

Senator Bradford Alstad was one of the primary critics of Senate File 5108, nicknamed "Becky's Law," a measure he opposed on grounds of enforceability. Maya had sought out his counteropinion to balance the piece.

In a week's time, Buck Morningside had dug up half a ream of financial-disclosure documentation that appeared to link Senator Alstad's personal assets to a holding company called Northland Enterprises. Northland, it seemed, held significant investments in long-haul timber trucking—an industry not apt to benefit from the criminalization of excessively fatigued drivers. And a clear conflict of interest for Senator Alstad regarding S.F. 5108.

Next came the second envelope. The thin one.

Here, Maya discovered a set of black-and-white 8x10 photo prints. The photos depicted Senator Alstad—who had served District 42 in the Minnesota legislature for the past twenty-odd years, espousing family values, fighting same-sex marriage, and sponsoring a number of school-prayer initiatives—conducting what appeared to be an intimate romantic relationship with a person who was not Mrs. Senator Alstad. A person who was not, in point of photographic evidence, a woman.

Maya still had Buck Morningside's mobile number in her phone. It was nearly midnight by the time she dialed it. When he answered, she said, "You've been a busy bee."

Morningside chuckled in her ear. "Shouldn't you be sleepin'?"

"Where did you get this stuff?"

"Thought I told you. Had some of my gals pull it together. Wasn't all that hard."

"Not that stuff," Maya said. She picked up the top photo, looked at it, put it back in her lap again. "I mean the other stuff."

"Oh, that stuff," Morningside said. He sounded pleased with the world.

"Well?"

"Hell, darlin', you should come have a look at my rainy-day files sometime," he said. "You'd be surprised what all you might find in there."

Unbelievable. "What am I supposed to do with it?"

"I'm sure I wouldn't know," Morningside said.

After he hung up, Maya sat for a long time, staring at the piles of incrimination in her lap. She thought of her old journalism-school professor. What would Gerry Slater have to say about all this?

She fell asleep wondering.

It finally felt like spring to Lily Morse. They'd gone a full week without rain, and the sun had been shining, and the whole world seemed to be abloom.

She met Wade at the cemetery on a Saturday afternoon in the middle of May. A few weeks later than normal, this year, but that didn't matter. These meetings of theirs hadn't felt court-ordered in ages, and they no longer took place only once a year anyway.

Wade's wife and daughter stood with him, as always. When Lily saw Juliet, she said, "Oh, honey," and wrapped her tight in her arms.

They put their flowers on the graves and stood there awhile, breathing the warm fragrant air. Everybody did their crying. They stayed about an hour, then pulled themselves together and left as a group.

It was Wade's idea to celebrate the Senate vote: 46–10, the final count had been. They were on the governor's desk at last. He took them all to a swanky steak place downtown that had been written up not long ago in the *Star Tribune*.

Chevalier, the restaurant was called. It was far too expensive, and Lily wasn't much of a carnivore. Still, the fish was delicious, and the wine tasted lovely, and her dessert was so rich and decadent that she felt a little guilty eating the whole thing.

But only a little. Life was too short not to enjoy a good meal.

ACKNOWLEDGMENTS

This book—in all its variations—owes special gratitude to the following folks:

Thanks to Rose Ann Shannon, Rob McCartney, Brandi Petersen, Jeff Van Sant, Marla Rabe, Farrah Fazal, and the entire dayside crew at KETV NewsWatch 7 in Omaha, Nebraska, for showing me the view from the other side of the cameras. Thanks also to Amy Dahlman, formerly of WLNS-TV 6 in East Lansing, Michigan, for hours of stories and unfailing generosity in the sharing.

Thanks to Carol Durham, assistant jail administrator, Pottawattamie County Sheriff's Office, for arranging the tour.

Thanks to Rick Crowl, attorney at law, and to Detective Craig Enloe, Overland Park PD, for patiently answering breathless questions about all sorts of cocka-mamie things.

Thanks to Danielle Perez, for telling me what I knew, and for protecting me while I figured out what I didn't.

Thanks to the great Kate Miciak for faith, mercy, and the steeliest of editorial eyes. No editor knows more about the care and handling of the common writer.

Thanks to David Hale Smith, turbo agent and friend.

Thanks to Jordan Global Media for years of support and lasagna. Thanks to Victor Gischler, Neil Smith, and John Rector for sound-boarding.

Thanks and love, as always, to Jessica, who endures hardships.

And to Brian Hodge, for the road trip, and for the ignition of heavy machinery. Figuratively and literally.

3 1252 02328 5422

PHOTO © SCOTT

SEAN DOOLITTLE is the author of five previous no
the Barry Award–winning *The Cleanup*, as well as *Ra*
Dogs, Burn, Dirt, and *Safer.* He lives with his wife and
children in Omaha, Nebraska, where he is at work on
his next novel.